A CHRISTMAS MYSTERY

Cambridge Murder Mysteries

by Charlot King

The Cambridge Murder Mysteries Series:

Book 1: *POISON*

Book 2: *CURSED*

Book 3: *BLOOD MOON*

Book 4: *A CHRISTMAS MYSTERY*

Book 5: *VALENTINE'S DAY – KISS OF DEATH (coming soon)*

First published 2019

Published by: Beautiful Day Cambridge

ISBN: 978-0-9934083-5-9

Illustration: Robin Howlett

DEDICATION AND THANKS

I'd like to thank my good friends, Penny and Robin, for their helpful reviews, and Robin Howlett, my illustrator, who once again has produced an illustration I love. And a big thank you to my son, who has endured endless conversations about Christmas throughout his summer break. Also, the animals I share my home with. Without them, writing from home would not quite feel the same.

PREFACE

Oxford has so many wonderful places to visit, such as the Ashmolean Museum, the University Parks or the Botanic Gardens. Wander the old part of the city and you will find so many beautiful buildings. Part of my heart belongs to Port Meadow, near where I used to live once upon a time.

PROLOGUE

When someone you love more than anything or anyone dies, everything stops and you can see a bottomless hole widening under your feet, ready to swallow you up. All colour disappears, replaced with black void. When someone you love dies, you lose purpose. You lose drive, ambition, but most of all hope. The sea of days ahead swirl around your head like a threat. When someone you love more than yourself dies, you know the true meaning of not only being alone but being lonely. It's as if some force rips your heart and your stomach out and leaves your carcass beating as the blood flows out through the holes. You find it hard to stand up, you don't want to eat, you can't stop the noise in your head. When someone you love more than the world dies, you will stop at nothing to end it.

1
SEEDS ON THE COBBLES

Father Christmas emerges from an alley, bent over and loaded down by a heavy sack of presents, his red jacket flapping in the icy wind to reveal his rotund belly, his tall boots scuffing their way into the historic New College Lane of old bricks and muted colours. It is not long past four o'clock on this Oxford city centre afternoon, the sky a winter black framing the eighteenth, fifteenth and older century College and university buildings. Despite a cold chill in the air, Oxford is still full of tourists milling, hoping to take that perfect snap of the Bridge of Sighs. Lights sparkle from streetlamps, Christmas trees and bicycles. When Santa's white whiskers are spotted, random strangers can't resist pulling at his buttons, expounding how good they've been over the past year then proceeding with their verbal lists of material and physical expectations. The merry figure kindly smiles but refuses photographs, instead melting into the mist of the narrow and well-trodden Brasenose Lane.

Brushing past this rosy-red figure are the black robes of a grim-looking Don clipping Santa with his elbows, as he huffs and frowns at the audacity of someone getting in his way. Unlike a jolly Father Christmas heading off to spread good cheer, the Don reluctantly scurries towards Catte College, a scowl on his face. His raven gown flapping as he strides past carol singers beside the Bodleian Library - beating out a confident 'Good King Wenceslas', the notes hitting the circular building and echoing around Radcliffe Square. The Don disappears under the brick arch of the Porters' Lodge. Cheerless behind his thick black eyebrows, he checks his watch and raises an eyebrow.

"Have I missed the wretched drinks?"

"No Sir, Fellows Room," the Porter replies, peering through the Porters' Lodge heavy teak door now framed in vintage tinsel and a line of Christmas cards sent by over-enthusiastic undergraduates who, if they really understood Porters would have known they'd have much preferred a bottle of port or whisky. The Porter's spindly finger points in the direction across the quad.

"Right you are," the Don sighs, dutifully pulling out a conference itinerary from his pocket, but in haste dropping an open packet of seeds which scatter across the cobbles beneath his feet. "Damn it!" The Don bends down, now angry, as the Porter peers over the reception counter to watch him scrabbling in the gloom.

"Have you any sticky tape, Porter?" A woman leans into the Lodge archway, picking up some tape and before the two men can decide what she is doing she proceeds to pull a long thread of the tape and apply it to the uneven cobbles. "See? Look, there they are." The Don, looking at the seeds caught on the tape, is surprised by her speedy action and shakes his head, irritated nevertheless that this woman has intervened without being asked.

"Have we met?" He glances at the woman, taking an immediate dislike to her reindeer party boppers and flashing Christmas badge, and trying to ignore her very long legs and curvaceous figure.

"Sandy Starborneck. I don't think so. I'm heading to the conference drinks. You?" Sandy continues to pick up the seeds using the tape but holds out a hand to shake.

"Ah, an American. Here, I should be doing this," The Don now looking up properly at the face of this woman with a small scar between her eyebrows on her forehead and tries to take the tape from her, "I'm Professor Resander," he replies, incredulous she doesn't know who she's talking to, and ignoring her hand and continuing with the seeds.

"Well, I think we have most of them," Dr Sandy Starborneck replies, then spotting a group of academics heading towards them she hurriedly speeds up her recovery operation, handing strips of tape to the professor to fold up. The Porter hands them a large envelope and shines a bright torch on the cobbles. Professor Alexander Resander fumbles with the envelope, the sellotape sticking to the side until Dr Starborneck helps him.

"Right," Alexander replies, as he watches Dr Starborneck go back to deftly retrieving more seeds from the cobbles. "Give them to me!" He shouts, wanting this woman to disappear.

"Right exactly, well I'm going," and Dr Starborneck points towards the drinks, "I think I need one."

Moments later the Porters' Lodge alley is full of Fellows and visiting academics wandering towards the Fellows Room, having spent a full day at the Conference on Botany and Biological DNA, and now with parched lips looking to wet their whistles.

*

The Fellows Room at Catte College has been somewhat minimally decorated for the Christmas period. A small tree with white lights and a trail of holly across the mantelpiece are the only signs of Yule joy in this high-ceilinged, oak-panelled room.

Dr Sandy Starborneck and Professor Alexander Resander join a packed room of thirsty academics, expounding loudly on the day's talks, a few hurrying over to congratulate Sandy Starborneck on her prize awarded earlier today, which came with a large research grant.

"Order, order!" Shouts a tall, balding man with a pointy nose, in a very loud cyan coloured suit, a cravat and a very large black hat, now standing on a chair. "Will everyone hush for a moment!" The man waves his hands for people to quieten. "Thank you." And then he leaves an uncomfortable pause before starting to speak.

"Get on with it, Michael," Professor Alexander Resander mutters under his breath.

"As you know, I love organising these events for you, which are so popular. I'd like to thank all those who've found me and told me how much you're enjoying it. It's very touching. Just make sure you sign up for next year and tell the Master how much you value it!" Michael Pussett says, unaware of Professor Alexander Resander's irritation, "We look forward to seeing you back here next year, and although I haven't spoken to the Master, I'm confident that he'll welcome us all with open arms." Michael looks to the Master in the corner of the room, a portly man who doesn't move any facial muscles apart from his eyes which he shifts to the window, already bored by this insignificant man. "So, enjoy the complimentary drinks and make sure you're back here for supper tonight. The College has a wonderful menu, and you'll be able to continue conversations about plants to your heart's content! Enjoy!!" And Michael jumps off the chair and starts to applaud the room, encouraging others to join in without much success. They are Oxford academics, after all, and don't suffer fools.

2
TINKLING THE IVORIES

Wearing a green velvet jacket with a silver brooch in the shape of a robin, cream blouse and black corduroy trousers, Professor Elizabeth Green peers over the top of her spectacles at the piano music right in front of her nose, her beady eyes locking onto the notes. Not a fan of big crowds, Elizabeth Green had already abandoned the Fellows Room at Catte College, Oxford, a short while ago and snuck her way into the adjacent and empty Master's Lounge and is now sitting at his piano, knowing far too well how her irritation levels creep up after being subjected to too much banal wine-induced chatter. Nobody ever had a good idea inebriated.

Conferences are not on Elizabeth's top ten list. Not that she makes lists, but if she did they would undoubtedly be on the list of things to avoid at all costs. However, this time Elizabeth had unfortunately drawn the short straw. There had indeed been paper straws pulled at tea last week in the Plant Sciences Department staff room on Downing Lane, at the University of Cambridge, for this particular Oxford trip, and the decision was made. When Professor Elizabeth Green picked the stubby end, the Department Head suggested to his team that it might be worth having another go, as it would be foolhardy to send her. He did this mostly with eye contact and glares to his colleagues, but others just patted him on the arm and said the straws don't lie. In the end, the Head had bribed Elizabeth with the very best in accommodation and the minimal number of days required attendance. All he asked of her was that she turned up to some of the presentations, and "mingle at dinner, that sort of thing. We can't be seen to be letting the side down. So, hide your normal face, you know, pretend to be happy about it."

So, having hidden her face for a while now in an altogether more peaceful place, and being close enough to conference attendees to defend against any who might accuse her of absence, yet for all intents and purposes being a continent away, Elizabeth breathes a sigh of relief for the isolation. She is sitting at a gleaming baby grand and knows that if she plays, she can disappear into the music. At least this room feels very Christmassy. The lighting is lower, scented candles are burning, as is a real fire, and the tall Christmas tree in the corner has white lights twinkling right up to the angel. Elizabeth picks '*Christmas Time is Here*' from her Guaraldi sheet music in her bag and is immediately caught in the tune and begins to relax. She tilts her head back and shuts her eyes, her brown curls, which have grown a little this past Autumn, dropping down her back.

After some time, her peaceful play is abruptly interrupted.

"Hello." a friendly man peeps his head around the corner of the door, with scruffy blonde hair and a large frame, his pink trousers and Christmas jumper bringing in good cheer as he enters the room, but Elizabeth tries to ignore him as he walks, trepidatiously to a chair and listens. She continues to play, while he looks up at the Christmas lights. She glances at him; his large blue eyes are open and friendly, but Elizabeth finds his interruption unwelcome. When the tune has finished, and before she can start another, he continues, "You know there are drinks in the Fellows' Room? Would you like to go? It might be fun. There were some good lectures this afternoon. Might be some interesting conversations?" Elizabeth shakes her head. Then the man lifts his bag, "Well, I brought everyone truffles," and pops a box on the piano, along with a card.

"No, thank you."

"They're vegan. A dicky bird might have mentioned." He smiles. Elizabeth looks up at the truffles. They look impressive.

"You're giving chocolates to everyone?"

"For the people I like. It's Christmas. I'm trying to make an effort this year. You know, get into the spirit. Not my thing but determined not to be a bah humbug." he replies. "Gabriel Deersman. We've met once before, a long time ago. I came over to Cambridge. Was fleeting, it's okay if you don't remember, but I saw your research at the Botanic Gardens on giant hogweed."

"And what do you think about giant hogweed?" Elizabeth's ears prick up.

"Completely misunderstood. Unfairly vilified."

"Precisely." Elizabeth smiles for the first time and looks again at the box of chocolates, not remembering this man with red cheeks and a warm smile from his Cambridge trip. "Vegan?" she asks. Gabriel nods, then she pops one into her mouth, trying to remember her own special man.

"Are you coming in then? Might be fun? Dinner later too?"

"Perhaps dinner." Elizabeth looks at him to make it clear she'd like him to shut the door on the way out.

"See you later then," Gabriel replies, but Elizabeth has already started to play Coots and Gillespie's '*Santa Claus is Coming to Town*'.

She shuts her eyes and thinks about Gerald. She remembers how he always used to wear the hat from a cracker for most of Christmas Day, and how he would bring her breakfast in bed, and light a fire in their bedroom so that they might read books until elevenses. Then they would mill about in the kitchen making all kinds of mess cooking up everything before a walk along the river arm in arm. They'd stroll back and cosy up and watch an old film while cracking nuts and drinking sherry. Elizabeth used to make a Christmas cake, and Gerald would always lie and tell her it was delicious and have seconds, even though she knew it was dry and a little bitter. Then they might play a game of Scrabble, and he would always cheat and try to sneak words past her that didn't exist. Finally, they would sit at the piano, and he would sing while she played. He was the best company, her best friend, the man she had started to grow old with, the one who left her over a year and a half ago.

And now she doesn't feel anything at Christmas. Her fingers know the notes of his favourite Christmas songs from muscle memory, but her ears don't translate the happy tune. They fall hollow. He was gone where she would never find him. Elizabeth couldn't feel more alone, more meaningless. Now, what was she supposed to do during the yuletide?

3
BACK TO WORK

Back in Cambridge, at the Police Station on Parker's Piece, Inspector Bob Abley takes his putt, causing Sergeant Goodey to jump out of the way. The little white ball shoots across the room, heading along the green felt and into the indoor golf hole, a small piece of metal made especially for enthusiasts who have time to practice while at work.

"Hole in one!" Abley shouts as Sergeant Goodey hurries over to the hole and lifts out the ball. Goodey's trousers a little too short, revealing odd socks. His glasses steamed up, his hands bright red with the beginnings of chilblains, having chased a previous ball outside and into the snow after it went through an open window minutes before – the first of many this morning.

"Well done, Sir!" Goodey claps enthusiastically. Inspector Bob Abley, the popular Inspector at Cambridge Police Station, takes the ball from Goodey's sweaty palms and looks out of the window at the people skating on the rink, throwing snowballs; there is a blanket of white covering the Piece.

"It's the only way I'm going to keep my form. Can't play in that," says Inspector Abley, huffing about all the snow fallen on the grass outside. Abley looks longingly at the sky, the kind creases around his eyes crinkling down his cheeks to meet the smirk breaking all over his face. "Still, this is fun!" Abley swings his putter like a samurai sword, then turns to pick up another ball, his bottle-green tank top with a little golfer on the side peeking through his fawn-coloured bomber jacket. Unlike the pasty face of his junior, Abley's skin is still honey coloured from a long weekend trip to the Canary Islands to play golf a month or so before.

"That's a shame, Sir. I bet you're terrific."

"Goodey, I am. Feel free to disagree with me on any case, but not on my golf. Or we shall have to part ways."

"Right you are, Sir."

"Come out with me for a round, when it's quiet. Lemon wasn't a fan. But, you have to try everything once. Don't you agree?" Abley says, but Chief Superintendent Raynott interrupts, walking into the room, breaking up the conversation, his huge eyes, darting around the room, his sneer as if he's about to bite.

"With that logic, perhaps I should try being a murderer for the day. Who would be my first victim? Hmm…" Raynott looks around, then confiscates Inspector Abley's golf ball from Goodey, but Abley doesn't give him the satisfaction by revealing his frustration. Instead he replies, "I'm sure we could see to it to look the other way for you Sir. Make an exception."

"You make it all the more tempting when you fail to read my memos. Did you not pick up my order for you to check out the Peter Ridleton file?" Raynott walks over to the window.

"You looking forward to Christmas? Got anything fun organised?" Abley takes his next putt with a new ball from his pocket, ignoring the Superintendent's question.

"I'm just deciding at the moment, actually. Currently, I'm down to work the whole of Christmas," Raynott says gloomily.

"Oh, right. Keeping the streets of Cambridge safe. You'll be all right. Nothing happens over Christmas, anyway, so it should be fun," Abley replies sarcastically.

"How about clearing the Peter Ridleton file from my books, as an early Christmas present. The damn woman keeps calling me," the Super suggests.

"The Peter Ridleton file? It's hardly a fair secret Santa, Sir. I got you something much better."

"What's that?"

"You'll ruin the surprise." Inspector Abley touches his nose.

"When will you learn that I don't like surprises," says Raynott, pocketing the second ball.

"How could I forget, Sir?" Abley glances at the drawer behind his desk, which is open but out of sight of Raynott. It is full of golf balls. He gives Goodey a look to shut it before Raynott spots it. But Raynott clocks this and follow's Abley's eyes to the drawer. He walks around the desk and pulls the drawer out, the golf balls rattling, and carries it out with him.

"The Peter Ridleton file, if you want your confiscated property. And don't stuff it up." Raynott leaves, then Abley looks at the space where his drawer was. Superintendent Raynott comes back and pokes his head in the door. "Oh, and actually, I've had a think, and I want to say how good it is of you to volunteer to work the entire Christmas and New Year instead of me. You shouldn't have. But, as you say, you'll be all right. Nothing happens over Christmas, anyway, so it should be fun." Then Raynott disappears.

"There's a good lad," Abley hands Goodey twenty pounds, "up the Grand Arcade. Get the yellow ones from the sports bargain bucket. I can see them better."

"What have you got Superintendent Raynott for Christmas?" Goodey asks his Inspector.

"Chop chop." Abley ushers Sergeant Goodey out towards the shops.

"But what about the Peter Ridleton file?"

"Be gone with you." Abley pushes Goodey away, but

then frowns to himself, examining the hole where his golf ball drawer used to be and the news of his imminent Christmas shifts. He'll have to think of something super special for Christmas for Superintendent Raynott.

4
LET SLEEPING DOGS

Professor Elizabeth Green is still seated at the piano in the Master's Lounge, her fingers brush along the keys, finishing another festive tune. For a while, once the music has come to an end, Elizabeth stares at the twinkling tree. Lost in her thoughts of Christmases past, she can't quite muster her next step, instead spots the vegan truffles and decides to let sugar revive her. It does the trick, and as she stands, she notices a landline telephone in the corner. Elizabeth sits by the fire and reaches over to pick up the receiver, clearly meant for College business and perhaps for a Porter to forewarn the Master of an impending guest's arrival. However, Elizabeth has an altogether more useful purpose for it. She places her fingers in the little holes and dials home — anything to avoid having to mingle.

*

In Professor Elizabeth Green's Cambridge home, Foxes Haven, and buried under two extremely muddy Afghan Hounds, Hector and Monty, and an Old English Sheepdog, Clive, her favourite grandson, Godric, is lying on the settee in the drawing-room, still in a jacket from walking the dogs earlier, when he hears the piercing trill of the telephone from the hall. He knows full well that no one, except his Nanna or her best friend Emily, uses this bakelite antiquity. He often smiles to himself as he listens to the two women, glued in conversation sometimes for whole evenings, unbudgeable from their telephone seats beside their beloved telephone tables with address books which flip open alphabetically - at least Emily also has a mobile phone. The ringing continues, and although Godric is surprisingly comfortable, he knows it won't stop until he answers.

His Nanna's home is cosy and ready for Christmas. Before Professor Elizabeth Green left for Oxford, she put up the multicoloured lights on the Christmas tree outside the French patio doors. They sparkle behind Godric, as do the twinkly lights running along the mantelpiece, shining between the holly and the limes dangling on pretty ribbon, cloves stabbed into their sides. The two cats who share this home, Bertie and Soot, are asleep on the mat by the fire, oblivious to anything other than the warmth emanating from the crackle and hiss of the flames. And Godric had been very comfortable doing nothing. Something he has taken years to perfect, and today was being helped on by a dram of rum and a muted Christmas film showing reindeer sauntering through the snow. Yet everywhere is in turmoil around him, with dirty boots, mud, dirt on the sofa, wet soaked dog towels, mud up the window.

Godric knows the force of his Nanna is stronger than any desire to rest, so he chucks the dogs off his legs and shouts, "I'm coming, I'm coming!" at the telephone as it continues to burst his eardrums. He knocks his way through takeaway boxes and cola bottles scattered on the floor, with crisp packets and half-eaten pizzas strewn about the table, just out of reach of the dogs. Godric is also covered in mud, resembling a man who has not washed for a week. His usual white linen replaced by brown corduroy and green jumper, which has taken on its own less than subtle smell. Anyone who caught a glimpse of Godric, however, would only notice his shiny blonde curls, huge grey eyes and the lithe physique of a Cambridge rower. To say he resembles a man of privilege would be to understate the extraordinary levels of rude health he exudes. As if a god, his name aptly suits him from the tip of his toes to the curl of his overly long eyelashes.

As Godric is about to pick up the phone, Ben opens the front door and puts the keys on the telephone table. In his oversized duster jacket, carrying a sack into the hallway and with a big grin, he kisses Godric. Godric puts a finger up to shush Ben as he picks up the telephone receiver and stands beside the elegant Georgian telephone table. Godric watches his boyfriend walk into the drawing-room, his brown hair tousled with white flecks of snow, his tall stature only just making it through the door.

"Hello, Bunny!" Godric says before he listens to who it is. He looks at Ben and shakes his head as Ben picks up the TV remote and is about to unmute the Christmas reindeers. Ben comes back and kisses Godric instead. "Yes, everything is wonderful here," Godric replies into the phone. Ben raises his eyebrows at the tip the place has turned into in just the one day since he last visited Godric.

The dogs rush up to say hello to Ben, who hugs them back, mud flying off their coats onto the walls. They fidget and jump around him, almost knocking all kinds of fragile objets d'art off their respective perches, as Ben makes his way to the cats lying by the fire. He pulls out a few badly wrapped presents and places them under the tree. Godric clocks this as he listens to Elizabeth in his ear. He knows Ben is relatively poor and notices the wrapping looks a little shabby. Godric watches as Ben empties his stuffed coat pockets to reveal a couple of pies and some Christmas cake, as well as an opened bottle of port, and knocks the pizza out of the way to make room on the table. Godric knows full well that Ben has pilfered these items from College.

Ben walks over and hands Godric a port, but Godric points to his rum precariously perched on the arm of the sofa. Ben retrieves it for him. "Thank you. Yes, no, I'm listening. Just the normal zoo." Godric pauses to listen again and decides to sit down on the little seat, his long legs and tall frame far too big for it. Ben hands him a mince pie.

"Compliments of St James's Christmas lunch. They were only going to throw them away." Ben swigs some of the port straight from the bottle.

"It's just me, Nanna. Don't worry. Yes, I've walked them. Yes, I wiped their feet. Yes, I'm only giving them one treat a day. Yes, the nice ones. No, not those. I know they are not good for—" Godric shakes his head again at Ben and hands him back the mince pie. Ben comes back over with Stilton and biscuits. Godric makes a thumbs-up sign, grabs some and then shoves them in. "Yes, it's been coming down heavy since you left."

*

Elizabeth, still sitting on the sofa in the Master's Lounge, is twirling a small piece of tinsel between her fingers as she speaks to Godric.

"It's not even snowing here. I thought it was the other way around – Oxford always gets far more rain." She listens to Godric, then replies, "Yes, but you have to take the ice balls out from between their feet. Have you checked?" Elizabeth listens again. "No, it's very dreary. Why they send me to these things, they know I hate them." Elizabeth stands up and walks to the window as far as the cord from the telephone will allow, "No, I haven't given it yet. I will leave as soon as I've presented, believe me." Elizabeth rolls her eyes. "I left you with a full fridge … already? Well, another reason for me to come back soon." Elizabeth walks over to where the telephone was initially placed, still listening to Godric. "I forgot my boots, so I jolly well hope we don't get snow here. I'm back tomorrow evening. Two nights away is long enough. Is Bertie okay? He doesn't like the cold." She listens and smiles. "Well keep it alight. That's the safest place for him." Elizabeth hears the door open to the Master's Lounge "No, don't cast a spell. I don't want the snow here, thank you. I hope you've been keeping things tidy over the past couple of days. All right. Bye-bye." Elizabeth holds the receiver. It starts to make a noise, as Godric has already hung up the other end, but she delays putting it back on the telephone. It is a line to home.

Gabriel comes back into the room.

"I felt compelled to bring you a drink. No one should be alone at Christmas." He hands Elizabeth a mulled wine and notices she has been using the landline. "Perhaps someone should buy you a mobile for your stocking?" Gabriel laughs, but Elizabeth frowns, refusing his drink. "I mean for the stocking over the fire," Gabriel smiles nervously.

*

After the call with his Nanna, Godric stands to survey the mess in the house. He peeps his head into the kitchen and feels slightly nauseous. Every counter is covered in dirty plates, saucepans, frying pans, empty food packets, food stains. The sink is stacked full of washing up, and the dishwasher is open and full, though the mud from the dogs is masking the stench of rotting food.

"How could you have made this much mess in one day, Ben? She's coming home tomorrow," Godric says jokily.

"I thought we had the week?" Ben shakes his head; they both know Godric makes all the mess.

Godric looks at Ben, wondering what to do.

"We need to hire professionals."

"I don't have the money for that," Ben replies.
"What were credit cards invented for, darling Benny?"

5
UNDER THE MISTLETOE

Professor Elizabeth Green is finally prised out of the Master's Lounge, by the very rotund Master who wants to make a call in private, although Elizabeth suspects he might also be after a quiet place to hide as well, and somewhere to gorge on the plate of scones he has in his hand.

She begrudgingly leaves with Gabriel, who picks up the chocolates and the bag which came with them and puts them in his jacket. The Master suggests they join the others, but Elizabeth walks away as slowly as possible, stopping to admire the wall art or look at the view in the Hall or Chapel. She even manages to stare for five minutes straight at a rather large metal sculpture of a horse placed in the middle of an enclosed quad, Gabriel checking his phone behind her, her shushing him as he tries to interject with words to encourage her to the drinks. Anything other than rejoining a room packed full of over-enthusiastic adults wanting to share their particular research ambitions in such microscopic detail it would even stop fleas from wanting to jump.

As they amble along a third corridor, Gabriel being instructed by Elizabeth to talk her through the history of the College "in as much detail as possible", and him explaining to her that he's been a Don here for over fifteen years, they can't help but notice through the windows that it has started to lightly snow outside.

"There you have it. It's official. Christmas has started," Gabriel says jollily.

"I just hope it isn't deep enough to maroon me. I have to get back to Cambridge." Elizabeth looks worriedly at the sky. "I can't be stuck in Oxford."

"Some people think Oxford is pretty special."

"Indeed, as it is. Yet, I can't help but save space in my heart for the most special place of all," Elizabeth says. As they continue to walk they spot Michael Pussett, the conference organiser, in a passionate embrace with one of the attendees, a drink still in her hand, taking sips between kisses.

"A rather particular style of hosting at a conference on botany. Still, we are in Oxford." Elizabeth winces.

*

In the Porters' Lodge at Catte College, a woman wearing tie-dyed trousers and carrying a bag in the shape of an elephant's head and all in rainbow colours, stands in the Porters' Lodge window, having arrived late.

"Excuse me. I'm looking for Dr Sandy Starborneck. I wonder if you might have seen her this afternoon?"

"No, Miss." the Porter tries to mask a frown at the woman's clothing. "Are you lost?" The hippy notices him staring, and so feels the need to explain her amazing wardrobe, waving her hands with rings on every finger in the shape of wild creatures. The Porter thinks one looks remarkably like a big cat, perhaps a cougar, given her accent.

"I didn't know whether to wear the blue sarong, or I have this purple pavada and choli. Oh, you would have loved it, and I am irresistible in it, but then I know you know that. I can see you are a highly perceptive man with strong chakras." The woman smiles and winks at the Porter, who coughs, unsure what a pavada is but hoping it is modest. He observes the long pea green jacket that the woman is wearing, which is covered in what looks like quilt squares with knitted flying doves. He also can't avoid staring at her long wavy hair, as it has streaks of pink all over as if she were an eighteen-year-old punk rocker instead of a middle-aged academic that he fears she might well be, judging from the badge on her handbag he has just spotted.

"Perhaps she is at the drinks, Ma'am. Over in the Fellows' Room? Might you like to try? I see you are at the Botany and DNA Conference? From your badge on your, erm elephant?"

"Oh, I don't let the man stick it to me, or on me. Mr Mugway here said he would wear it on my behalf." The woman looks at her bag and then back at the Porter "You know, Mr Mugway has cousins in Nairobi. I could bring one over for you, next time I go?"

"Please don't go to any trouble," the Porter eyes the bag uncertainly.

"Oh, it's no trouble, ask for Haven in a few months, and I can make sure I bring one back. I mean, I might not be coming back here. Are you planning any trips to the States? That's also if I go, which I might, but I might not. Well, anyway. Ask for Haven. That's me. I will hear you." Then the woman takes out her card and gives it to the Porter, pulls out her water bottle and takes a sip of water, then walks off towards the Fellows' Room, and the Porter follows her with his eyes until she is out of sight, and then opens his eyes wide as he looks down at her card. It has a photograph of the woman riding a camel and her full name, Haven. And that's it: no phone number, no email.

As Haven turns the corner into the front quad of the College, she notices two people embracing in a passionate kiss. At first, she is charmed by the festive show of love.

But then, as she nears, she pulls out an apple from Mr Mugway and throws it at them as hard as she can when she recognises the lovers as the conference organiser, Michael Pussett and Dr Sandy Starnborneck.

"Turncoat! I've a good mind to report you to pest control. They'd hose you down and make you stop doing that, or better put you down. Oh, my eyes. My eyes!" And Haven rushes across the quad covering her eyes but also pulling out more food to throw back at the pair. Michael momentarily pulls away from Sandy, then smirks.

"I think your friend might be jealous," he says, watching Haven rush away, and picking up an apple that has rolled under his feet and rubbing it on his trousers before taking a bite. He notices Professor Elizabeth Green and Dr Gabriel Deersman emerge from a door, and he nods a greeting. Elizabeth frowns and tries her best to ignore this odiously tall man in his loud suit, as Gabriel follows Elizabeth into the Fellows' drinks. She spots mistletoe over the door and senses the conference organiser has followed them and is now close behind.

"Don't even think about it, Mr Pussett," Elizabeth shouts back curtly to the conference organiser, most unhappy about spending any time with this odious man, as she heads into an hour of obligation and doom.

6
BUSY WITH PRESENTS

Across the street along Brasenose Lane, a little way from where Professor Elizabeth Green is presently trying to avoid small talk at the Botany and DNA conference drinks at Catte College, Father Christmas is emptying a sack of presents and loading them into the boot of his 2CV van. His sack is full, and he neatly takes some out and stacks them into the back, before picking up different presents and putting them back into his sack and slamming the doors. He walks up Brasenose Lane and back into Radcliffe Square. From now until late evening when he will be finished, Father Christmas knows that he will be so busy with work, but also that he won't be able to escape the attention of tourists. When too many start to circle he throws sweets behind him onto the cobbles. This brings laughter and slows the tourists down, just enough for him to make his escape down St Mary's Passage and onto more colleges. He has presents to sort out.

7
MINCE PIES AND MULLED WINE

Now in the conference drinkies, Elizabeth observes how everyone in the Fellows' Room is significantly more relaxed than earlier. Ties have been removed and stuffed into pockets. Voices are louder as the crowd successfully decompresses from the sessions today, lubricated by copious amounts of Catte College's own collection of wine from their cellar. For those choosing to remain sober, catering staff weave their way through with offers of tea and crumpets.

Gabriel removes his jacket, making his Christmas reindeer jumper all the more prominent. Elizabeth notices the conference organiser, Michael Pussett, and the woman he was over-enthusiastically attacking with his lips, both leaning on the wall at the edge of the room, her holding two drinks.

"Hello," a man says from behind her.

"Oh, hello," Elizabeth replies.

"You're standing on my foot," he sneers.

"I feel a little crushed in here."

"So you thought you'd punish my foot. Seems fair.

Please, may I have it back?" He says sarcastically. Elizabeth looks down at her foot on the man's shoe and tries to see where she might stand instead.

"This is ridiculous," is all she can muster, regretting her return to this chaotic room.

"No, don't go. Here," Gabriel offers Elizabeth the mulled wine he retrieves from a tray. Elizabeth shakes her head. "Oh, sorry, what do you like?" he asks, putting it back.

"I have to go," Elizabeth says again, "I can see you at dinner."

"That would be good. Can I have my foot back?" the other man adds dryly. But then, Elizabeth is accosted by a loud leggy American woman wearing reindeer party boppers.

"Oh my god! You're, I mean, is it really Professor Elizabeth Green? I've read all your papers!" The woman grabs Elizabeth's arm and stops any hope of escape.

"Who wants to know," Elizabeth asks, recognising her as the one being kissed by the organiser moments before in the quad, and the woman who won the prize this morning. An American.

"Ha! Sandy, Dr Sandy Starborneck, but you won't have heard of me. I mean I don't think so?" The woman looks into Elizabeth's eyes, hoping for a glimmer of recognition. But Elizabeth shows increasing displeasure at being here, so Sandy Starborneck continues, "I'm on sabbatical in Oxford to pick up a prize. It's so quaint, isn't it? The Queen, Buckingham Palace, black cabs, alright guv'nor." Sandy Starborneck does a poor impression of an East-End London accent. "I mean I know I'm supposed to be professional and all, but we've all had a drink, right?" Sandy hiccup burps. Elizabeth withdraws back as far as the crowded room will allow, but Sandy keeps hold of her arm and tries to focus on Elizabeth's face, "You've got such intelligent eyes. All those lines around them. And haven't the English got unusual teeth? Like fangs?" Sandy looks at

Elizabeth's mouth carefully, then stumbles. Michael notices this and starts to make his way through the crowd to reach her.

"Everything all right?" he asks Sandy Starborneck.

"How did you get that scar?" Elizabeth looks at the old scar on Sandy Starborneck's face, slightly insulted by her teeth comment.

"From a big mistake," Sandy Starborneck says, now looking at Michael.

"Are you drunk?" Elizabeth asks, stating the obvious.

"Everything's wonderful," Dr Starborneck twirls around, finally letting go of Elizabeth, who starts to walk away, but Sandy chases her. "Here. Wait!" Sandy shouts at Elizabeth, who stops momentarily, "Sorry," Sandy says, "Shush, wait. I just wanted to say that I'm looking forward to your keynote paper you're giving on plant diversity and climate change, the new toxi–, toxi–, you know, I've memorised it, hang on," Sandy says frowning as she tries to say 'toxicity', but she is swaying too much.

"Come on, I think we need to get some coffee down you." Michael Pussett tries to grab hold of Sandy. But she flails about and manages to break free.

"Toxis–, tox—,"

"Oh, you idiotic woman!" From a parting crowd, Dr Haven Usrey rushes over to Sandy. "How much have you had? What on earth are you doing? You're embarrassing yourself. You sure you deserve a prize?"

"Get off me." Sandy pulls away from Dr Haven Usrey.

"When did this sound like a good idea? What's got into you, Sandy? Let's go." Dr Haven Usrey reprimands Sandy.

"I'm enjoying the fine wines of College life, isn't that what you Dons all do?" Sandy pokes a Don standing beside her in the stomach and then rubs his cheeks. "Look at that nose! Bet you top that up daily." Dr Starborneck tweaks the Don's nose, which is indeed bright red and would suggest heavy alcohol dependence, although perhaps better tolerance than this loud American woman.

"Very festive. Very now." Dr Sandy Starborneck pokes it again.

As Elizabeth watches the argument unfold in front of her between Dr Sandy Starborneck and Dr Haven Usrey, she can't help but hear another conversation going on behind her, with Gabriel speaking to the man whose toes she previously stood.

"No, no, leave it, let them play it out, Alexander," Gabriel says.

"We can't have a catfight in the College. Get them off the premises," Alexander replies firmly.

"Let's give it a moment, please," Gabriel urges. But Elizabeth watches the expression of Alexander, and he looks straight at her, partly still irked at her earlier standing on his foot. Alexander raises his eyebrows but otherwise is entirely expressionless. Elizabeth notices the particles of food dropped down the front of Alexander's jacket, his hair salt and pepper, and although he looks unhappy, his eyes are a beautiful fiery green. In that split second, Elizabeth can tell that perhaps he might be almost as intelligent as she is. Almost. Then she notices the mud on his trousers. Speaking over the continuing commotion Dr Sandy Starborneck is making behind her, Elizabeth listens to Professor Resander.

"Whippet. Just a bit lighter than you on my feet." He acknowledges her observation of the mud and scowls at the women arguing.

"A man with a dog." She nods and smiles, noticing his nicotine-stained fingers.

"Here." Gabriel gives Alexander a Christmas card.

"People still do this?" Alexander opens the envelope shaking his head and slips out a card, handmade with seeds embedded into the paper.

"You plant the card, and it brings wildflowers in the summer for the bees," Gabriel nods. Elizabeth begins to regret she left her card on the side of the piano until Gabriel smiles again at her and pulls hers out, without her noticing having retrieved the bag with chocolates and her card earlier.

"Thank you, what a lovely idea and—" but Elizabeth is interrupted by a scream, as Dr Haven Usrey has hold of Dr Sandy Starborneck's hair, with Dr Haven Usrey shouting, "It's for your own good!" and Sandy replying, "Have you met Haven, everyone? Haven and I are working on a project together. And yes, we are both loud Americans." Sandy laughs, her party boppers finally falling onto her face, as Haven boots her out of the room. There are gasps, soon broken by the caterer.

"Anyone for a mince pie?" the caterer asks, as she pulls a trolley through the gap the two women have created, accidentally bumping over Professor Alexander Resander's foot with the trolley, while Elizabeth is left wondering whether this room is full of friends or enemies.

8
ROOM SERVICE

Professor Elizabeth Green is relieved to be back at her hotel, the St Giles' on Beaumont Street. She upgraded rooms from her Head of Department's university budget and booking to secure a larger suite, and well worth the extra pennies as she sits back on her sizeable four-poster bed against the softest pillows purveying the sumptuous room while looking out into a heavy snowy sky and eating the dark chocolate left on her pillow. She picks up the telephone and dials her friend, Emily.

"Hello, yes. I'm still here. It makes me want to stick knitting needles in my ears. No, of course not." Elizabeth rolls her eyes, listens, then replies, "Yes, I will, but I'm sure he is responsible enough to walk them." Elizabeth hears a knock at the door. "Just a minute." Elizabeth answers the door and room service brings in a silver tray with a pot of fresh mint tea, a cake stand with tiny cucumber sandwiches, cake, mince pies and a little flag with a Father Christmas on it sticking out the top of the stand with the word 'vegan' written on it. Also on the tray are some Christmas lights, woven around the teacup and plate, as a festive decoration. Elizabeth spots the small bottle of liqueur with a crystal glass she doesn't remember ordering and points to it.

"Complimentary, Madam." Elizabeth smiles at the room service, tips him and shuts the door. "Sorry about that, Christmas afternoon tea has just arrived," Elizabeth cuts a piece of cake using a fork and pops it into her mouth. "Lemon drizzle."

*

Emily stands at her telephone table in her home. Down the corridor she can see her husband, Cuthbert, sitting on a barstool at a large kitchen island reading the paper. Everything in Emily's home is colour-coordinated in cream and grey. Emily covers the phone and tells her husband, "It's not easy without Gerald, at Christmas," then shakes her head and speaks to Elizabeth. "Hmm, eating cake before sandwiches?" Emily asks Elizabeth. "Nothing changes."

*

Elizabeth stands by the window, having poured a cup of tea. She looks into the sky some more and sees that it is releasing more snow. She speaks to Emily down the phone.

"It just started to snow. I hope it doesn't delay my return tomorrow. The Talbot isn't exactly the right car for this weather." Elizabeth listens to Emily, saying how the snow is magical and to try to enjoy it. "How can I enjoy it when I'm cooped up with all those academic climbers?" Elizabeth listens as she takes a sip of tea. "Gerald used to like Christmas. He always took me to see a show in London," Elizabeth says, thinking about how they'd go away for a long weekend after Christmas. Somewhere like Paris or Vienna.

*

"Well, you're still coming to us on Boxing Day this year, and New Year's Eve?" Emily looks at Cuthbert, who nods agreement. Anything for a quiet life. "Good."

*

"Coming to yours will be an antidote to Christmas with my daughter," Elizabeth says, adding, "They're sending a car for me on Christmas Eve evening, can you believe it? They must be back from America by now." Elizabeth listens, "No, just for a few days, apparently the weather is better in L.A." Elizabeth shakes her head. "I suppose it will be good for Godric to see his mother and sister." Elizabeth listens to Emily. "All right, yes, speak later. You go, and yes, he's a good chap." Elizabeth puts the phone down, thinking how lucky Emily is to still have Cuthbert.

Elizabeth takes the tray of afternoon tea and places it on a corner of her bed. She sits back in the silent room and clicks on the television. She flicks until she finds an old Christmas movie and puts it on mute. Then, Elizabeth shuts her eyes. In the quiet, she hears screams. At first, Elizabeth thinks they must be coming from the television and checks again that the sound is turned down, soon realising that she had already successfully muted the black and white, she listens intently. There it is again.

She jumps up off the bed, knocking the cake stand over and rushes to the window. She spots two women in the snow, which she is quite surprised has come down heavily very quickly. The women have come out of an exclusive restaurant on the opposite side of the road. One of them has hold of the other in a headlock grip. Elizabeth looks closer and sees that it is the two women from her conference. She can't believe it, academics acting like misbehaving children.

Elizabeth bangs on the window, and one of the women

looks up. There are no cars, and the snow has made everything quiet. She shakes her head at Dr Haven Usrey. Haven lets go of Dr Sandy Starborneck, who falls to the ground.

"This is what I have to deal with!" Haven holds her arms stretched out and hands upturned. "You work with what you've got, lady, this is what I've got, a drunk friend! Who knew?" then Dr Haven Usrey looks at Dr Sandy Starborneck who has sat on the kerb and is rubbing her head. Somehow the snow slows everything down. Dr Haven Usrey looks up to the sky and shuts her eyes.

Elizabeth spots Michael Pussett, the conference organiser, watching the two women from the door of the restaurant, putting on his coat and lifting a cigar to his lips. He starts to walk over to the women, and Elizabeth observes his seeming tenderness as he eventually bends down to Dr Sandy Starborneck on the pavement and pulls her up. He puts his arm under hers and starts to walk her back into the restaurant. Elizabeth raises her eyebrows as Dr Haven Usrey looks back up at Elizabeth and waves goodbye and a "See you at dinner!" and walks off in a different direction. Elizabeth tries to bury her Head of Department's words about needing to 'mingle' by running through ideas in her head about how to get out of dinner. There must be a way to avoid having to mingle.

9
OBSESSED

After the drinks and before supper, Professor Alexander Resander has gone back to the lab. Like Professor Green, he isn't keen on attending the conference either, but given that it is his College hosting it, he has no option. Despite all undergraduates having gone down for the holidays now, the laboratory still has half a dozen PhD and post-doctoral researchers working this late up to Christmas. Alexander nods at a few and continues through the lab until he gets to his own research desk.

Professor Alexander Resander takes the seeds from the sticky tape that he dropped earlier and unlocks a little fridge to put the envelope inside. He then takes out a bowl of much larger seeds from a shelf, and places just one of them into one small pestle and mortar. Alexander gently grinds the seed and drops it into a test tube and puts that into a laboratory centrifuge. As the machine spins, he hears the door open. Dr Gabriel Deersman pokes his head around the door and then walks across the laboratory to say hello.

"I had the same plan. I didn't get to give you these." Gabriel leaves Alexander some chocolates on the workbench.

"Chocolates too? Are you feeling okay?"

"I just want to try to be normal this year."

"Normal, huh. Normal people don't give everyone chocolates. Only Father Christmas does that, Gabriel."

"Okay, not normal. I wanted to get in the festive spirit."

"I hope the whole ruddy thing is over as soon as possible. And I shall be spending Christmas here. Only time I get some peace," Alexander looks at his post-docs listening to the radio playing Christmas tunes and asks, "Who's changed it from classical?" But they all look guiltily away.

"Do you think we should ration the College wine? Some don't appear to be able to moderate their behaviour this year," Gabriel comments, attempting to make conversation with Alexander.

"Just don't. Awful people."

Gabriel walks over to his research lab and through a door. Inside his lab, through a glass partition, he walks into a greenhouse. It has simulated natural light lamps in strips. Underneath are tomato plants.

"And now we have to dine with them. Want one?" Gabriel picks a tomato and pops it in his mouth. "Extra pep in these,"

"Has it worked?"

"Looks like." Gabriel looks at his tomatoes. "Daily vitamin and mineral shots in just one tomato," Gabriel smiles.

"Easy to overdose then," Alexander replies, "if you eat as many tomatoes as I do. Go on then," Alexander adds, catching a tomato Gabriel has just thrown at him.

"That's not my job, that's why they have marketeers," Gabriel replies, then shrugs, asking Alexander, "and you, have you found them yet?"

"Yes, but they may be infected already with fungus, we'll see, I may have to go back."

"The Yunnan Wilde banana, *Musa itinerans*, is certainly a

beauty in the photographs. I still think you will be successful, and we will see one yet," Gabriel replies.

"Who is that annoying woman who wouldn't get off my foot?"

"Ah, watch out. You don't want to make an enemy of Professor Green?"

"Why the hell not?"

"She's only the most intelligent woman at Oxbridge."

"You don't know many women." Alexander looks at Gabriel and immediately regrets his last comment. For different reasons, Gabriel raises his eyebrows and is just about to explain why Professor Green is the biggest boffin when they are both interrupted.

"Knock, knock." Standing by the door is Michael, not knocking anything, just making the noise. "Hello."

"This laboratory isn't open to the public. Can you telephone through the Porters' Lodge if you need to reach us please." Alexander is cross that Michael has interrupted their sacred Departmental territory. Not liking this oily man, he'd prefer to use his university privilege and kick him out when he can. Alexander picks up a knife he uses to open seeds and moves a seed pod resting on the bench ready to slice.

"I thought you might like to know the time of supper. After all, most are looking forward to you being there, what with your research being so interesting." Michael tries to flatter Alexander, but it falls on deaf ears. Gabriel wonders if Michael might be attempting just a little sarcasm. Alexander points the knife at Alexander.

"I told the Master I will attend and attend I will. But I do not take kindly to unannounced interruptions," Alexander retorts, knowing full well how Michael was just worried that numbers don't drop at dinner so he can keep his precious conference running next year. "You know, conferences are rapidly becoming more of a hindrance than a help to my research, Michael. I have to warn you that I'm unlikely to attend next year. I can do all the networking I need on my computer."

"That is a great shame to hear. Is that for me?" Michael tries to make light of the knife Alexander is now directly pointing at him. Gabriel walks over and takes the knife from Alexander's hand. Alexander shakes his head.

"This bloody conference!" Alexander shouts.

"Well, please don't make up your mind now. It's a long time before the next conference. Anything could happen. Dr Deersman, thank you for the chocolates. Look forward to seeing you later too."

"Pleasure," Gabriel replies. And with that, Michael makes a nervous departure, his tall figure now spotted outside the window, walking back across the cricket green to Catte College. Alexander looks out of the window and watches him talking to another Fellow.

"Look at him, schmoosing his next victim. And you bought him chocolates. And I thought you said you only gave them to people you like. What I'd give that man bears no repeating," Alexander sneers.

"What can I say? It's the new me."

"There is no new you, just the old one. Chocolates won't stop you being a lonely old man," Alexander rebuts. Gabriel frowns at his words, slightly hurt.

10
CHRISTMAS DINNER

Elizabeth could find no good excuse for avoiding tonight's conference supper. She thought about saying she overslept from a nap, or that she was feeling a little unwell. Perhaps a family emergency. But she liked to save those excuses for when she needed them most and eating supper didn't quite feel, well, severe enough to warrant wasting a 'white lie'.

Her decision wasn't easy though, as she was far from hungry, having eaten all of the sandwiches and most of the cakes on the stand on her tea-time tray – perhaps having succumbed to a little boredom. She was always telling Godric that a little boredom, emphasis on the word little, never did anyone any harm. Indeed, a little boredom was good for the brain. And it had been so for her this afternoon, as after taking a short nap Professor Elizabeth Green now feels altogether much better than she had just a few hours before. Her mind crisply alert.

So, she has put on her gown and joined her peers as they wander towards their late supper in Catte College. Elizabeth had already mentioned to her friend that she had forgotten to pack her snow boots. But unlike other peers she could now see kicking their shoes, Elizabeth's feet were not wet from the snow. The two shower caps from her hotel bathroom had come in handy, as she'd already slipped them over her shoes.

The College Senior Choir sing Leontovych's '*Carol of the Bells*' in the quad to supper guests arriving, their white and red gowns bringing smiles to the guests as a young soloist with a very high voice enchants everyone. Elizabeth finds it hard not to enjoy the music and stands watching them for a moment as others walk by. Eventually, the carol comes to an end, and they start singing Mateo Flecha's '*Riu, Riu, Chiu*'.

Just as Elizabeth is beginning to relax and taking off her shower caps, Michael sneaks up and stands right in front of her, blocking her view of the carol singers. Thinking he is the cleverest magician, he pulls a bunch of mistletoe out of his jacket sleeve. A few Fellows gasp as it is rather large, and they are unsure how he managed to hide such a huge bunch. Michael is just about to kiss Elizabeth without permission, having lifted the parasitic bunch of white berries above her head when, quicker than he, she lifts her handbag and with it swipes him across the face. It is at the point when he drops the mistletoe on the floor and puts his hand up to his cheek and shouts "Ow!" that she gets a proper look at his ridiculously loud suit and is about to shout at him when Gabriel pulls her away.

Dr Sandy Starborneck is close by and so to save face, Michael grabs Dr Starborneck's shoulders and leans her back for a full-on kiss. It looks far too intimate to occur in public. Michael then leaves abruptly, without a word to Sandy, jumping in front of the queue forming to go into the dining hall, his hat towering above everyone else as it disappears around a corner.

Just as Elizabeth is checking that she hasn't broken a strap on her bag, Haven joins her and Gabriel in the corridor outside the Dining Hall, the carol singers still pelting out their carol.

"I like your action lady," Haven says to Elizabeth, having seen Elizabeth whack Michael with her bag, "Haven. Pleased to meet you properly, and up close and personal. Not just waving from a window. Nice digs lady by the way. I'm Haven," and Haven gets out her water bottle and takes a sip of water before replacing it back in her bag.

"Hello," Elizabeth replies, "What were you doing earlier?"

"Sometimes a Haven headlock is called for. And believe me, when I headlock you, you will do as Haven says. I am afraid to say that Sandy isn't used to the juice. Gave it up years ago. And now for some reason, she's back on it with force these past few days, since this conference started. I think her threshold has plummeted too. It's all very odd. Making all kinds of shaky decisions. I'm just here to keep her on the straight and narrow, if you get my meaning."

"I'm not sure that I do."

"Friendship, it's thicker than gin. Merry Christmas!" And with that, Haven decides to check in her umbrella and elephant bag and loses her place in the queue.

"Quite the character," Gabriel offers.

'You're quite the character, Dr Deersman. Bringing everyone gifts. What are you hoping to achieve?" Elizabeth observes Gabriel, wondering why he is trying to be her friend.

"Christmas spirit. Please, it's Gabriel."

"We're not your children," Elizabeth replies as she wanders through into the College Banqueting Hall. From the ceiling, giant gold baubles hang from red velvet ribbons above the line of long dining tables. The tables are all heavily dressed with white linen, poinsettias and large green crackers. A tall Christmas tree emits scents of the forest, as blue lights sprinkled all over the boughs slowly pulse. Following the last straggling diners, the carol singers walk in, stand in a corner by the tree and start to sing 'We

Wish You A Merry Christmas', as Elizabeth and Gabriel walk towards a table. Before being able to choose who to sit with, both Sandy and Haven plonk themselves down opposite. Sandy's glazed look reveals she has not spent between afternoon tea and now sobering up. Far from it.

"You can come and look at my tomatoes, Professor Green, if you might be interested?" Gabriel tries to hold a sensible conversation with Elizabeth, nervous and aware that their table companions could ruin any reasonable discussion this evening.

"I love tomatoes! Can I come?" Sandy replies.

"I'm not sure you'd be interested," Gabriel says, "I only mention to Professor Green, as these tomatoes have been engineered to contain vitamins."

"I'm not sure I'd like to. Perhaps Haven might be more interested," Elizabeth suggests.

"GM crops, I don't think so!" Haven raises her voice.

"No, that's the point. These are natural–" Gabriel starts to explain his research, but Sandy thumps the table interrupting.

"Can we talk about something more interesting? I'm bored. Lady, lady." Sandy chips in, doing an impression of Haven, "What do you call that?" Sandy grabs a napkin Haven has been sketching the Christmas tree on. The tree has a face and the tree is covered in cars. "That's a terrible doodle."

"I'm allowed to dabble."

"It's like a kid's drawing," Sandy slurs. She picks up a cracker joke from the dining table and reads.

"What do you get when you cross a snowman with a vampire?" then waits for a response. But when she gets none, finishes the joke, "Frostbite!" Sandy laughs loudly. Haven groans, so Sandy defends it, "It's for the kiddies, isn't it? Christmas. For the kiddies."

"Do you have children?" Elizabeth asks Sandy.

"Lady, tell me everything about you, there's nothing to tell here. No husband, no family, free as a bird," Dr Sandy

Starborneck says to Elizabeth, almost not recognising her.

"That's Professor Green you spoke to earlier," Haven rolls her eyes and grabs Sandy's hands, which seem to be covered in icing, so they can't touch Elizabeth's gown. "Did you not drink any of that coffee?"

"Yes, and I had afternoon tea, and the port, and the sherry and the wine," Sandy hiccups, "you were there, lady."

"You really should pull yourself together, Dr Starborneck, or perhaps someone might take it the wrong way," Gabriel glares at the drunk academic, cross that she was interrupting his attempts at conversation with Elizabeth.

11
PETER RIDLETON IS MISSING

Despite being dark outside, the snow brightens everything as Inspector Abley is pulling up outside a house on Owlestone Road, Newnham; a quiet part of Cambridge where some might say a more mature community who like to think of themselves as a wiser generation have chosen to settle. They might tell you quietly that they are looking for peace, away from the tourists and a thousand bicycles, for a place where everyone still knows each other in the post office. And of Newnham, this is undoubtedly true. One could also reasonably surmise that if it is nightlife on a Friday evening being sought, it would not be sensible to stumble down Eltisley Avenue or Grantchester Street looking for it either. For although residents might tell you that they see their fair share of dancing and wild life, upon closer inquiry their regaled stories are merely of four-legged creatures dancing on their long lawns seen through their wildlife night-video-camera birthday gifts, which keep them entertained for hours. And this evening will be no different to many other evenings, with food left out for hungry foxes.

It was this place that Superintendent Raynott had taken great pleasure in sending Inspector Abley along with his new Sergeant, Sergeant Goodey, to investigate the disappearance of Peter Ridleton. Indeed, the Superintendent's last words were, "And, don't come back until you've found him!" Which would have been a tall order, had Peter Ridleton been buried in concrete shoes in the Cam by the mob, or cut into slices by an angry butcher wanting revenge over being jilted by his wife. These were things Sergeant Goodey was picturing in his head, having been helped along the way in his imaginings by a somewhat bored Inspector Abley, looking for ways to entertain himself in the car on the way over. Unfortunately, this case was nothing so glamorous.

Peter Ridleton indeed lived at this address. Mrs Ridleton, however, was in her nineties, deaf in one ear and deafer in the other, and not so spritely these days on her legs. So, hardly the glamour case most coppers might long to work on. Though, having been given a mobility scooter Mrs Ridleton was quite the whizz around the streets of Newnham, building up to a speed of at least twenty miles an hour when visiting Grantchester along the river path to run the community library. Which she still did, single-handedly. So most definitely not to be underestimated.

And now Peter Ridleton, as she had explained on the phone to Superintendent Raynott a good few times over the past twenty-four hours, had just disappeared into thin air. But Mrs Ridleton had not murdered Peter, nor had she buried him in the garden, or locked him out of the house. No, she had been phoning the police every hour, as Peter Ridleton was still missing and it was a complete mystery to everyone. And when Inspector Abley came round the first time, she had told him as much, over a slice of carrot and walnut cake and a cup of tea.

Now they have returned, and Sergeant Goodey jumps

out the car. Sergeant Goodey is not from Cambridge, and so his local knowledge is a little sketchy. He stretches and yawns loudly, and an elderly man walks past and tuts at him for causing a disturbance at this time in the early evening. Aside from this small encounter, Sergeant Goodey immediately notices the quiet in the air. He feels like he has stepped into a chocolate box picture with a Christmas tree in every window, curtains still open, fires burning and pretty Christmas wreaths on many of the doors. Some homes have fairy lights tastefully up in magnolia and willow trees. This part of Cambridge feels like a film set, Sergeant Goodey thinks, particularly when he sets eyes on the snowmen lined up in front gardens, adorned with very healthy-looking vegetables.

Inspector Abley steps out, having mildly enjoyed his harmless fun with Goodey in the car on the way over, and starts to rub his tummy as he stretches. When Mrs Ridleton opens the door, she is clutching some drawings.

"I saw your car, I've been waiting by the window you see, as my ears aren't what they were." She wobbles a little on her feet and shuffles back, beckoning them into her kitchen at the back of the house. Sergeant Goodey has taken off his hat and looks very sorry. He also notices her enormous ears.

"We will do our best, Mrs Ridleton, to find Peter," Goodey offers.

"Yes, I know you're from the police, I recognise our lovely Inspector Abley, but it is very late to be calling. Has something happened? Do you have bad news about Peter? Oh dear, let me sit first." Mrs Ridleton clutches Sergeant Goodey's hand in hers and won't let go. Sergeant Goodey is a little confused until he looks at Inspector Abley who points at his ear and shakes his head.

"It must be so hard, losing Mr Ridleton and just not knowing where he has gone," the Sergeant shouts this time.

"What? Yes, yes, but it is very hard not knowing where

Peter has gone," Mrs Ridleton says, not having heard a word Sergeant Goodey just said, and waiting for the Sergeant to answer.

"We will find him," Goodey replies, hoping something is getting through as they walk through the hall.

"I hope you find him," Mrs Ridleton continues, "I have sketches which I thought might help the case? Here, let me put more lights on. It's so dark in here." Inspector Abley is keeping remarkably quiet, hanging back as they enter the kitchen, his eyes skimming along the surfaces and wooden table in the middle, full of fruit and a teapot.

"Do you have any more of that lovely cake you made?" Inspector Abley finally asks loudly, also making eating signs, aware that there have to be some advantages to this trip.

"Oh, Inspector. Yes, how rude of me. Sit down, sit. Let me get a slice for you. Have you eaten your dinners yet? I expect so. I don't want to spoil them. Now let me think…" and she goes off to open a cupboard on the wall, putting down the sketches on the side, face down. Sergeant Goodey glares at Inspector Abley, for thinking about his stomach at a time like this.

"May I look at the sketches of Mr Ridleton?"

"Oh, yes dear." Mrs Ridleton hears Sergeant Goodey this time, as he has shouted very loud indeed. Sergeant Goodey turns over the sketches to see if he has seen Mr Ridleton before.

"I get about quite a bit. I might have seen him," he says as he turns the sketches and tries not to show his surprise.

"My great-grandson, little George, drew Peter when he came to visit in the summer. I knew I had them somewhere," Mrs Ridleton replies, opening a tin to reveal the tastiest looking coffee cake.

Sergeant Goodey stares down at an infant-aged child's drawings of a big ginger cat.

"I'm sure the Inspector has filled you in. It's so strange.

Peter went out yesterday morning to perform his ablutions, and never came back? I haven't seen him since! Dear, he is hard to miss. At first, I thought Peter had abandoned me for three doors down and that young couple. Well, he has such a large retirement pension, he can afford tasty treats. I've seen them buy it countless times in the local shop. But after the third time of stressing to me that they have not taken Peter hostage with promises of salmon, I have to accept that someone must else have kidnapped him. He is, after all, such a handsome fellow."

Sergeant Goodey looks at the childlike drawings again and up at Inspector Abley, who nods and tucks into the largest slice of coffee cake.

"Tea, Inspector?"

"That would be lovely, Mrs Ridleton. Thank you."

"Would you like some tea, Inspector?"

Inspector Abley nods and smiles.

"When exactly did Peter go missing?" Sergeant Goodey asks again, still with a raised voice.

"Shall I make some tea?" Mrs Ridleton looks at the Inspector, and he nods again, not hearing Goodey, so she continues, "Well, I was making a cake. This cake in fact," Mrs Ridleton smiles at Inspector Abley, shovelling in cake, "can I tempt you with another slice, Inspector?" the Inspector, with a mouthful of cake, nods back and smiles, watching Mrs Ridleton start to shakily cut another slice with an unnecessarily large knife. "Yes, and I was cooking, and then once the cake had baked, I didn't see him again all day yesterday. Or today. It's very distressing." Mrs Ridleton's eyes start to spike with tears, and she pulls out a handkerchief and wipes them away.

"You were cooking when Peter went missing?" Sergeant Goodey asks.

"Would you like some cake, Sergeant?" Mrs Ridleton says, not having heard Sergeant Goodey.

Sergeant Goodey looks around the house and spots a

pantry in the corner of the room and puts two and two together. He walks over to it and opens the door.

"Sergeant, that's my pantry! The cake is over here, please, I have all my jams stored in the cold in there. Don't let the heat in." But Goodey doesn't listen to Mrs Ridleton; he has his own hunch. He opens the door, and out runs a very bored and angry ginger cat.

"Peter!" Mrs Ridleton shouts. "Where did you come from?"

"The pantry, Mrs Ridleton," replies Sergeant Goodey.

"Good idea, I'll put the tea on. Yes. Oh! Peter! Sardines for you. Now, where did I put those sardines?" She picks up a tin and gives it to the Sergeant to open. Peter runs back under the Sergeant's feet. As the stinky fish gets all over Goodey's shirt as it bursts out of the tin, it makes Abley chuckle.

"You solved your first case," he smiles at Sergeant Goodey, who spoons out the tin of sardines to a purring cat. "Purrfect!"

12
CLEANING FOR CHRISTMAS DAY

Godric feels so Christmassy! He watches the dogs play in the snow in the garden in the dark. They are covered in snow clumps. He's not sure he can let them back in. But then again, the house is a mess, so what difference would it make. Ben is cuddling next to him, pulling a half-eaten banana from behind him out of the sofa, aware that they'd better start tidying up soon.

"Is your Nanna coming home this evening?"

"Yes, she said straight after her talk. So this evening," as the doorbell tinkles.

"What if that's her?"

"Nah, it takes a while to drive back in the Talbot."

Ben opens the front door to his Nanna's home in Cambridge and drops his jaw. Standing outside on the gravel drive in the evening snow are three Father Christmases. But there is something altogether not quite traditional about their attire. Ben doesn't know where to look, but cannot stop staring at their chests, bare to the world under long white beards, or their legs, trouserless down to their snow boots, save for their modesty being covered in white tinselly pouches. Godric comes bounding up, hugs him from behind and smiles.

"Why make cleaning dull? Bunny doesn't have to know, remember?" Godric touches his nose. "In you come, boys, boots off." Three Father Christmases walk into Professor Green's house just as the next-door neighbour, Mrs Cloud from number twenty-four, walks by, eyes wide open as she gazes upon three bare-cheeked bottoms. Clearly, the Father Christmases are not wearing Santa briefs either!

"Evening Mrs Cloud."

"Good evening, Godric."

"Bit chilly, isn't it?"

"Yes, er, yes. A lot of—" Mrs Cloud's eyes nearly pop out of her head as the three Santa's are now bending over to take off their boots. A couple pull out cleaning equipment from their Santa jackets.

"Snow?" Godric finishes Mrs Cloud's sentence for her, looking at her open jaw.

"Yes."

"Happy Christmas!" Godric says and smiles as he ushers everyone in and waves goodbye to Mrs Cloud, who hasn't had such an eyeful for a number of years, what with Mr Cloud having taken a liking to wearing thermals.

13
FATHER CHRISTMAS DAY

Everyone has been seated in the banqueting hall in Catte College for some time. The noise of chatter and clinking glasses blend in with catering staff to-ing and fro-ing with additional courses, more wine and fresh cutlery for those that have dropped their own. Professor Elizabeth Green and Dr Gabriel Deersman have tried their best to enjoy Christmas supper. Gabriel is wearing a red cracker hat. Elizabeth has been given a very tasty vegan Christmas dinner, and she is now extremely full.

However, both Sandy and Haven have done their best to bring both of them into every conversation, no matter how dull, about the machinations of their lives, whether it is Haven having repeatedly told Sandy that she needs to stop drinking and help her with her research while they are in Oxford, or Sandy telling her friend, Haven, to chill and that she is the most uptight hippy that Sandy has ever met. The final straw for Elizabeth is when Dr Sandy Starborneck falls off the back of her chair.

"Oof, haha. Oh my god, these chairs are so flimsy," Sandy says, from a very unladylike position, having bumped her arm and calling out a delayed "Ow!" about the pain emanating from her elbow.

"Here, c'mon," Gabriel rushes around the table to help Haven pick Sandy back up onto her chair. Haven then tries to take Sandy's drink away, but Sandy grabs it back.

"Hey! I need that. Painkiller!" She takes a swig and rubs her elbow.

"Are you having a good Christmas, Sandy?" Gabriel asks, trying to calm things down.

"Methinks my enemies are circling. Christmas isn't a happy time for everyone, you know," Dr Sandy Starborneck replies.

"Shush, everyone." Michael, sitting on the top table with the Master, taps the side of his glass with a small spoon and says, "I just want to say a few words."

"Can this get any worse?" Elizabeth mutters under her breath, and Gabriel hears her and replies, "Depends on the length of his speech."

"Ah, fabulous!" Dr Sandy Starborneck shouts and claps for Michael. "I've always loved Oxford. The Colleges always know how to put on an after-dinner speech! Speech!" But Michael glares back at Sandy for interrupting him, and shakes his head slightly, which Elizabeth notices.

"As many of you may know, I have been running these conferences now for ten years," he continues, "so this year is a special anniversary. Plants might not be rockets or fast cars, but they sustain us. They are thankfully still everywhere, though we are doing our best to destroy them and deplete the rainforests—"

"Boo!" Haven shouts. Michael glares at her, but her interruption encourages some to use it as a cue to start talking among themselves.

"As I was saying, plants are important." Michael pauses, then continues to waffle on about how he knew he was doing the right thing organising the conference series, and if it wasn't for him, blah, blah, blah, but people have already started to tune out.

Elizabeth spots the Master of Catte College wave at the

carol singers, milling in the corner waiting for instructions, to start on their next carol. They begin '*We Wish You a Merry Christmas*', finally interrupting Michael's umpteenth speech to everyone's relief. Dr Sandy Starborneck gets up to dance by her chair to the carol. Some watch with disdain, disappointed in the loss of proper decorum. Elizabeth is just pleased that this signals that the evening is nearly over, and she can retire to bed.

It is at this point that Dr Sandy Starborneck spots Father Christmas, as does everyone else, coming into the room with a sack of presents. She can't contain herself and rushes over to the tree to await her gift as he approaches.

"Santa! Santa!" Sandy shouts.

"Oh, dear god," Haven utters from the table behind. "Sandy! Come and sit down for chrissake!"

Gabriel, Dr Haven Usrey and Professor Elizabeth Green wonder which of them should get up to bring Dr Sandy Starborneck back to the table, as they and many others now notice that she has grabbed Father Christmas's hands and is trying to dance with him.

Father Christmas struggles with Dr Sandy Starborneck, and then everything happens in slow motion as Dr Starborneck falls backwards, grabbing the Christmas tree. But the tree comes down on top of her. She hits her head on the wooden floor, and those closest hear the crack as they see her strewn across a pile of Christmas presents already under the tree. Father Christmas takes one look at the commotion, and Dr Sandy Starborneck's motionless body, looks up at the dinner guests, and then turns and runs out of the room before anyone can prevent him.

"Stop Father Christmas. He's getting away!" shouts Michael. He looks at people for a split second, but no one is moving, so he starts to run towards the exit. He shouts back, "Someone, help her. Call an ambulance!"

Dinner guests rush over to Dr Starborneck and lift the tree from her body. Baubles have shattered, and the tinsel and lights now hang precariously close to Dr Sandy

Starborneck's face as Gabriel joins in and tries to bring order to the area so that there is more space for Sandy. Elizabeth bends down to Dr Sandy Starborneck.

"Is there a doctor?" Gabriel shouts.

"I think it might be too late for that," Elizabeth replies, holding her fingers against Sandy's neck, and watching the blood trickling from behind her skull, her eyes fixed on something far away.

14
A FRIEND IN NEED

Elizabeth has reluctantly returned to the hotel, as she had wanted to stick around and interview everyone about Dr Sandy Starborneck's death. What they'd seen, what they'd heard. How well they knew her. The Master of College, however, had other ideas. She knew he was determined to have as little fuss and gossip about the incident as possible. Everyone was escorted out and the College closed for the evening. Elizabeth had indeed walked out with the choir, who inappropriately perhaps, continued to sing '*We Wish You a Merry Christmas*' as everyone started to leave the College and disappear off into the night, possibly disappointed that they didn't get to finish their set-pieces.

Elizabeth presumed the Master had then called the police and her parting words were to warn him to cordon off the area. But he was having none of it. Michael jumped in deciding to be the Master's right-hand man, and although usually the Master would shudder at the thought, on this occasion it suited his interests, repeating that this was just a horrible accident and that it was sensible to call it a night, ushering people out, but they'd see everyone on time for the conference tomorrow, as normal.

Elizabeth couldn't leave it, however, and had to call the one person who would know what to do. So she picked up the telephone in her suite and dialled.

*

"What are you doing in the Free Press?" Elizabeth Green listens to Inspector Abley's excuses as he explains how he was only having the one at his Cambridge local pub and did she have a camera on him? How did she know? "That's what you used to say before, please go home." She listens again. "Please go home. I need to talk to you. I can't talk to you there. Yes, there should be a parcel as well. Godric helped me choose. I need to speak to you properly. Please, go home." Elizabeth fiddles with her coat, and despite the chaos that ensued after Dr Sandy Starborneck's death, she takes off her dry shoes, having not forgotten the shower caps.

*

Inspector Abley opens the front door to his rented flat in Prospect Row, his conscience having been guilt-tripped out of the Free Press by Elizabeth's voice. Though he was only washing down Mrs Ridleton's cake in his own mind, he was annoyed that she was probably right. Two pints had turned into three much quicker than he intended.

Inspector Bob Abley had rented a second-floor apartment in this quiet street as it was the closest he could find to the Police Station, which meant the longest time in bed. He also liked the lack of cars in this part of Cambridge - as only residents would use these roads. He loved the way the streetlights were hidden in the tall trees and the peace. And, despite it being a little hidden gem right in the centre of things, with three pubs in one hundred yards, in fact these days he was finding bed more appealing than staying out late. Sleep took all his troubles away, and thankfully he had no trouble finding it and was always in the land of nod as soon as his head hit the pillow.

So here he was. He looked around the room. His sofa, a TV, one armchair, a table and two chairs by the window from which he could see a little way down Warkworth Street, a stone's throw from his office on Parker's Piece. But he hadn't felt the desire to do anything with it, unsure what would happen with his family home on Park Parade by Jesus Green now up for sale. He found it hard to pass it and tried to avoid the area when going for walks, and he had no desire to buy it, with too many memories. So, for now, this was home. The important thing, he told himself, was he had his golf clubs and a putter in the living room. What more could he need? But he knew he was fooling himself and missed Maureen terribly. Somehow, nothing felt worth it.

Abley keeps the phone up to his ear. "Are you listening to me?" he hears as his lobe is currently being bitten off by Elizabeth's fretting that he has an empty stomach, he shouldn't drink, can't he ever learn, she can't help him next time he loses his job. He's lost one wife to his next-door neighbour. He won't get another in a hurry if he keeps up his bad habits. Abley is beginning to wonder why he is still listening when he picks up the parcel that came earlier and puts Elizabeth on speaker, putting his phone down on the table in his flat.

"All right, what's so important? I can't find my scissors. God, woman, you've wrapped it like it's a bomb or fine china." Abley pauses – "Tell me it isn't either" – then he listens to Elizabeth who is clearly growing irritated.

"Just open it. Have you opened it yet?"

"No, I'm looking for scissors!" Abley walks into the kitchen as the phone is still on the table. Elizabeth keeps talking, her voice travelling into his flat through his phone.

"I've told you that you need to organise yourself in that

place, make one of the bedrooms an office. Then you'd have all your essentials in one place. I'm not coming round to do it for you. But if you can't even find scissors, you're not getting on top of things." Thankfully, Abley hasn't heard a word of this and just comes in on Elizabeth saying, "Gerald bought me these lovely scissors. They were embroidery scissors, and the cutting mechanism was the beak. Blue-green and shimmering, like a peacock. I love them. Want me to buy you a pair?"

"I think I'm good, but what is it? Why the demand I go home? Was it the present?" Abley shakes his head, pulling a face at the phone.

*

Elizabeth lies down across her bed. She puts her feet up in the air. She has done this for many years, as her mother told her it was an excellent method of preventing varicose veins. She listens to Bob Abley through the telephone receiver.

"Yes, yes Catte College. She's dead – this woman at my conference. I can't believe it. I was just talking to her. It's horrific. She's gone." Elizabeth listens to Bob Abley, then continues, "No, they didn't have vegan custard, but the Christmas pudding was vegan and very fruity. Enough about the food, have you opened it yet? No, well listen to me while you do."

Elizabeth rolls her feet around in circles as she speaks. "I know it's not the right thing to say, but I still have my talk tomorrow, so I'm stuck here for another day. I was so looking forward to putting my feet up at home. It's such hard work here. You've no idea. I have to talk to people. People. They're everywhere! Why would anyone think I would want to do that? And now this?"

Elizabeth shakes her head. "How can I leave when there's a death right in front of me and, let me tell you, a suspicious one at that. It's ghastly." Elizabeth listens to

Inspector Abley. "Yes, that's what I was about to tell you. Well, if you spoke to some, you'd believe she just fell over and hit her head." Elizabeth listens to Abley. "I didn't want it to break, no, I always wrap things like that. Are you listening to me? I saw a woman die." She pauses. "Yes, yes. And now, no, I didn't have anything to do with it! Bob! Listen. One minute she was dancing about with Father Christmas, and the next minute she was stone cold dead. Then Father Christmas ran away."

Elizabeth listens to Inspector Abley, then replies, "No, I know there are two layers of wrapping, that's the fun!" She listens again. "Yes, he just ran. The consensus in the room was Father Christmas pushed her. They haven't caught him." Elizabeth stops twirling her feet and drops her legs to the bed. "I went to look for him on the streets with Gabriel." She listens to Abley. "No, he's not an angel. No! He's just a scientist at the conference. I'm being serious. No, I haven't been drinking. We looked everywhere, and Father Christmas had disappeared into the night. Well, the Master chucked us all out. The strange thing was, at dinner, just before she died, Dr Starborneck said 'Methinks my enemies are circling'. Plural. Enemies. What does that mean? She was a peer at my conference. It feels too close." Then Elizabeth pulls up her legs into the air again, her back on the bed, and starts riding an imaginary bicycle, her legs peddling in the air.

*

"You need me to come over and arrest Father Christmas?" Inspector Abley stops cutting with the scissors, waiting for Elizabeth to reply. There is silence coming from the phone on the table. "Just over a week before Christmas Day? I mean, there will be some unhappy children. Elizabeth?"

"No, no, I mean, maybe?" Elizabeth's voice comes out of the phone on the table.

"What's going on over there? I thought you hated conferences. What you even doing there?" Inspector Abley continues to cut at the box that Elizabeth has wrapped what now looks like a present in, as he has got down to the second layer of wrapping paper and is growing quite irritated by the amount of tape Elizabeth has used.

"What was odd was that as he ran away, he kept his sack of presents over his shoulder. You'd think if you were running from a crime scene, you'd drop them?"

"Who?"

"Father Christmas!" Elizabeth shouts through the phone.

"You can't go meddling over there, Elizabeth. Lemon's only just started with Oxford Police, Thames Valley" Abley shakes his head at the phone.

"He's here?"

"Yes, why don't you ask him to arrest Father Christmas? Ho, ho, ho. I'm sure he'd love you for that."

"Why's he here?" Elizabeth is surprised by this news.

"Couldn't work with me, apparently. I've turned him off Cambridge altogether," Abley says. "He's in Oxford now, put in a transfer." Abley throws the present in frustration.

"You haven't just thrown that present have you?"

Abley wonders how on earth Elizabeth could know that and looks at his phone to check he hasn't got video call on. But remembers Elizabeth doesn't even have a mobile. He scratches his head, then picks up the present and scissors again and cuts into the paper. He makes a hole in it and can finally see a string of fairy lights and manages to pull them out.

"Christmas lights! Thank you!" Inspector Abley smiles as they are uniformed policemen with Father Christmas hats on. He drapes them over the mirror above the mantelpiece and plugs them in.

"Godric found them on some weird internet site, custom-made. Have you seen the other present?"

"Cake, hmm, how lovely," Abley knows what Elizabeth's cooking is like and worries it is one of hers and she is going to make him eat it so she can hear. Abley grimaces to himself, then looks around in case she is somehow watching and breaks open the cake box. There is a small wooden knife on a white cake with a Father Christmas on it and a snowman. He cuts a slice and takes a tentative bite.

"Orange and Lemon cake," Elizabeth says. "Have you tasted it? Are you being quiet because it's nice?"

"I have to go now. Thank you. This is tasty," Abley lies, holding his cheek having hit something hard in the cake and almost breaking a tooth. He picks out the object. It is a burnt clove. "One thing – leave Lemon alone. Don't interfere. I've ruined his life already. Please don't make it worse. Please." Then he kills the call on his mobile on the table and turns it off.

Abley puts the TV on to the cricket channel. It's a repeat, but he needs to concentrate on calming down as his call has made him think about Lemon, and his guilt is bubbling close to the surface.

*

Elizabeth puts her feet down and ponders on the fact that Sergeant Lemon is now working in Oxford. Well, I never. She wonders whether to disturb him. She is itching to call Lemon. She looks at the clock. It has gone midnight. She will find him tomorrow. He's sure to find out anyway, as there will be a post-mortem.

In the meantime, Elizabeth needs to be somewhere. She pulls a serviette out of her bag and opens it up. Inside is a glass with lipstick around the edge and a tiny bit of nail polish on the side. Elizabeth wraps it back up, puts her coat on and leaves the hotel room. Snow, or no snow, she has to find out.

15
A DEAD DOCTOR

The next morning and Professor Elizabeth Green cannot stay away from Catte College any longer. She has dreamt about a laughing Father Christmas pushing over Dr Sandy Starborneck, and presents spewing out everywhere, knocking over all the carol singers like pins in a bowling alley. She is convinced something is awry. Elizabeth wants to speak to the Master and share her concerns. She must also find Sergeant Lemon and tell him about Father Christmas. She hears Inspector Abley's voice in her head telling her to leave Lemon alone, but Bob's not here, so he doesn't get a say!

Elizabeth pulls back the curtains to see an Oxford tucked up under a snowy blanket. Despite her room being lovely and toasty, she feels a chill from behind the windowpane. Dr Sandy Starborneck is dead, and this has changed everything about her trip. Elizabeth stares out into the darkness. No cars trundle up or down St Giles' this early in the morning, only a brave gritter coughing out its contents.

Elizabeth notices a sparkly tree on the island in the middle of the road, decorated with paper wishes by local children. It is now laden down with a heavy white load. It makes Elizabeth feel sad, that no one is looking at the burden it carries for others. For a moment, she thinks about Gerald. He'd go and shake it for her, understanding her peculiar empathies and anthropomorphism. Then Elizabeth remembers that she doesn't have any boots and sighs. No shower cap will protect her feet from the avalanche before her. She decides breakfast might be in order and picks up the room's telephone.

"Room service? Yes, I'd like the vegan cooked breakfast. Please, I'm in a hurry. Thank you." Elizabeth looks at her watch. Fifteen minutes past six.

*

Not long after demolishing some warm hearty food, and after a very kind member of staff has leant her two large bags, she wraps them around her shoes and up her legs, tying them with elastic bands over her trousers, then trudges through the snow towards Catte College, her snuggly duffel coat protecting her from the cold and her face almost hidden under a heavy hood, perfect for protecting against the snow coming down thick and fast. Once through the Porters' Lodge, Professor Green spots Dr Gabriel Deersman, in another Christmas jumper.

"Breakfast? I'm just going," he says, acknowledging her arrival, trying to see in under her duffel hood up over her head and scarf wrapped around her chin.

"I've eaten, thank you. Isn't the dining hall closed anyway? Surely, after last night's terrible tragedy? Aren't the police there?" Elizabeth's green eyes are poking out above her scarf and bore into Gabriel.

"True, undergrads have gone down, but a significant part of the college is post-grad. Far too many of them to take away their food, Professor Green. There'd be a riot. I have to admit. I think I'd be banging down the doors too. I'm famished! So, the show must go on. Terrible thing, though."

"How can you be famished at a time like this?" Elizabeth then remembers how much food she herself has tucked away this morning. "What do you think happened last night?"

"Perhaps the snow makes me hungry. As for the poor woman, you saw as much as I did. She seemed to hit her head. I think that's the consensus doing the rounds. You know there was no need to come in after the shock, the conference doesn't start until—"

"Hmm, doing the rounds." Elizabeth interrupts. "I was looking for the Master."

"Expect he's eating too." Gabriel slaps his belly indicating the Master's voracious appetite and rotund figure, and nods to the Banquet Hall, which doubles up as the regular dining hall.

Elizabeth and Gabriel walk past the conference room, with all the exhibition material still up. She pokes her head around the door, but the place is deathly empty.

"How has everyone known not to come in this morning? It's awfully quiet of conference attendees."

"Um, probably the agenda," Gabriel replies helpfully, "says a 3 pm start."

"I read that," Elizabeth lies.

"Of course you did," Gabriel chuckles, aware that Elizabeth has not been enjoying the conference, "but do check it to make sure you don't miss the keynote," he adds jokily.

"I'm giving that," Elizabeth replies curtly, glancing furtively at Gabriel. Surely he knows she has top bill. And why is he so cheerful, after what has happened?

"That's right," Gabriel replies, knowing all along and just teasing her. "But I see that Michael has moved it to the day after tomorrow. Did you see the amends online?"

"What? No, he can't do that. I'm leaving today after I've given it'," Elizabeth protests, cross that Michael has moved it without consulting her. She wonders, given what has happened to Dr Sandy Starborneck, whether she will be leaving at all.

Elizabeth walks into the College Banquet Hall, which is still dressed for Christmas, and spots a familiar face and the tallest man in the room, Sergeant Lemon. Lemon is standing near the uprighted Christmas tree, its lights and decorations looking a little like it's been redecorated by a small child after last night's topple. Lemon wears his crooked smile as he looks down at the Master's head, the two of them deep in conversation; the Master is holding a long baguette and eating from one end of what appears to be the largest sausage sandwich Elizabeth's ever seen, onions dribbling down his shirt. Elizabeth spots Haven, sitting alone at a table. Although she is tempted to rush over to Lemon, there is something about Haven's stare into the distance that pulls Elizabeth over.

"Hello, Haven. What a dreadful business," Elizabeth offers, her duffel hood still up.

"Oh, hello," Haven replies, in a half daze.

"You look like you haven't slept," Elizabeth observes, sitting down next to Haven, who is playing with a Christmas gingerbread Father Christmas. "And that's not a proper breakfast."

"How can I sleep?" Haven looks up at Elizabeth, with bloodshot eyes, still wearing what she had on last night.

"I'm sorry for your loss," Elizabeth replies.

"What did she expect?"

"I beg your pardon?"

"She was a drunk, I mean," Haven replies.

"Do you think that's to blame then?"

"If that Santa hadn't of pushed her. I want to rip his head off!" Haven takes the biscuit and rips off the head of Father Christmas and throws the biscuit back down.

"Where have you been?" Elizabeth picks up the biscuit from the table and places it back on Haven's plate.

"I don't know. My friend." Haven goes back to staring into space.

"What were you and Sandy Starborneck really rowing about yesterday?"

"Come again?"

"On the street, out on St Giles'?"

"There was nothing to see from your fancy-schmancy hotel, I already told you," Haven replies. "You're very English, aren't you?" Haven breaks a tiny smile, then thinks of her friend, "Oh, I can't remember, it doesn't matter now. My best friend is dead!" Haven thumps the table, and for a moment all those eating breakfasts in the hall fall silent. She doesn't say anything until the din of chatter starts up again around them, "I think you need to arrest Santa. From where I come from, he's more into giving the presents, you dig? We don't have Santa hitmen." Haven picks at her food.

"You think he was hired?" Elizabeth asks.

"Didn't you see what I saw? You saw what I saw, don't play games."

"What did you see?"

"Oh my god already, I saw Santa Claus kill my friend, lady. And so did you, don't deny it. I want to know what is happening to track him down." Haven looks around. "I'm not a big fan of the fuzz, but where are they?" Haven looks around but can't see any uniformed officers. Haven picks up the head of the gingerbread Father Christmas and crumbles it between her fingers.

"Sandy was drinking an awful lot last night, you said it yourself," Elizabeth replies.

"Yes, she was. I don't deny it. I was trying to keep her safe. It was so out of character. She doesn't drink. And then, all of a sudden, she starts again. But what of it?" As Haven is about to open up to Elizabeth, they both feel taps on their shoulders.

"Ah, Professor Green." Michael appears from behind Elizabeth. Gabriel walks over to listen. "Glad this dreadful accident hasn't kept you away. Please do help yourself to breakfast. Although the conference doesn't officially start until this afternoon, our caterers have joined forces with the regular kitchen staff this morning, and I'm thrilled to say that breakfast is complimentary." They all now watch the Master take another large bite of his baguette.

"Accident?" Elizabeth says, finally pulling down her duffel hood to reveal her unruly curls. "Whatever gave you that idea?"

"Well, yes, Dr Green. I mean, we all saw it. Dr Starborneck fell," Michael replies a little defensively.

"Some think she was pushed by Father Christmas," Elizabeth says and gives Michael Pussett a beady stare. "And it's Professor." Haven delivers a high five to Elizabeth's resting hand, which makes Elizabeth pull away a little, not liking high fives in general.

"Of course, you're entitled to your opinion, Professor Green. And I've heard you're a bit of a sleuth? But the fact of the matter is, what you're saying, well, I haven't heard that from anyone else. And it's not a good idea to go around stirring," Michael replies.

"She's not the only one who thinks that," Haven chips in. "Oh, it was Santa all right. And I'm going to find him," and she throws some bread at Michael.

"I haven't said what I think, actually, but we need to investigate. I think we may need to postpone the conference," Elizabeth suggests matter-of-factly to Michael.

"Oh, no, no, no. Look, it's nearly Christmas, and this was a terrible tragedy. But the police are treating it as an accident. The Master informed me this morning as such, and the conference will continue as normal," Michael stresses, adding, "I know what I saw. I saw a woman fall and hit her head. I appreciate you believe what you think you saw. But the accident happened. Let's focus on getting through the next couple of days. I really hope you don't disappoint your audience and are happy to continue to deliver the keynote speech. Do let me know if you decide to change your mind."

"Please don't tell me what you think I might be feeling, Mr Pussett," Elizabeth frowns at Michael. "One minute your tongue is caressing Dr Starborneck's tonsils, and now she's dead and, you seem unperturbed. All you seem to care about is your wretched conference. And I cannot give the keynote the day after tomorrow, as I will be leaving today. I didn't intend to be here for the entire conference. My Head of Department made a strict promise. Perhaps you should check with your keynote speaker before you move the date."

Elizabeth leaves Michael before he can say anymore, and leans into Gabriel and whispers, "Suspect numero uno," as she looks back at Michael, rubbing his head and Haven stopping him from sitting down with her.

"You're leaving?" Gabriel asks.

"I hate conferences, he broke the terms of the invitation," says Elizabeth, turning. "Now excuse me, Gabriel, but there is someone I must speak to."

"Professor Green, please," Gabriel replies. But Professor Elizabeth Green has already left his company.

*

Sergeant Lemon has spotted Elizabeth from the corner of his eye and given her the biggest smile. Elizabeth thinks how much better a welcome this is than that handsy overbearing two-bit conference organiser. The Master takes another bite from his sandwich and nods at Elizabeth.

"Good morning Professor Green, we welcome you into our humble abode. How are the fens? Norwich? Thetford?" the Master asks, inviting Elizabeth into this conversation with Sergeant Lemon, being a little bored of it himself.

"Morning Master. The fens are as beautiful as ever, thank you for asking. Teeming with biodiversity. How's Swindon, Reading and I mustn't forget to ask after

Aylesbury?" Elizabeth replies.

"Not a clue, good woman, not a clue. Not long for the big East Anglia flood if the IPCC has it right. You'll be beating our doors down then. No doubt about it." The Master is slightly more interested in the demise of Cambridge due to climate change than any trifle from the past twenty-four hours.

"They'll have to drag me away first, Master. I shall live on a punt before I leave. But yes, it might be an idea to turn off some of these lights." Elizabeth looks up at the prolific number of ceiling lights in the Banquet Hall. "Anyone would think you were single-handedly attempting to flood us all?"

"Touché. I was just telling the police here that Dr Sandy Starborneck was a little worse for wear last night. I've never seen anything so unsporting as a scuffle over presents with Father Christmas. Not the kind of thing one sees in Oxford. Perhaps you've been bringing some other place's habits with you, Professor? Perhaps they rubbed off on the attendees?"

"Dr Sandy Starborneck, I believe, was educated here and was returning. She has never set foot in Cambridge, nor will now sadly. Game and match." Elizabeth turns to Sergeant Lemon, who is used to this and has tuned out. "I wonder if they knew each other?" She asks him. "It seemed very odd that Father Christmas ran away. Had it been an accident, he would have surely stayed. It's so lovely to see you." Elizabeth smiles at Sergeant Lemon.

"I know, what a nice surprise." Sergeant Lemon smiles and then hugs Elizabeth, much to her delight. They have a moment where she looks him up and down.

"You look so well," she offers.

"I'll take that. So do you."

"We know each other from Cambridge, Master. An excellent policeman." Elizabeth smiles again, caught up in the joy of seeing a familiar face in this other place.

"Right, well, I'll leave you to it, Sergeant. Let me know

if there is anything else you need. Professor," The Master touches Elizabeth affectionately on the arm to indicate his admiration. But, now with plans for his busy day, he walks off, leaving the two friends to catch up.

"What are you doing here?" Lemon asks, "No, wait. You're at the conference. I'm a detective. Doh," Lemon is unusually relaxed in Elizabeth's presence and beams at her, clearly pleased to see his old friend.

"Where are all the other police? The SOCOs? Why such a small cordon?" Elizabeth looks at the police tape around the tree and presents, about ten-foot square.

"Oh, my Inspector thought it didn't sound suspicious," Lemon offers, adding, "they came and went last night. Took photos, few fingerprints. But the College had already tidied up. It was a busy night last night by the time they got here according to the station. I've been on lots of fights, and drunken incidents in Oxford before the police on shift could attend. Christmas eh? We're stretched everywhere." Lemon raised his eyebrows.

"Hang on, what do you mean?" Elizabeth asks.

"The area had already been cleaned."

"By whom?"

Lemon looks at his notes "I spoke to the conference organiser, a Mr Michael Pussett, and he said the College was keen to get the tree back on its feet, then they tidied up around it. The staff, he said. They washed around the blood. Our guys got to that, but everything else. He's an odd one. Really up himself, isn't he? Arrogant and smarmy," Lemon says. Elizabeth looks at the cordon and then at all the people coming and going into breakfast.

"There's no way any evidence could be used now from here."

"It's okay, we're still looking for the person dressed as Father Christmas," Lemon offers.

"He's hardly going to dress up again in that costume now, is he?" Elizabeth says.

"Did you get a good look at him? Could you identify

him if you had to."

"Of course," she replies.

"Terrific!"

"He was wearing a red hat with a white pompom on the top, had a large white beard and a red outfit. He was carrying a sack of presents."

"I've missed you," Lemon replies, looking at the blood. "Well, we're doing a post-mortem to confirm the cause. As I say, my Inspector thinks it was just an accident. Drunk woman falls and hits her head. So at the moment, we are not treating it as—"

"Murder," Elizabeth interrupts. Lemon rolls his eyes, knowing in his heart that if she has suspicions, they are probably founded. Here we go again.

16
LEMON

It is noon, and Professor Elizabeth Green sits outside the Vaults Garden cafe in the snow, drinking soup from a mug and looking up at the Radcliffe Camera. She watches her breath leave her mouth and can't feel her toes, but wants to speak to Sergeant Lemon in private, away from the Master and the conference organiser, Michael Pussett. As she waits, she wonders if Godric is walking the dogs in the snow and if he is making sure he melts the ice balls that collect in their feet when the dogs get home, so they don't get chilblains.

Liz blows her hot soup in a mug, and it isn't long before a police car shoots over the cobbles and parks just outside the cafe, leaving its engine running. Sergeant Lemon opens the door on the passenger side and gestures for Elizabeth to get inside. She picks up her soup and walks over.

"Don't you want a hot drink? Soup? They've got alcohol-free mulled wine, though I don't know what it's like." Elizabeth asks, but Lemon shakes his head. "Can I bring this in the car? Why the cloak and dagger?"

"One, it's cold. Two, this is my patch and people will

talk if I'm relaxing in a cafe on duty." Lemon regrets allowing Elizabeth to bring her mug into the car when fresh smells of vegetable soup soon flood his nostrils. "Don't spill it. My super will have my guts for garters," Lemon pulls up the handbrake, but leaves the engine running to keep the heater going, while they sit in Radcliffe Square, going nowhere.

"Guts for garters?"

"Another of Inspector Abley's overused sayings, now ingrained in my head. When will I be rid?" Lemon rolls his eyes at the sky.

"Bob told me to leave you alone, so I'm probably in his bad books right now," Elizabeth replies.

"Right." Lemon doesn't want to be drawn. He left Cambridge to get away from his old Inspector's drinking and having to make excuses for him all the time on the job. And yes, he missed Professor Green, but he wasn't ready to forgive Inspector Abley. He sure as hell didn't want to know how he was doing.

"Yes, he's still Bob. But I suppose he's got to start somewhere," Elizabeth offers.

"I must admit, I was surprised to see you here. Brought it all back." Lemon tries to change the subject again off Inspector Abley. "You didn't have anything to do with it, did you? I mean, did you know," Lemon gets out his notepad, "Dr Sandy Starborneck, did you know her?"

"First, no, I didn't cause her death. Second, I really do think it's a murder."

"It could still be an accident."

"Then, why are you here?"

"Because in all the time I've known you, you've never been wrong." Lemon blows out a sigh. "If it's anyone, it's that mad hippy."

"Dr Haven Usrey. Hmm. What's this new patch like?"

"Drunk Fellows, undergrad pranks, revelry from the local pubs. Home from home. No missing statues or poisoned apples though."

"Give it time," Elizabeth replies.

"Been quiet. Then you come over, and suddenly we're doing autopsies."

"Will you tell me what you find?"

"You're asking me to break the law." Lemon looks right at Elizabeth.

"Not really." Elizabeth stares straight back.

"Yes, really."

"Will you?"

"No. But if there is anything to investigate, I'll let you know,"

"That's the same thing. I'm at the St Giles' Hotel."

"Of course you are. And, no, it's not. I won't tell you if there's nothing. But if it is something, I will have to notify the College anyway, so I expect they'd cancel your conference."

"Hurrah!" Elizabeth sips her soup. "Want to hear about Bob?"

"No."

"He's back at work, getting grief – some might say justifiable – from your Super." Elizabeth corrects herself, "your old Super. I think he's sending him on the runaround. Small cases. Inconsequential open files." Elizabeth pauses. "You never said goodbye."

"I'm rubbish at it," Lemon taps the steering wheel, as he adjusts the heater.

"I didn't know you'd even gone."

"I'm here, aren't I?"

"No, it would have been nice to know. You're important to me."

"You'll say anything for post-mortem results," Lemon jests. But Elizabeth glares before taking another sip of her soup.

"Ordinarily, I wouldn't be suspicious." Elizabeth puts the finished soup outside the car now, aware the smell is overpowering, then shuts the car door again. "But at dinner, she said something strange: 'Methinks my enemies are circling'. What does that mean? And she also said: 'Christmas isn't a happy time for everyone'. I remember her saying it, as it resonated. What did she mean?"

"Is Christmas a happy time for anyone?" Lemon scoffs, "Having to eat the in-laws' roast potatoes instead of your own Mum's? Having to watch someone else's choice of television? Being told to sit down and enjoy yourself on someone else's couch while an uncle sitting next to you breaks wind from eating too many Brussel sprouts? When all you want to do is sleep, get up late and go for a walk with your dog? Like I said, we are not treating this as suspicious yet, but are going through normal routine. If the autopsy throws anything up, I'm sure you will find out. We will have to inform the Master."

"Come on, surely I deserve—"

"Okay, I'll phone you if I have to inform the Master, so you can coincidentally be there, and perhaps overhear. Anything else and I'm sacked. In the meantime, enjoy the St Giles'. I'm very jealous."

"And are you looking for Father Christmas?"

"I already said so," Lemon replies.

"I really do think it's murder, you know," Elizabeth muses, asking "may I borrow your telephone, Sergeant?"

Sergeant Lemon hands his personal phone to Elizabeth and has to show her how to dial. Then he blows out air and shuts his eyes – murder, just what he needs just before Christmas.

17
PAMPERED POOCHES

Having been spared Elizabeth's expected return yesterday evening, and despite the sparkly home cleaned by three partly-dressed Santas, Godric knows that Elizabeth will express horror at finding three stinky dogs, so sodden, muddy, caked in goodness knows what, the only clean thing remaining about their personages being their eyes. That is why Godric has rushed to get them pampered this morning.

Saying rushed might be exaggerating somewhat, having let them out in the garden and gone back to bed until noon. But his intentions are honourable, he tells himself, and leaving Ben to prepare a hearty luncheon, Godric is in a Cambridge pet parlour on King Street with the Afghans, Hector and Monty, as well as Clive, the Old English Sheepdog.

Some might wonder how he managed to squeeze three big dogs into a pet parlour at such short notice. One can only surmise that the six-foot-plus leggy blonde with the looks of a male model might have fluttered his eyelashes and told them a desperate tale. Godric was good at this and could manage the impossible frequently, just by gazing into someone's eyes.

All the dogs are up on grooming tables now, having been previously washed. Studious groomers have their heads under their bellies or are tackling legs as the dogs stand, unamused, while they are combed and dried. Godric is laughing with one of the groomers as three dryers blast out full pelt, and the radio blares. Godric, already a head full of grips himself, tries to brush one of the groomer's hair with a dog brush and chases her as she squeals.

"What you doing for Christmas?" one of the groomers shouts to Godric while she brushes Hector.

"Oh, just a nice quiet one. I'm spending the day with my Nanna and my folks. These are my Nanna's dogs."

"Any siblings?"

"Sister." Godric's telephone vibrates in his pocket and barks like a dog. "Hello. Who's this? Oh, hello Bunny." Godric turns to the groomer. "Excuse me, it's my Nanna." Godric walks into the corner of the room to answer and the groomer pulls an 'aww' face and turns down the local radio. Godric shouts over the noise of the dryers, pleased to hear from his favourite relative. "When are you arriving?" He listens with a finger in his other ear, "What? No, it's just windy, yes, walking the dogs. Yes, I'm taking the ice balls out. No! Really? Oh my god. No. Were you there? That's crazy. Won't he come for you? Sorry, no of course. I was just... Be careful." Godric hangs up the phone and stares at all the groomers' hard work on the dogs and wonders if it hasn't all been for nothing. He walks over to the groomer who earlier put grips in his hair. "Father Christmas is a murderer."

"What, babe?"

"And my Nanna …" Godric looks worried and looks into the groomer's eyes. "I was getting the dogs ready to see her. But she's not coming. I'm going to need to book another wash at short notice. Maybe in a couple of days."

"Let me look at the diary," the groomer takes the brush

from Godric's hand and replaces it with a cuppa. "We normally leave it four to six weeks?"

"What can I say, we live a rock n' roll lifestyle," Godric replies, knowing he can never resist splashing in the biggest puddles with the dogs. A habit his nanna is always trying to wean him out of. "Bunny could be in danger from Father Christmas violence."

"Two sugars." The groomer points to the drink now in his hand. "You look like you've seen a ghost. Sit yourself down. What's this about Father Christmas being a murderer?"

"This is my resting face," Godric replies. "She's dead, and she wasn't dead before he pushed her," Godric mumbles.

"Wait, Father Christmas killed someone? Will she be all right?" the groomer asks.

"I don't know, says she wants to stay until she hears," Godric replies, misunderstanding the question thinking the groomer is asking about his nanna.

"What?"

Godric shakes his head.

"Father Christmas didn't murder my Nanna," he whispers.

Another groomer mishears.

"Father Christmas murdered your Nanna?"

"What?" Another says. Joining in.

"He's killed this boy's Nanna," the groomer who gave him tea chips in, having missed Godric's last comment while being in the kitchen.

"Oh my god, I'm so sorry. Are you going to be okay? Has Santa been arrested?"

Godric raises his eyebrows, too lazy to correct them.

"He ran away, with the presents too. Took everything."

"What? You have no presents? Grooms are on the house, least we can do."

Godric pulls a sad face, pleased he doesn't have to have an awkward conversation about putting it on Bunny's tab or part with any readies for the dog grooms himself, being skint from his last gambling escapade. He begins to wonder what else he can get for free in town if he says Father Christmas killed his Nanna. A very lucrative story.

"I don't suppose you have anything stronger, do you?" Godric shakes his mug.

"Sharon!" The groomer who was being chased by Godric a moment ago screams out the back for a colleague. A moment later, the work experience girl, soaked from washing the dogs earlier, appears with a broom in her hand. "Get the vodka and the orange from the back fridge. Get the freshly squeezed. Let's help this boy drown his sorrows." The groomer rubs Godric's arm, lovingly, then puts the tub of Christmas chocolates from the reception onto his lap. Godric flicks through and chooses his favourite and unwraps the chocolate.

Yes, he must drop the dogs off home shortly, and pay a visit to his tailors. They make the best coffee. He can sober up there later. A large tumbler of vodka and orange is placed beside him, and he downs it in one, much to the groomer's shock, who takes the glass and hands it to Sharon, the work experience, for a refill.

"Perhaps, if they can't find Santa, they should look for his sleigh, and ask around in costume shops," Sharon suggests.

"Maybe you could write to him and leave it by the chimney," the most innocent looking groomer says to everyone. "Was it a real beard he was wearing?"

"I don't' know," replies Godric.

"There are a lot of impersonators out there," the innocent groomer chips in, adding, "maybe he will strike again, and they can catch him in the act."

All of a sudden Godric has a tinge of real worry for his Nanna.

"Maybe he's an out-of-work actor," another groomer suggests, "they can lose it sometimes. Could be on the loose."

Suddenly, Godric stops thinking about tailors and freebies. His Bunny really could be in danger. He looks at the dogs. What would they do? Then he takes the second vodka from Sharon and downs it in one.

18
A CHRISTMAS WALK

Directly after seeing Lemon, Elizabeth decides to take a walk down by the river alongside Christ Church Meadow. The temperature has dropped dramatically in the past twenty-four hours. Folly Cathedral looks breathtakingly beautiful in the snow. Kind strangers are feeding swans and ducks. Cyclists flash to and fro far too fast on their way to something no doubt important as Elizabeth turns the bend from the River Cherwell towards the Thames.

She stands and stares at the water for a while, the carrier bags around her legs, getting a few looks. Everything is still this winter, the snow has settled on the reeds, and the surface looks close to freezing. Then she sees the rowers, all wearing reindeer hats, followed by another eight, this time with tinsel and flashing Christmas tree hats. As she turns to leave the biting cold for the shelter of Poplar Walk, she looks up into the trees sparkling with festive lights. It is so pretty; Gerald would have loved it.

As she wanders into Folly Cathedral, hoping to view the sun streaming through the stained glass windows, she spots Gabriel up high, playing the organ in what sounds like a rehearsal, given the absence of any audience, save a few tourists who like herself have wandered in from the cold. Elizabeth perches and listens to the choir sing their rendition of '*O Holy Night*'. The choir then stop, perhaps to take a break, so Elizabeth walks to the bottom of the steps to say hello to Gabriel once he descends.

"That sounded beautiful."

"Yes, quite angelic. Gives me a warm fuzzy feeling. Did it make you feel Christmassy? Nice to see you," he says.

"A bit, but you're looking at an atheist, I'm afraid."

"Me too, but you can still enjoy the music."

"Gerald preferred jazz, but my grandson is in a choir. So, I suppose—"

"There you are then," Gabriel interrupts, "I've only five minutes now, but the rehearsal will be over in half an hour. We're ready. It's just a technical for the lights. We have concerts all next week. If you want to come, I'd be so happy. If you'd like to wait, perhaps we could find some food together? Vegan, of course."

"Good. We can discuss Dr Sandy Starborneck and what happened."

"I was rather hoping we could talk about something more pleasant. Maybe about what you're doing in Cambridge at the Botanic Gardens?"

"I've been wanting to go to the cafe on the corner of Little Clarendon Street. It has a wide selection of vegan dishes on the menu, according to a brochure in my hotel room. I think it's called 'Kick the Habit' or 'Kinder Habits'?"

"'Killer Habits', I'm happy to go wherever you like. Okay, see you shortly, looking forward to it." Gabriel gives Elizabeth the biggest smile, and she nods in return, unsure he was right about the name of the cafe but with no opportunity to correct him. Then he walks off in what looks like the direction of the toilets.

As Elizabeth returns to her pew, she feels uncomfortable with Gabriel's over-enthusiastic friendliness. There is something about it, needy perhaps. How can she judge a person well if they are so keen to be her friend yet don't even know her? People like that are odd, she thinks. But if it means she can cross-examine another witness for half an hour and perhaps find something out about why Sandy died, a spot of lunch is worth it. Elizabeth makes a mental note to make sure she eats with her mouth open, and burp when they go to lunch shortly. Anything to make sure any interest Gabriel has in her is killed, quick smart.

*

As Gabriel and Elizabeth walk into Kinder Habits, the vegan cafe on the corner of Little Clarendon Street, they are greeted by a friendly maître d'.

"Hello, welcome into our cosy cafe. Please come in and sit." The maître d' ushers Elizabeth and Gabriel to a table ten feet from a roaring fire.

"That might be a bit hot. Would you mind if we sit on the sofas over there by the window? I always prefer fresh air. If it's too hot for a plant to grow, then it's too hot for me," Elizabeth says. "I do like to people watch, I can't help it."

"Of course, Madam." And they all walk over to a huge sofa with a clear view of both snowy St Giles' and Little Clarendon Street. The maître d' hands them both menus.

"I came over here once, from Cambridge, for a year, to work," Elizabeth explains to Gabriel.

"Did you? When?"

"After my PhD. I took a one-year lectureship but decided not to take a College. Somehow it felt disloyal to Granta. I don't know why. So, I never really felt part of it," Elizabeth explains.

"I never knew that about you," Gabriel looks into Elizabeth's eyes.

"Lived in Summertown, in a beautiful house. But

Gerald was still in Cambridge, and so it was all too much travel for both of us. I felt myself again when I returned to Cambridge and took up a permanent role."

"So you know the place."

"I don't like to broadcast it, but yes. I suppose I do." Elizabeth looks out at her favourite part of the city. "A little. I will certainly remember it more vividly now, with the past twenty-four hours making such an impression, for all the wrong reasons. I will admit I'm a little homesick." Elizabeth thinks of Hector, Monty and Clive, of Bertie and Soot.

"Awful thing that happened to the American," Gabriel agrees. "I wonder if you were here when I was then?"

"Oh, I doubt it. I think I'm a little older than you," Elizabeth is irked by Gabriel digging. "What you're studying is very different from my field. You're engineering, aren't you?"

"Researching the ripening of tomatoes, both genomic and biochemical. RNA and looking at cell death."

Elizabeth is saved by the maître d' who walks back over, "Can I get you a drink?"

"I'd like the apple, lime and ginger smoothie please."

"Oh, I'll have one of those too." Gabriel smiles and the maître d' nods.

"Just give me a shout when you're ready to order."

"Thank you, Dave," Gabriel sees the cafe owner's name badge. "We are the lucky ones," Gabriel replies, genuinely, "thank you."

Elizabeth finds herself slightly irritated by this pointless exchange and opens her eyes a little wider.

"What did you know of the American?"

"I didn't really. I knew she was formidable. Working on biodegradable plastics. Turned it around really," Gabriel shook his head, "I think her colleague will still be able to carry on, I suppose. Not sure how many postdocs Sandy had."

"Do you think she had any enemies?"

"No idea, though don't we all have one or two?"

"No," Elizabeth replies, surprised by Gabriel's answer. "Who are yours?"

"Well, I sometimes wonder if my brother-in-law blames me for my wife's—" Gabriel interrupts himself, "not an enemy, I suppose."

"I just want to know who would do this to her," Elizabeth says, looking at a menu.

"Come on. You're in Oxford now. Isn't your detectiving saved for Cambridge?"

"Isn't Father Christmas supposed to dish out presents?" Elizabeth asks.

"Yes, it was odd that he seemed to be picking up presents at one point," Gabriel replies.

"Did he? What do you mean?"

"Oh, nothing really. I was half watching him before Sandy started to grab him. I thought he might be leaving some presents for the College staff, so thought it odd that he started to pick up presents and put them in his sack."

"You know, I'm quite relieved this is the first time I've made it over to this peculiar conference. This sort of thing doesn't happen every year, does it?" Elizabeth has chosen her food and places the menu in the air to catch the attention of Dave.

"As it happens, there are a lot of new faces this year. Sandy for one, and you. Even Alexander usually gives it a swerve."

Their conversation is interrupted by the appearance outside of a dozen or more Father Christmases who all appear from Little Clarendon Street and seem to be congregating outside the window, spilling into St Giles'. Elizabeth waves back Dave, the maître d'.

"What's this?"

"The Santa Fun Run – 5k. Are you ready to give your order?" he asks, bringing over the smoothies.

"I'll have the spinach parcels please."

"Would you like chips or rice?"

"Chips are the devil's work. Rice will suffice." Elizabeth hands the menu back to the maître d'.

"What do you recommend?" Gabriel asks.

"The Christmas dinner is delicious, nut roast and all the veggies."

"Sold!" Gabriel snaps the menu shut.

Elizabeth holds her hand up for Dave to move out of the way, as she tries to get a look at all the Father Christmases dressed up, in case she recognises any of them.

"His suit was more old fashioned. A better fit. Our Father Christmas."

"Yes, I like a traditional Christmas," Gabriel says trying to be helpful.

"Do you have a big family?" Elizabeth asks.

"I did have. I live in College now." Gabriel doesn't want to say more.

"What do you mean, did have? That's cryptic."

"You know what academic life is like, very demanding. But I was looking forward to meeting you. Professor of Poisons. What a title your students give you."

"They don't dare say it to my face."

"It's flattering," Gabriel smiles. "Better than the 'King of Tomatoes'."

"Don't you think it's a bit odd that she just collapsed like that?" Elizabeth asks.

"Yes, though she did say she was feeling a little unwell for the past day or two."

"Did you tell the police that?" Elizabeth asks.

"No, why, do you think it is relevant?"

"Of course."

The food arrives, as Gabriel looks a little stressed, while Father Christmases still congregating outside notice the food and start to claw at the window and laugh. Elizabeth looks them in the eye and pokes out her tongue.

19
MISSING YOU

It is late afternoon, and Elizabeth goes back to the St Giles' Hotel and collapses into luxury. She picks up messages that Godric has telephoned her five times, so calls him back.

"Is everything all right?"

*

"Yes, I just wondered when you were coming back?" Godric sits in a tidy home, with three fluffy dogs and his handsome boyfriend, Ben. He walks the landline as far as the cord will allow, sitting down on the edge of the settee in the drawing-room. He hears his Nanna say that she is not sure she will head home because of the death, and how Sergeant Lemon is now looking into it. "Sergeant Lemon? But you have to come soon, while everything is clean."

Godric looks about at the clean house and the clean dogs. "And, I've no one to stroke my hair," Godric adds, and Ben hits him jokily, "or run me a bath." Ben hits

Godric again, clearly irked as he's always running Godric's baths. Godric listens as Elizabeth says something about how she never runs his baths. "I live in hope, Bunny, you'll be my favourite Nanna when you do," Godric sighs, then looks at the book on the table, still in its wrapper. "Yes, I'm halfway through it. Will you read to me, Bunny, at bedtime?" Godric jokes. "Oh, I'm so bored. Why are the terms so drearily short? Am I seeing Ben? Not much," Ben lightly hits Godric again, this time Godric says "Ow" silently. "He's far too violent to see often. What about me?" Godric pines. "Yes, the animals are fine." Godric looks at Ben and covers the phone and speaks to Ben. "She doesn't know whether to come home," he says, whispering.

"Good idea if she does, as I'm off this evening, to my Mum's for Christmas," Ben says.

"Your Mum's?" Godric's not used to the word. Ben nods.

"Not back until term starts, was going to tell you," Ben smiles.

"What?" Godric is quite surprised by this news that he will be alone. "Yes, I'm still here." Godric answers his Nanna on the other end of the phone. "Yes, you have my undivided attention. Okay, see what they say. Yes, do something Christmassy while you wait. Go shopping. I like scarves, single malt," he tells his Nanna down the phone. Godric then whispers to Ben again, "What am I going to do on my own? Even Pinkham's buggered off," then Godric switches back to talking to Elizabeth, "Keep warm, stay safe Bunny. If Father Christmas is killing people, no one is safe. Love you, darling," he says, then hears the call being cut. Godric walks back to the telephone table to put the phone down.

"I love you, Goddy," Ben grins, grabbing Godric. Godric feels awkward. He told Bunny he loves her, as he says that a lot. But he really hopes Ben doesn't expect him to say it back.

Thankfully, there is a knock at the door. Godric rushes to be the first to open it, praying for a diversion. When he gets there, he is greeted by a very large, very intimidating hulk of a man, who looks like he ate two bouncers for breakfast and they are still straining to get out.

"You know why I'm here."

"Stilton and port?"

"You owe Mr Reggie. He wants it by tomorrow."

"He's sending you out for small amounts, it's only a nickel," Godric replies scoffingly.

"Don't get smart with me. I'm on a sandwich run. You're on my way. I'm hungry. Grrr," the man growls at Godric.

"I'll drop it off. Don't come here again."

"Mr Reggie told me to tell you that he's getting a little fed up of your delayed payments. Stick to the plan!"

"Toodle pips," says Godric, shutting the door in the gorilla's face.

"You all right?" Ben asks, extremely worried by the size of the man dishing out threats.

"Oh, that? Just Stan, he's harmless. I shouldn't have got drunk and gone into Dicers. I'm always in debt to Reggie," Godric yawns.

"Gambling?"

"I like to call it entertainment. The early hours can get so dull without it, dear boy. Normally play the cards and come out on top. I'd had one too many mojitos. Don't worry your pretty head." Godric ruffles Ben's hair and smiles, remembering Ben's words about loving him and being more concerned about that.

*

Elizabeth has already picked up her phone again as soon as her conversation with Godric was over. She is now on the line to Inspector Bob Abley.

"You can't play in the snow. You've got time," She

listens to Bob complaining about not being able to play golf. "You shouldn't have given me your new mobile phone number if you didn't want me to call. I'm just saying. This is more important. Listen." Elizabeth listens to Bob, still talking about golf. "Can't you do that in the clubhouse? And by the way, yes, I saw Lemon, and he is looking thin, and there are black circles under his eyes. It might be an iron deficiency. He looks like he has grown. How tall can he get? And Gabriel said Dr Sandy Starborneck had been feeling unwell for a couple of days. How does he know that? And why was she feeling ill?" Elizabeth listens to Bob Abley's question. "Yes, he's at the conference. No, I don't know him well." She listens again. "It's not about trust, he's just shared that information with me, and I think it's important. I'd be interested to know what you think," Elizabeth listens, "No, I don't know what the forecast is. I'm just saying, we need to find Father Christmas, and we need to find out who killed Dr Sandy Starborneck. And Lemon is going to help me." Elizabeth listens to her friend berate her intentions, then continues, "Well, there's nothing you can do about it." She hangs up, pleased with her conversation.

Elizabeth falls back into the comfy pillows and does a star shape on the bed. Grateful that she has some time to herself, she picks up the phone again, speaking to room service: "Have you got any more of those lovely afternoon teas? I'm going to need sustenance for what is coming."

20
CLOCKS

The day has gone and the night has crept over Cambridge. Inspector Bob Abley fully expected to be fast asleep by now, but his Superintendent had other ideas.

"Stolen clocks." Inspector Bob Abley shakes his head, as he drives out on dark country lanes leaving the city lights behind. "That was so clever of you to do the digging on this and tell the Super about it." Abley does his best to encourage his new Sergeant, Sergeant Goodey, although every cell in his body aches to be anywhere else in the world.

The hedgerows scratch the side of his car, with clumps of snow dropping on the lane behind. A fox crosses in front of them then disappears into the farmer's fields.

"Oh, was just a hobby really in my spare time. I was so thrilled the Super let us come to investigate my hunch," Goodey replies excitedly. Inspector Abley tries not to roll his eyes, doing his best to support this new police officer. Goodey continues, "Did you know that time is a man-made construct? It can't be proved to exist. And, there is a Norwegian island that wants to get rid of time," Goodey adds, trying to cheer up his Inspector with this bit of trivia.

"How would they know when to meet?"

"I don't know. Shadows cast from the sun?"

"What if it's cloudy?"

"And if it doesn't exist, why get rid of it?" Goodey agrees, continuing, "Personally, I like a good clock."

"Bit of an expert, are you?" Abley asks as he watches the road ahead, just lines of white snow and black tarmac.

"I studied history of art before joining the force, specialised in home antiquities later – know a thing or two. Not an expert. Though I could tell you about the most valuable clock in the world–"

"Save it for when we get there," Inspector Abley interrupts. What living hell has Superintendent Raynott sent him on now? He guesses the Super knew Sergeant Goodey was into clocks before they left and is having a private laugh all tucked up cosy at home, as they drive in the middle of the night to the absolute middle of nowhere in the fens.

"Is now a good time to tell you that I have a collection of clocks at home?" Goodey smiles, excitedly.

"Now is never a good time to tell me that," Abley replies, hoping the journey will be over soon and they can arrest someone and go home. The lane starts to narrow as snow falls in clumps onto both sides of the car from the hedgerows.

"I wanted to give you a lovely cuckoo clock I've been refurbishing, as I think it would look good in your new flat you said you have now. A bachelor needs a good clock," says Goodey, trying to make an effort to bond with Abley.

"That's very kind," Abley replies, unable to tell Goodey that he'd rather drop such a clock from a high height into moving traffic than watch a cuckoo burst out of a wooden box every hour, sending him cuckoo.

Inspector Abley and Sergeant Goodey arrive at the barn surrounded by countryside in total darkness. As the Inspector's car approaches, Abley turns his lights off before parking up outside on a stretch of gravel. They sit in the car in silence for a moment, before Goodey opens his window and listens. He holds his finger up to stop the Inspector from saying anything,

"Shush, do you hear that?" Goodey asks.

"I hear you shushing me."

"Shush," Goodey says again. Abley is peeved but then hears a clock chime. He looks at Sergeant Goodey, who then nods. They both get out of the car quietly and walk to the door of the barn. Sergeant Goodey slowly pulls back the door as Abley gets ready to pounce on anyone who leaps out. But all they find are clocks, chiming on the hour of midnight. Inspector Abley looks around the room at the cacophony of clocks. There must be about three hundred stolen clocks. Goodey starts to film them on his phone.

"I think it's about time we woke the Super up, don't you, Sergeant? Give him a call."

"Now?"

"Yes, and quickly, before this ends. We want him to know how successful you've been. So he can hear the ringing in of a new day!"

21
INSPECTOR'S BAR

The next morning and Sergeant Lemon and Professor Elizabeth Green sit in the Inspector's Bar at the St Giles' Hotel.

"Thank you for coming. I've ordered tea. What have you found out?" Elizabeth asks.

"I can't stay long. I have to go home for breakfast or Rosie will not be happy." Lemon looks around. Framed photographs of Oxford line the walls. Small table lamps throw a warm glow across the room, a Christmas tree with blue lights sits in the corner by a real fire. Lemon spots advent calendars on each table, picks up the closest, opens a window and eats the chocolate, "I've not been in here yet. Isn't it great?"

"What are you doing, still working?" Elizabeth asks.

"I started my double shift at 8 am yesterday. With one catnap I'm shattered. Thank god it's over."

"Well, a nice cup of tea will help, and a crumpet." Elizabeth starts to pour. "So they've got you on the graveyard shifts?"

"Please. And as for still working, I wasn't the one who suggested we meet here," Lemon smiles at Elizabeth.

"You told me you had news."

"I do." Lemon picks up the cup of tea takes a sip and nods.

"What?"

"A nice bit of goss," he smirks.

"Please don't let Oxford turn you into an oik with crass language," Elizabeth frowns.

"Whatevs," Sergeant shrugs, rubbing his eyes from fatigue.

"No," Elizabeth shakes her head.

"How's Cambridge?" Lemon asks.

"White, just like here. I haven't been on a case since you left, so I presume all things are quiet at Parker's Piece."

"Nothing is ever quiet in that place."

"You know, if you want to find out how Bob is, you should call him," Elizabeth suggests. Lemon says nothing. He's not going to tell Elizabeth that his old Inspector broke his heart and that he has been avoiding his countless emails. No, Lemon is trying to make a clean break. It's weird enough that he's now sitting with Elizabeth. Again. Though this feels more relaxed today. Like old times.

"What are the Inspectors like here?" Elizabeth asks.

"They're okay. It's all very professional. I like it."

"Bob is apparently turning up and putting in the hours. He only plays golf at the weekends."

"That's because it's snowing. And did you really say 'putting'?" Lemon takes another sip of his tea and shuts his eyes from the comfort it brings.

"He's come to terms with his marriage being over. He's quicker at getting to the point than you are, too," Elizabeth replies.

"Dr Sandy Starborneck was arrested three nights ago, for a street brawl. Michael Pussett made a complaint against Dr Starborneck some time afterwards. I don't think she knew he did that from the notes we got from witnesses after she died. I think they were still lovers?" Lemon takes off his shoes and rubs his tired feet.

"What did I tell you? Something isn't right. What more do you know?"

"I know, your hunch is sounding less crazy, about murder, but not much," Lemon says, adding, "Two women were seen fighting with a man. Someone phoned it in. Then when we got there, we arrested Dr Sandy Starborneck. She was very drunk. The other woman must have run away. Well, my colleagues did anyway. I wasn't working that particular night shift. Just gleaned from reading the notes this morning. What more can I tell you? That she was wearing a Santa hat?"

"There's something new about you," Elizabeth looks more closely at Sergeant Lemon, narrowing her eyes.

"Yeah, I'm more tired," Lemon says, still rubbing his feet.

"No, it's not that."

Lemon shakes his head, then takes another sip of his tea.

"There's something new about you too," he replies.

"What?"

"You've expanded your geographical meddling," Lemon chuckles.

"You see, the Cambridge Lemon wouldn't have called it meddling. He would have been grateful," Elizabeth sips her drink.

"Again, lack of sleep."

"No, you've come out of the shadows." Elizabeth studies Lemon's face.

"That's all I do, work in the shadows. If they put me on another night shift, I swear I'll turn into a bat."

"Perhaps the absence of Bob has done you good. So what else do you know about Dr Starborneck?"

"I can't tell you everything. It'd break all the rules."

"Yes, but this new Lemon, breaking all the rules. Reminds me of someone I know."

"I'm not like anyone else you know."

"Exactly as he would say. Come on, we make a great team, you and I. We solved a multiple murder case," Elizabeth reminds him about last time.

"This is different. I could get the sack here. You're not on the payroll."

"You could put me on it?" Elizabeth stares at him straight.

"Beyond my pay grade, I'm afraid."

"Who am I going to tell?" She leans in.

"Do you ever not get what you want?" Lemon asks.

"Of course! But you need to spill if you want to solve this."

Lemon pauses. Why does he feel the weight of responsibility to tell Elizabeth all, when he knows it is the wrong thing to do? It could cost him his career. And yet, if they catch the murderer, if this woman was murdered, before they strike again, then it has to be worth it.

"It goes no further."

"Of course!" Elizabeth wants him to get to the point.

"Dr Sandy Starborneck had been drinking in The King's Arms and having a merry old time. According to witnesses she was slurring her words and was with her friend who was only drinking green tea. She was on her way home when she got into this fight. Michael Pussett was the man involved as I've mentioned. The person who phoned it in reported him being beaten up by Sandy yet didn't want to press charges initially. It was only later he changed his mind."

"Perhaps because he didn't want it getting out when he was holding his conference?" Elizabeth suggests. "Dr Haven Usrey said that Dr Sandy Starborneck's drinking was out of character. That she didn't usually drink alcohol?"

"That's all I can say."

"Rubbish. Where does she live?"

"She's dead, but Haven lives in Summertown. She used to live there."

"Come on then, chop-chop."

Lemon frowns and looks at his half-drunk cup. He could stay here all morning. He starts to finish it.

"Leave that." Elizabeth smacks it out of his fingers. "We can't sit around here doing nothing. We need to act before something else happens!" Lemon scrabbles to put on his shoes as he watches Elizabeth march out of the bar.

22
MORNING CAKE

Michael Pussett waits in the room with all the academic display stands. He cannot believe his conference has been jeopardised like this.

"Can you make sure we have extra coffee and cake put on tomorrow morning. I'd like two rounds, not one. So you will need to go out and buy more provisions today, from my budget. Nothing can go wrong tomorrow," Michael tells the caterer, Linda, while scoffing a piece of chocolate cake she had brought him.

"Any particular cake? And the scones?"

"This is nice. More of this, and the scones, yes. If you have those Christmassy ones, with cinnamon and fruit, they're festive."

"Why don't you skip the cake and go straight to the rum. That would be more fitting." Haven walks in on the conversation.

"Can you not make everything so dramatic?" Michael says viciously to Haven, adding, "Sandy slipped. She's dead. You being a pain in the arse isn't going to bring her back."

"Can you not sweep everything under the carpet like

Sandy never existed?" Haven shouts at Michael.

"Thank you, Linda, that will be all," Michael says to the caterer.

"Linda, no, that will not be all. Can you bring me some soap and a cloth to wash this man's mouth out," Haven demands. Linda stands waiting for the next instruction. Michael shakes his head, indicating she can go. The caterer turns to leave.

"Why do you have to embarrass yourself all the time?" Michael looks Haven up and down with disdain.

"Oh, I don't know. You used to like it. Thankfully for me, you were distracted elsewhere. Funny how quickly you move on. Did you hire Santa to kill Sandy?"

"You're a crazy woman."

"You're trying to build an empire. Was she embarrassing you, with her drinking?"

"You look after yourself and stop fussing about what I'm doing." Michael puts the rest of the chocolate cake down, his appetite gone.

"What are you doing? Should I be worried for my safety? Perhaps I should talk to the Master. Tell him about your fight with Sandy?"

Out of nowhere, Michael turns and grabs both of Haven's wrists.

"Look, missy. You are beginning to annoy me. Stop. Just stop. Or, I won't be responsible for my actions."

23
SUMMERTOWN

Having persuaded Lemon not to go straight home, but to extend the length of his torture, as he dreamt of his bed, Professor Elizabeth Green and Sergeant Lemon are now sitting outside Dr Sandy Starborneck and Dr Haven Usrey's rented home up in leafy Summertown.

Elizabeth is impressed by the large houses on the broad avenue – Georgian leviathans outside most peoples' budgets, with their extensive front gardens, tall trees and quiet pavements. She wonders how two visiting Fellows can afford such riches until Lemon explains they only had the ground floor.

"I can't believe I let you persuade me to bring you up here. I'm going to get in so much trouble if we're spotted," Lemon says.

"We won't be spotted.

"We're in a police car." Lemon shakes his head.

"So no one will want to come closer than a hundred yards of you. Perfect cover."

Lemon takes out a crumpet from a serviette he grabbed earlier from the hotel's Inspector's Bar and starts to munch.

"If you waste time eating that crumpet, then you might blow our cover. We need to move swiftly."

"I'm hungry. What are we doing here, anyway? You had a look. Now we should go." Lemon takes a huge bite and chews. "Hey! Where are you going? Get back in," he shouts through a mouthful. But Lemon cannot stop Elizabeth from getting out of the car and marching up to the house. She tries the front door and then disappears around the back.

Lemon decides to move the car out of sight, just in case, then jumps out of the vehicle, crumpet still in hand, and races after Elizabeth, just in time to see her pushing up an open window and climbing in. He finishes his crumpet before disappearing through the window after her.

"We have to get out, I'm getting doubts about this," Lemon hisses to Elizabeth, who is now pulling out drawers and lifting papers in the open-plan kitchen dining room.

"In a minute,"

"I'm in so much trouble," Lemon worries.

"Calm down. We're already here. We might as well have a look," Elizabeth picks up a handbag and tips the contents out on a kitchen island. She grabs a lipstick from the marble worktop without Lemon noticing and pops it in her pocket. Lemon looks around the house; never having been inside he is impressed by the high ceilings and muted colours. There is a modern-looking Christmas tree tucked into a corner of the room, decorated with grey and white bows.

"Who lives like this? Everything is white and grey?" Lemon says.

"Someone with too much time on their hands. You said they were renting though. And what's this artwork? It doesn't fit with the décor. I wonder if they're Haven's handicraft? Perhaps this one isn't popular." Elizabeth and Lemon look at the floor of the dining room. There is a smashed painting. The glass spread all across the floorboards. Elizabeth observes the art, in blue and green, of a woman holding a chicken, floating in the dark starry sky. With initials in the right-hand corner.

"I P, is that it?" Elizabeth asks.

"Yes, probably," Lemon replies, looking at the mess on the floor.

"It doesn't strike me that they spent much time here, judging by how sparsely decorated it is. Though it's obvious Haven still lives here." Elizabeth points at the scarf over the lampshade, to the gonk on the sofa looking out of place and burnt joss sticks on a bookshelf. "I suppose they've only rented it for the Christmas period perhaps. Can you check, Lemon? Hang on, what's this?" Elizabeth looks at a coffee table and points at the corner. There is blood on it, and the carpet below. It doesn't look fresh.

"Blood." Lemon looks more carefully, "We have crossed the line. I have to call this in. I'll have to admit you drew me here. I'm going to be in trouble."

Elizabeth spots a black leather driver's glove in a wastepaper basket by the fire and goes to pick it up, curious.

"Why does someone throw one glove away?"

"I dunno, because they lost the other one? Don't touch it. Oh god, our DNA is everywhere," Lemon says. They both hear a car door go outside and men's voices coming up the drive. Lemon peeks through the curtains. "You've got to be kidding me; it's my Inspector." Lemon grabs Elizabeth's hand and pulls her to the open window at the back, virtually pushing her out. She falls into hydrangeas and looks up at him before he hurls himself out and almost on top of her. They run around the side of the garden and hide until they hear the policemen shutting the front door. Lemon and Elizabeth crouch in the bushes out the front for what seems like ages.

"Why don't we just walk away?" Elizabeth asks.

"You'll see."

"I haven't got all day."

"That's rich," and with that, Lemon pulls Elizabeth out of the bushes and to the front door. He knocks on the door, and a Constable opens it. Lemon whispers to Elizabeth, "Just remember to pick up the bag. Whatever you do. Pick up the bag on the counter, and put it back down, all right?"

"All right." Elizabeth is not sure what Lemon is up to, but any chance to go back in and take another look is worth going along with.

"Hello, Inspector," Lemon smiles as the front door opens.

"Sergeant Lemon, why are you not in bed? Your shift finished two hours ago."

"Double shift, Sir. Yes. I bumped into Professor Green, and she told me she was going to come here. And I had an inkling it might be a crime scene. But, no matter what I tried to do, there was no stopping her, as you can see," Lemon turns to Elizabeth and says, "I told you, you're not allowed to come in here," and back to his Inspector, "Professor Green thinks there is something suspicious about the death of Dr Starborneck. She was at the same conference when it happened." Lemon whispers to Elizabeth, "the bag. Pick up the bag."

"Yes, I saw her pushed by Father Christmas," Elizabeth says to the Oxford Inspector, "But apparently, she wasn't herself for a few days before this. According to Gabriel Deersman, that is." Elizabeth walks over to the kitchen island and picks up the handbag.

"Put that down, don't touch anything," the Oxford Inspector instructs Elizabeth, "and you are?"

"Professor Green. I'm at the conference that Dr Sandy Starborneck was also attending, as your Sergeant just told you," Elizabeth says, just realising Lemon has come back in so their DNA is legitimately inside the house, and thinking how clever he is.

"Have we questioned you?" the Oxford Inspector

looks at Elizabeth as if she could somehow be guilty of something.

"I would love you to question me, as perhaps then I could ask you why you didn't treat this as a murder straight away?"

"I beg your pardon?" The Oxford Inspector asks.

"This is very suspicious. You must think so, or else why would you be here?"

"As it happens, the autopsy is showing signs of poison, but we're not sure what yet," the Oxford Inspector replies, irritated he gave the information away to this annoying woman, "so perhaps you know something about that?"

"I knew it!" Elizabeth shouts.

"Lemon, who is this?" The Oxford Inspector has no time for Elizabeth and starts to walk over to the kitchen. Lemon hisses at Elizabeth, "touch the window, the window," as Lemon himself, goes over to the window and looks out. Lemon then deliberately falls out of the window.

"Sergeant Lemon, what are you doing?" The Oxford Inspector rushes over to the window as Lemon calls up to Elizabeth.

"Professor Green, Professor Green!" Lemon shouts. Elizabeth wanders over to the window and puts her hands on the windowsill. "Oh, nothing. I must have hit my head," Lemon adds.

"You need to go home and go to bed," the Oxford Inspector looks down at Lemon, now in the hydrangeas. "I'm not getting into trouble for keeping you on a treble shift!" Then the Inspector turns to Elizabeth. "And I don't know why you're here, only that I find it more than a coincidence. So I ask you not to leave Oxford until I can question you."

"Like I say, I look forward to it," Elizabeth replies.

"Now please leave, we need to cordon off this flat. There may well be evidence here." The Inspector turns to the constable behind him. "Call the SOCOs, let's sweep this place for fingerprints." Then the Inspector spots the blood on the coffee table. "Looks like we have a crime scene here. You, out!" The Inspector has no tolerance for a meddling middle-aged woman getting in the way of his investigation.

Elizabeth steps out the front door, and Lemon appears from behind the house.

"Let's get out of here before you get me into any more trouble. Hopefully, by going back in, they won't question why our prints are everywhere. But first, come and lay in the bushes," and he drags her back into the back garden and quickly in the bushes then shouts up at the Inspector who looks back down at them.

"Sorry she was helping me find my phone. Got it!" Lemon shows the Inspector leaning out of the window.

"Get her out of here. It's a crime scene!"

Lemon nods and drags Elizabeth back out of the garden.

"Can you stop shoving me? Did you hear him? Traces of poison found in the autopsy. Poison."

"Yes, I heard," Lemon sighs, tired and now covered in mud.

"Where's the car?" Elizabeth asks.

"Around the corner," Lemon replies, exhausted.

"Luncheon beckons," and Elizabeth follows Sergeant Lemon along the avenue and towards the car. As they amble along, Lemon overtaken by Elizabeth as soon as she sees the car, him now watching a twig from the hydrangea bounce in Elizabeth's curls, they both spot a familiar face on the other side of the road. Gabriel Deersman.

"Hey, isn't that the Professor from your course?"

"Yes. What's he doing up here?" Elizabeth asks herself.

They both watch him from behind a van as he heads towards the avenue where Sandy and Haven's house is. Elizabeth is tempted to follow him, but Lemon grabs her jacket.

"C'mon. I'm already in trouble. Let's not make it

worse."

24
SILVER SERVICE

As the snow falls thick and fast outside, back at the hotel Elizabeth is now enjoying a silver service luncheon in her room. With a trolley cart packed with delights next to the table by the window, she puts down her napkin after eating a nut roast and potatoes, watching a few people scurry from building to building, all wrapped up in coats, hats and gloves.

She decides to leave the Christmas pudding for later and thinks she might have an afternoon nap. But before she uncurls the sheets and switches off the lights, she telephones Inspector Abley. With the phone piece to her ear, she hears the ringing.

"Hello? Yes, it's me. No, not again. I have news." Elizabeth is irritated by Inspector Abley's lack of interest. "This is important. Sergeant Lemon and I—" Elizabeth stops talking, her ear being chewed from the other end of the phone. "He is involved on the case anyway. They found traces of poison in the victim. What did I tell you? No, I won't. Oh, come on, I have to find out more about it now, you can't blame me. Sandy must have already had poison in her body before she was pushed. The chances of dying are slim from just falling over. Whereas, if you've been poisoned, you're more likely to hit your head. It's murder."

Elizabeth nods as she agrees with Abley who congratulates her down the telephone on her hunch, "I have to speak to the pathologist now," she says. But she is then disappointed as Abley tells her to stay out of it. "But why would I do that?" she asks. There is nothing from the other end of the telephone. "Have you eaten all the cake I made you yet? Open the next box if it's there. You have more Christmas presents. Someone has to look after you now."

There is a knock at the door in Elizabeth's room. "Hang on a minute,"

*

Inspector Bob Abley has been in the pub again, this time in The Elm Tree on Orchard Street, Cambridge, a stone's throw from his flat. When Elizabeth called, he had to walk out with his pint so as not to give the game away and is now standing in the snow without a coat and with a cold pint of bitter in the other hand. To say that he is worried that Elizabeth is going to get Lemon into trouble is an understatement. He feels helpless, and without a hope of warning his favourite Sergeant, he shakes his head at the thought of Elizabeth butting in and rubbing the Oxford Police up the wrong way.

Inspector Bob Abley decides to call time on his luncheon drinkies. He finishes his pint and puts the glass down on a table outside the pub. He walks back to his flat, a few doors down on Prospect Row, and wonders what delights he has waiting for him in Elizabeth's second package, which he can see propped up by his door – who would steal from a policeman's front step?

Inspector Abley picks up the parcel, then turns the key to his home. He feels ready to throw himself on his sofa and fall asleep before his late shift already organised by his Super again. If he could only hang up the phone, he's still holding to his ear. He thinks about his work over the past week. Inspector Bob Abley is done with midnight jobs to find clocks, and Newnham visits over missing cats. He needs to sink his teeth into something meaningful. Like the murder, Elizabeth is talking about. Why is everything happening in Oxford? He feels jealous. Jealous of Sergeant Lemon working on a murder case, jealous of Elizabeth for being in the right place at the right time. But then he stops in his tracks. What is he thinking? Of course, he shouldn't be jealous of that. He doesn't want anyone to be murdered. He's just nervous of what the Super has in store for him next.

"Are you still there? Hello!" Abley waits to hear from Elizabeth and puts his mobile on speaker on the table by the window. He walks over to the fridge and takes out a beer. He mutes the phone while he opens the bottle, then unmutes again. He just has time to turn on his electric fire and huddle in front of it, a little cold, before Elizabeth chirps up again.

"I've just had a delivery of boots and flowers," he hears her voice say from the phone speaker.

"Good?" Abley wonders why he's being called for this.

"Very thoughtful. The card says they are from Dr Gabriel Deersman. From the conference," Elizabeth explains.

"What is he doing giving you presents?"

"I went to lunch with him. Sat next to him at dinner. I suppose you could say we are new friends."

"New friends? You don't have time for your old ones."

"Bob. Have you opened your second parcel yet? It was sent by your friend."

"No. But if you don't know this Deersman chap, be careful. If there's been a murder, as you suspect, then you need to keep your distance. And don't jeopardise Lemon's career."

"Bob. D'you not remember what I did for Lemon while you were unavailable? Open your next present."

"I've got you something too, you know," Bob Abley tells a white lie.

"Have you?" Elizabeth asks excitedly.

Abley looks around his flat. He hasn't bought Elizabeth anything but knows he has time to find something before her return. He walks to his table and starts to open the box, which is next to the cake he was given yesterday which is still intact. All but the slice he tried and nearly broke his tooth on.

"I'm opening it." Abley finds some gingerbread men and women on strings.

"For your tree," Elizabeth suggests.

He doesn't like to say that he doesn't have a tree. He bites into one, but it is very hard.

"Lovely, thank you," Abley says as he crunches.

"You can hang some over your mantelpiece as well," Elizabeth explains. Abley lifts out a gingerbread woman on a string and walks over to the mantelpiece where his old electric fire is propped up below. He hangs the gingerbread over the fire, and it starts to burn. Abley smiles and shakes his head.

"Delicious," he replies.

"They're for decoration. They're too hard to eat. Did you see the other little gift?" She asks.

"Oh, there's something else?" Abley nervously places the biscuit on the coffee table and looks inside the box. Inside the box is another box. He opens it to find a snow globe, with Father Christmas on it. He shakes it.

"Wind it up," Elizabeth says.

"Later."

"I want to hear it."

Abley rolls his eyes and winds up the snow globe. It starts to make a "Ho, ho, ho" noise. Then he looks for an off button as the Father Christmas sings *'I'm Dreaming of a White Christmas.'*

"Is there an off button?"

"No, tee hee."

Abley can hear the uncontrollable laugh in Elizabeth's voice. She's gleeful.

"That's not funny."

"How spooky it is that the snow globe is Father Christmas. Almost as if I knew the murder was going to happen. Hang on. There's the door again." Abley hears Elizabeth say from the speaker on his phone.

*

Elizabeth puts the receiver on the bed while she gets up to open her hotel room door. She is somewhat enjoying this chat with Bob, knowing he's there on his own and cheering him up like this at Christmas time. As Elizabeth twists the handle and pulls, three dogs bound in. Her eyes widen.

"Surprise!" Godric shouts, throwing open his arms.

"Who is feeding the cats?" Elizabeth asks.

"Mrs Cloud," Godric replies, smiling. "Boy, the trains were packed. We had to sit in the aisle at one point. People were stepping over us all the time until this very cute ticket inspector let us in first class. He said we were far too handsome to be sitting on the floor. I took his number. Hector stretched out across two seats after that!"

"You shouldn't impose on Mrs Cloud."

"I put her in touch with a good service I think she's going to use while Mr Cloud is away. She's very happy."

"So long as you haven't pressed yourself on her."

"You won't find me doing that. She's got a service now for that." Godric smirks, thinking of the naked Father Christmas cleaners and Mrs Cloud's face.

"Well, how lovely is this?"

"Exactly!" Godric jumps up and down on Elizabeth's

bed, the dogs jumping up on it too.

"Get off. The hotel won't like that."

"We have to sleep somewhere."

"This is my suite. You're not thinking of staying here, are you?"

"Exactly, I'm thinking of staying, right here. When there's a murderer on the loose."

"Oh, Bob," she lifts the phone to her ear again. "Stop it," she says to the dogs now jumping up. Elizabeth tries to untangle the telephone lead from Clive's leg as he throws himself at her, so pleased to see her. "Bob, Bob, are you still there?" Elizabeth listens to Bob Abley asking her if she's okay, "Yes, it's Godric and the dogs. They've come to keep me safe apparently." Elizabeth pulls a face as Hector and Monty jump on her, making the telephone conversation far from safe and Elizabeth's bones bruised as always. Then Elizabeth spots the concierge behind Godric, carrying Godric's huge rucksack. "Bob, I'll have to go." She hangs up the phone and turns to her favourite grandson. "Godric, are you planning on staying a fortnight?"

"Christmas in Oxford!" he shouts while bouncing.

Elizabeth shakes her head and pulls out her purse to tip the concierge - who has followed Godric up from the reception, rather taken with him – now politely ignoring Godric jumping on the bed with three large dogs.

"Get down!" Elizabeth shouts, then to the concierge, "Do you have any other rooms?"

"I'm so sorry, Madam, but I am pretty certain we are full. I can double-check if you like. But this settee is a sofa bed." The concierge walks through to the sitting room and points.

"Great! Cosy!" Godric shouts, still bouncing.

"Would you like housekeeping to make this up for your companion?"

"My grandson, and please do check if there are other rooms first," Elizabeth knows her privacy is very likely over and clings to the hope Godric can stay in an adjacent room. "It doesn't have to be this luxurious."

"Hey! I heard that!" Godric shouts as the concierge smiles and is the height of professional service, going back into the corridor to bring the dog beds. "May I have a hot toddy and some mince pies, please? And this, same again?" Godric looks at Elizabeth's half-eaten lunch.

"Of course, Sir. Vegan?"

"If you like."

"Thank you," Elizabeth says, pleased the concierge remembers her dietary choices. She shuts the door behind the concierge and stretches out her arms to Godric, who stops bouncing and hugs his Nanna. "I have everything neat in the room," Elizabeth looks over his shoulder, smiling.

"Neat is boring," Godric replies, "and we were lonely without you. All of us have been to the parlour to spruce up for our big visit. Don't we smell nice? And, by way of nothing, isn't the bellboy cute?"

"If you're staying then you need to earn your mince pies. And he's not a bellboy. He's part of the concierge team at the front desk."

"Ah, don't spoil it. It's such a becoming title." Godric starts to bounce again. "bellboy! bellboy!"

"Do you fancy a night out in Oxford? We have to go and investigate a brawl."

"I'm in."

With that, the concierge has sent room service for Godric's hot toddy and mince pies with a knock at the door, and a silver tray is put down on the table with lunch, puddings, pastries and a hot toddy.

"I'm afraid we're fully booked, but we can make up the double sofa bed in the other room," room service informs Elizabeth.

"If you can stretch my sheets, I'd be grateful." Godric smiles. "Where's the bellboy?"

"Pardon?"

"Thank you," Elizabeth ushers the room service waiter out. "Tonight, we pay a visit to Broad Street. I hope you bought your snow boots."

25
CANTEEN CHRISTMAS

The day has run away from Inspector Abley and, after his snow globe stopped making that god-awful racket, he finally had a snooze on the sofa. When he woke, it was dark, and he worried that he was late for work. So, he jumped up and ran the three hundred yards to the Police Station.

Now, he can see rows of uniformed officers wearing hats from crackers line the tables in the Cambridge Police Station canteen for a Christmas teatime treat. The tables are festooned with old tinsel, and paper snowflakes pulled out of a box and reused for many years. A small plastic tree hides in the corner vibrating its way off the table to the beat of a weak sounding boombox playing an old CD of Christmas songs on a loop, which is itself being drowned out by plates clanking, cutlery jangling and general chatter and laughter from many officers who could call today their last day before the Christmas break. Others, with less of a smile, still in uniform, and their police radios on the table, have their bums half on, half off their seats, ready to rush to their squad cars and race off to this or that.

Among this crowd of Christmas cheer, Inspector Abley decides to sit down, just glad he made it in time. Unfortunately, however, his choosing a table with spaces on has left an opportunity for Superintendent Raynott to join and pull up a chair directly opposite. Abley feels the gravy curdle. Constable Goodey joins them. Abley is not sure if this makes things better, or worse. Goodey is far too cheerful for Abley's temperament tonight.

"How nice it is to see everyone enjoying themselves, in moderation of course." Superintendent Raynott says, then smiles with a mild sneer at Abley, then looking around the room notices people looking away from him, avoiding eye contact. He sighs a little, as his large saucer eyes fix back on Abley. The table grows just a little quieter now Raynott has sat, those coppers in close vicinity not wanting to be picked on by their boss's boss. "I have decided to take two weeks over Christmas in a modest cottage in Cornwall, and no one is going to pluck me out. Thank you for standing in, Abley."

"Right," Abley says, looking straight back at Raynott, and through gritted teeth, "it will be such a pleasure."

"Yes, I shall enjoy the entire holidays knowing the force is in safe hands," Raynott smiles. "So if you want to take a few days now before I'm gone until the sixth of January, then do so as I'm going to expect you to be here from eight until eight right through. Duty calls, as they say. I know you'll step up to the plate."

Abley detects a slight hint of sarcasm in Raynott's tone.

"Do I have a choice?"

"There's always a choice."

Goodey chips in, seeing how devastated Inspector Abley looks at this news.

"I'm working Christmas too, Inspector. We could catalogue all those clocks together and chime in the New Year. It'll be fun!"

"That does sound like good work. I will think of you while I'm on my long walks along the Penzance coast,"

Raynott says, pleased with his manoeuvre, "but I will check in with you every day, mind, to make sure everything is shipshape. The WiFi down there is excellent, you know."

"Great," Abley is rapidly going off his food.

At this point, some radios start to flash, and a table of police officers get up and rush out, probably to an RTA, burglary or even a public act of disorder. At that moment, Abley is jealous as hell.

"More cordial, Inspector?" Raynott pours himself some squash and tucks into the roast potatoes going cold in the dish in front of them, while the taste in Abley's mouth has turned sour.

For what seems like forever, Abley sits with Raynott, listening to stories about Raynott's time in Africa, how he's plotted out six walks in Cornwall, and hears him recount every pit stop and tourist site along the way that he's hoping to see.

Abley starts to watch Raynott's every mouthful, praying for no cheeseboard as he observes Raynott shovel in the Christmas pudding. Finally, Raynott is interrupted by a call.

"Excuse me. I have to take this. You'll be taking these in a few days for me." Raynott gets up, the phone hard against his ear to block out the canteen chatter, "Hello? Yes, this is Superintendent Raynott. Yes, I was just speaking to him. That's right. Inspector Abley will be the main contact point through the Christmas and New Year period. Great. No, he's not taking my parking space. Wait a minute. Let me check that. No, it's back at the office. Wait a minute. While you're on the phone," and with that, Raynott is gone.

"Fuck it." Abley can't help himself.

"Inspector, you're welcome to come back to mine after our Christmas shift," Goodey offers, seeing his Inspector is a little down. "Mum already knows I'm working, so she's saving me my Christmas dinner. And I'm supposed to be getting the new wiring system for my set up in the loft."

"Your set up?"

"Choo-choos. I have five-hundred metres of track. You could help me lay the new wiring if you like. I've got music up there and everything."

Abley wonders how Sergeant Goodey has lasted this long here but doesn't want to sound ungrateful.

"Well, that does sound like the perfect way to spend Christmas. I expect I won't get time though. But will make sure you get to put tools down in time yourself." Abley thinks about booking those few days off pronto before he's put on any more trivial raids by Raynott in his last remaining days of relative freedom. What a Christmas this is turning out to be. No wife, no home and no murder to solve. But more important than all of that, as he looks out the window at the snow which has been relentlessly falling heavily all afternoon, no golf!

26
DRINK AND BE MERRY

Later the same evening, despite the snow making it preferable to stay indoors and huddle close to a fire, Godric and Elizabeth head towards the King's Arms pub. This journey takes them down St Giles' and along Broad Street. A few tourists are still out, looking in lit shop windows, pouring over artworks and teddy bears wearing College crests on their knitted jumpers staring back up at them from the displays. Post-doctoral students and Fellows mingle between College gates, sharing papers, arranging dinners to analyse new mathematical calculations.

The dogs attract attention, as always, slowing down Elizabeth's mission, although recently Elizabeth has taken to putting small signs on their harnesses with the necessary information, so as not to be interrupted by the constantly repeated banal questions about age, name and whether the dog is a dog or a bitch. The signs answer these points. Elizabeth wanted to add and extra statement: 'my human companion is fed up of explaining these things about me to every Tom, Dick or Harry'. But Godric stopped her, so instead it just reads 'Happy Christmas!' If people now ask Elizabeth she points. She is a little irked when Godric uses the new signs to talk to men when they stop and laugh. She hears Godric behind her now, explaining to someone that the dogs are very friendly.

Elizabeth is holding Clive's lead, as Clive is still missing his human companion after his heart attack. And Elizabeth is looking after Clive, while Ed the old Lock Keeper recuperates, although recent correspondence with Ed would suggest that Clive might be staying with Elizabeth for longer than she anticipated. So Elizabeth allows Clive to get away with things that she doesn't tolerate from Hector or Monty.

Inside the King's Arms, Elizabeth makes a beeline to the bar to speak to the manager, while Godric finds a table big enough to accommodate the dogs around it. He is immediately surrounded by people coming up to say hello, including a group of academics in Father Christmas hats and flashing tinsel. Elizabeth, on the other hand, has to wait her turn in a busy pub. When she is given some time, the manager knows nothing about the brawl out in the street the other night. Instead, she gets pulled into a game of Scrabble taking place at the bar when she spots over a man's shoulder a space for the word 'maximize' and is welcomed onto a team immediately. No matter how hard Elizabeth tries, she cannot resist next placing 'quixotic' before apologising that she has to go.

The dogs come to find Elizabeth and she returns to Godric with half a stout for herself and a martini for him.

"Vodka martini?"

"I'm not buying you whisky this early."

"No complaints," Godric sees the olive in the pretty drink and stabs it.

"I learnt nothing," Elizabeth sips her stout while stroking the dogs, "that's no good, is it Clive?"

"It's okay, as we learnt a lot. See those four over there?"

"Which ones?"

"In the fabulous dresses."

"Ah, yes."

"As it happens, they saw a fight out on Broad Street recently, between two women and a man," Godric nods.

"Can they show us where?"

"Let me finish this, and I'll go over," but Godric sees his Nanna's impatience, so he sighs, hands her the leads and gets up to walk over to the drag queens. Elizabeth can't hear what Godric says, but she can see the queens looking over at her and pulling faces. Then Godric shakes his head. The whole thing lasts far too long, and then Elizabeth watches as Godric puts his leg up on the chair and starts to sip his drink he took over while brushing his thigh. For goodness sake. She hasn't got time for watching him flirt, so she gets up, and lets go of the dogs. They run and jump at Godric, who manages to lift his drink out of the way just in time.

"Would it be possible to show us where the skirmish was that you saw the other night?" Elizabeth bluntly asks the queens.

"Yes, darling. But hold your horses, we can't rush our cocktails," one drag queen says, eyelashes fluttering at Elizabeth. "I just love your curls, girlfriend."

"Someone has died actually. There has been a murder," Elizabeth replies.

"What? No, I'm not getting involved in that. I can't go out there if it's dangerous," one of them says, wearing a bright pink dress, with a pink tiara.

"Don't be silly. This woman is a living legend. Her dogs will protect us, and she can sing any evil people away," says another. Elizabeth looks at Godric, wondering what he has told them. "Without her, we'd be knee-deep in hate crimes. Thank you for all your hard work."

"You're welcome. Shall we go?" Elizabeth waves her arms for them to stand up.

"Let's go. You'll protect us, won't you, Goddy?" Says a

queen in blue sequins.

"I will most definitely go down fighting," Godric says, throwing around an imaginary sword.

"You will not," Elizabeth replies.

"Don't spoil the illusion," Godric whispers.

"What did you say I did?"

"You play the piano for a travelling band, and the dogs sing for you. It felt realistic."

"Of course, that makes complete sense." Elizabeth rolls her eyes.

"You're called Professor Strict and the Fuzzies." Godric looks at the dogs. "I was thinking on my feet. Look, they're putting on a panto. It felt apt."

*

"Oi, darling," shouts one of the drag queens as Professor Elizabeth Green, Godric and the drag queens now stand in the middle of Broad Street. "It was here. We just saw three people fighting," the drag queen says, having tottered up Broad Street and is now standing opposite the statues on the pillars outside the Sheldonian Theatre. "They were punching him."

"Where were you?"

"We were on our way to Jerry's club for some drinks, and this man approached the women from the Sheldonian," one says, pointing.

"And did you see their faces?" Elizabeth gets out a local paper, which has a photo of Sandy who died in Catte College. The story headline reads 'Have You Seen Santa? – Don Dies Under Christmas Tree'.

"Yes, that's one of them. The other looked like she camped in the woods. You know the type."

"Are you stereotyping?" Elizabeth asks.

"All the time. You're not Professor Strict or whatever, are you? You're an academic!"

"I'm very strict."

Some of the other drag queens titter.

"I'll let you off, but only because I like your dogs." Then the drag queen turns to the rest and shouts, "Why don't we put on a show, a crime scene recreation?" There is some whoop whooping and enthusiasm, and two of them start to pretend to pummel Godric. They lift him gently onto the snowy pavement and begin to hit him. One strikes him with their handbag, gently. "It was more violent than this. They were all going at each other."

"Hey! Stop this!" Godric laughs and protests.

"No, this is useful," Elizabeth replies, "keep going. Then what did you see?"

"We saw the man jump on one of the women, then lie there for a moment. The other hit him with her handbag." The drag queen is standing out in the snow, wearing next to nothing in green lace, reenacting the brawl, still looking like a million dollars.

"No, I think she was on the floor too," another says, pushing over the drag queen who had just been speaking. There is a lot of falling in the snow and throwing snowballs, as they break into play. Elizabeth tries to bring it back.

"C'mon, then what happened?"

"I wasn't even playing her. Divina May is playing her."

"No, honey, I'm playing the taller one, as I'm very leggy."

"So, let me get this straight. You saw two women, one with the bag with all the penises sticking out of it, hit the man. What did he look like?"

"Oh, he looked sleazy. I thought you go, girl, when I saw them. I mean, they weren't hurting him. I didn't see any kicking to the crown jewels," another says.

"Yes, but he sat on her. Almost straight away."

"Who did?" Elizabeth asks.

"The one with the penis bag. Lots of sparkly rings, proper knuckle dusters." Elizabeth nods her head. She is not sure she is going to get much more out of the reenactors. "Could the bag possibly have had elephant trunks and not penii on it?"

The drag queens just stare at Elizabeth, so she continues, "Well, would you mind sharing your contact with my grandson, in case we need to get hold of you again?"

"Your grandson can get hold of us any time," then to Godric, "Come back with us, we're hosting auditions down Ship Street. We've lost a cast member for our show." A drag queen beckons Godric to join them as they start to walk down Broad Street.

Elizabeth watches as Godric waves to her and shouts, "I'll ask for more evidence if they have any." Before her 'helpful' grandson puts his arm around two drag queens, then disappears into the snow.

*

Elizabeth ponders on how the evening has taken an unexpected turn. She holds the dogs. She searches the area for anything. Then she spots it, next to a snowman wearing a saucepan for a hat. A black leather driver's glove on one of the metal spikes between the Sheldonian pillars. Just like the glove in Sandy's home in Summertown in the waste paper basket. Could it be the other glove of the same pair? Elizabeth searches for something to put it in. She finds a poo bag.

She looks down at the dogs as they stand in the snow and enjoys the moment, as her heart skips a beat with joy at remembering that they are all now together. That was what was missing. She smiles to herself and is pleased with her find of the glove. So there was a fight where Sandy and Haven were attacking a man? Elizabeth can't believe it. She decides to abandon the warmth of the King's Arms, with its glowing lights and inviting smells, even though she knows she could thrash them all at Scrabble if she returned. Instead, she takes the dogs back for a rest and some food.

As Elizabeth takes a different route home, away from people on Broad Street, she heads up Parks Road where the trees reach up to the sky. It is silent, and there are no people. The dogs sniff and read the pee-mail, as Elizabeth's mind finally has some peace. She ponders on the fight described. It doesn't sound like Dr Haven Usrey, beating up a man, or beating up anyone. She is willing to believe that Haven might act out of character, but not with Dr Sandy Starborneck. As far as she can tell, Haven was well aware of Sandy's flaws and happy to point them out. So unlikely to be led like a sheep into doing something she didn't believe in. And, as for Sandy, she hardly seemed the type for aggression. But, then again, Elizabeth was now holding a glove, just like the other one at Sandy's home.

Elizabeth turns left into Museum Road. Memories of her time here as a lecturer rush back as she remembers how she would cycle along Lamb and Flag Passage to get to her research laboratory every day. She had not been happy, away from Gerald. And now, she was parted again. Her heart sinks a little until she feels the hair of Clive between her fingers, all snowy and soft. Hector and Monty, together with Clive, seem impervious to thoughts of the past or the future, although she knows that isn't true. She knows Clive is missing his own friend, Ed. She will hurry back now and bring treats for all.

As Elizabeth has thoughts on her mind about what she is convinced is a murder, someone taps her on the shoulder. It makes her jump a little. But when she sees the face, she smiles.

"Hello," Gabriel says. "I was on my way back from the lab, and I thought I'd go for a quick pint in the Lamb, and here you are. You appear to have acquired rather a lot of dogs. Are they all yours?"

"We're just heading back from stretching their legs."

"They're beautiful. How are they so clean?"

"My grandson arrived with them. Apparently, he missed

me. He took them to the parlour before he came. Which probably means my house is a mud bath and that's why he's evacuated and decamped here."

"Would you let me accompany you? It's rather quiet on the streets. Be good to know you're back safe."

"It's only ten-thirty."

"It's just an excuse to spend a little time with you. Indulge me," and Gabriel gives Elizabeth the largest smile, "perhaps you could join me for a nightcap?" Elizabeth nods, and they walk the very short distance to St Giles' and then pop into The Lamb public house. The very kind barman has dog treats and water, so Elizabeth starts to relax. It is only then that she decides to probe Gabriel a little further.

"You know, Sandy had poison in her system. The police said as much." Elizabeth watches Gabriel's face for any flicker of guilt, "I'd like to find out what."

"Poison? Isn't that your area?"

"Yes, the police might come knocking before long." Elizabeth raises her eyebrows, not pleased that she has been right all along.

"But, it could still be accidental?"

"Unlikely." Elizabeth sips her stout, as Gabriel feeds the dogs treats. "Not too many." Then Elizabeth narrows her eyes, "What were you doing in Summertown, near Sandy Starborneck's house?"

"What?"

"Earlier today. We saw you, Sergeant Lemon and myself. You were in Charlbury Road."

"I was just out walking. I'd been up by the Cherwell, heading across to get something to eat in Summertown, yes."

"In the snow?"

"It's so rare and so beautiful. I see you got the boots I sent over," Gabriel replies. They both look down at the rather smart boots.

"Thank you."

"Pleasure. Will I see you in the morning?"

"Yes, Godric will have these loves."

"They're special, aren't they?" And at that moment, a member of the public comes over to ask about the dogs. Elizabeth points at the signs on their backs and looks back at Gabriel.

"Apparently, they still haven't found Father Christmas. He might be a murderer, after all. But it makes no sense. First, he poisons, then he pushes? Just to be sure?" Elizabeth says, almost to herself. The member of the public listens to Elizabeth's words about poison and murderers and frowns and goes back to her seat at the other end of the bar. Elizabeth continues, "Father Christmas, a murderer?"

27
UNIVERSITY PARKS

The next morning and Elizabeth leaves Godric sleeping on the sofa bed in the other room, still wearing his clothes from the night before, a Christmas brooch flashing on his jumper. She writes him a note and throws on a coat before taking the dogs out for a walk in the University Parks. The snow is deep, but the sky is a clear blue. Elizabeth places her sunglasses on the end of her nose and crunches across to the Cherwell. Hector, Monty and Clive spot another dog and run over to say hello. A few ducks scoot across the freezing river, which is beginning to ice over at the edges, looking for treats. She has snuck a bread roll from breakfast, although she knows this isn't good for them, breaks it into tiny pieces and drops it in the water. The ducks hoover it up and then watch, with one eye, in case she has more.

Elizabeth has had poison on her mind since that Oxford Inspector let it slip. She can't wait to talk to her friend, Inspector Abley, again, to see if her suspicions have been confirmed. Elizabeth looks at the tall bare chestnut trees covered in snow, at the grasses and old thistle heads all white. She tries to think how Sandy would have been poisoned and by whom. Sandy had eaten dinner, some of it. She had seemed fine. Not perfect, and most definitely drunk, but functioning. Haven said that Sandy had not been herself for a few days. Granted. But she was functioning. Not curled up in a ball, complaining of stomach cramps. Elizabeth knows this was deliberate. But it might have been something that perhaps the killer would have got away with had there not been such a thorough autopsy and she hadn't died in College with all the eyes on her.

Elizabeth heads to the Plant Sciences Department on the South Parks Road, where she pops her head around the corner of Professor Alexander Resander's laboratory.

"You haven't come to stand on my feet again, have you?" he asks, with a straight face, as she walks in finding him at his workbench already.

"Thought I'd see what all the fuss is about. Had a lot of funding for this," she replies.

"It might be shinier than yours," he says. "And, get those dogs out of here!"

"Our laboratories are exceptional, as well you know. Was Dr Sandy Starborneck working here with you?" Elizabeth asks.

Alexander shakes his head and frowns.

"No, she wasn't here, or next door. I don't know where she was. The dogs, Professor Green."

"Biodegradable plastics apparently," Elizabeth says, trying to get more information from Alexander.

"So, not plants."

"Yes, plants."

"Look, she probably upset Father Christmas as much as she did us. Who can blame him for losing his rag."

"She was poisoned. What are you working on?"

"I know actually. Gabriel told me the news this morning." Alexander stops and looks at Elizabeth.

"Well, if the police said they found traces of poison in Dr Starborneck's body then it could be murder. What are you working on?"

"Ha! Subtle segue. If you want to know did I poison Dr Starborneck, I'd say you're asking the wrong question. What on earth would be my motive?"

"So you're not denying it?" Elizabeth presses.

"Hello!" Gabriel comes out of his laboratory, pleased to see Elizabeth. "Good walk?" He pats the dogs.

"I'm just asking Alexander if he knew anything about the poison they found in Dr Starborneck's autopsy."

"And I said no. Dogs, out now." to which Alexander walks off, turning before he disappears with a parting shot, "I'm looking forward to your keynote speech. Wouldn't miss it for the world."

Elizabeth had momentarily forgotten all about her speech. Damn it.

"Right, right. That's not today, though. I thought it had just been postponed because of the murder?" she says to Gabriel, with Alexander already gone.

"Yes," Gabriel reminds her, "they delayed it to today. Sorry, that wasn't a secret, was it? We were just talking about her death this morning, and it came out," Gabriel says. Elizabeth sighs, thinking about the keynote. Speaking to her peers is one of her least favourite things. She enjoys lecturing students, as they want to learn. But her so-called 'equals' just want to find holes in her research.

"Do you think he will mind if I borrow his laboratory for an hour?" Elizabeth asks Gabriel, looking around at Professor Resander's lab.

"Yes, especially with these cuties, but I don't. I'm leaving, so you can use mine." Gabriel smiles and shows Elizabeth into his laboratory. "What are you doing?"

"Oh, nothing. I just want to run a few tests," Elizabeth says vaguely.

"Into the poison?"

"I don't work for Oxford Police."

"Okay, I'll leave you to your mysterious work. See you in College shortly?"

Elizabeth nods and waits for Gabriel to leave, then she gets out a poo bag with the glove in it that she found outside the Sheldonian Theatre on the railings. She knows she must give it to Sergeant Lemon if she is right, so puts plastic inspection gloves on. The dogs lie down by her feet as she steps over them. She is not sure if she is looking for blood or a clue. But she is determined that this glove might have the answer.

28
YOUR SLEIGH BELLS ARE NICKED!

Professor Elizabeth Green has made her way to Catte College to deliver her keynote speech. She is not surprised to see a bleary-eyed Godric standing in the Porters' Lodge, still in his dressing-gown under his coat, with his pyjamas tucked into his socks and his shoes getting wet in the snow. She had expected he wouldn't read her note, so had tipped the concierge to bang the hotel room door. That would wake Godric.

"I've been asked to star in a pantomime!" he sleepily tells an impatient Elizabeth.

"If you're intent on paying a visit while I'm on my work trips, at least maintain some illusion of punctuality, Goddy. I have to give a keynote speech, and I'm late." Elizabeth hands Hector, Monty and Clive's leads to Godric. "They have been for a good walk, but they will be hungry, so if you can take them back to the hotel before you do anything else," Elizabeth pulls some poo bags out of her pocket and hands them to her grandson.

"I might need to use the dogs to help me publicise the panto today. I've been given a sandwich board and everything. I'm Buttons!"

"Just take the dogs." Elizabeth turns to leave.

"The dogs can be reindeer," he whispers as she starts to walk away.

"No, no way. They are not being used as entertainment." Elizabeth turns back, having heard his whisper. Godric tuts, and then looks down at the dogs as Elizabeth leaves.

"We'll find a way," he tells them quietly, "I know you'd like your moment in the spotlight. Giddyup," Godric slides on the soles of his shoes across the ice back to the hotel.

*

As Professor Elizabeth Green makes her way into the College lecture hall, in preparation to give her keynote, she can hear a pin drop. Her peers have packed out the intimate velvet blue chairs in sloped seating, with standing room only at the back. She wishes she'd prepared something to say, having been an unwilling participant to this whole event; Sandy's murder is the only thing on her mind. As she walks up the steps to the stage and is met by technical support in his white coat, who attempts but fails to put a microphone on her lapel as she nears the lectern, she brushes him away. Elizabeth doesn't need electronic aids, as her booming voice can travel across the largest hall. As she pauses to gather her thoughts, Michael steps on stage to make an introduction. Again, she gestures for him to leave, so he nods and keeps it short.

"Professor Elizabeth Green, who needs no introduction!" he shouts. Then she stares at the audience. She surmises they are all approximately her age. Where are the young, eager Readers and Junior Lecturers of Plant Sciences? Elizabeth answers her own question in her head. They are in their departments, with no budgets to travel. Hmm. Elizabeth decides she is going to talk about the murder and poison and is just about to open her mouth when there is a loud kerfuffle at the back of the lecture hall.

The two doors fly open either side of the aisles and two uniformed police officers barge in. They stop suddenly, and stand very still, surveying the room. Then apologetically, they step out slowly, before everyone can hear them rushing along the corridor outside. Muttering in the lecture room now grows louder. "What was that?" and "The police?" can be heard uttered. Just as the room attempts very hard to refocus on the woman on stage, another intruder flies in. Father Christmas!

Father Christmas, dressed in full regalia and carrying a large sack of presents, runs down the aisle and, before anyone can stop him, attempts to duck behind the curtain left of the stage. But then he reverses as a policeman appears from nowhere. Another uniformed officer opens the back door and starts to head towards the stage, which causes Father Christmas to rush up the side of the audience and then begin to run along the backs of the chairs to the exit, presents falling out of his sack as he goes, causing chaos as the audience attempt to grab the presents for themselves, some even starting to open a few. Father Christmas disappears through the 'Exit Only' door then reappears as another uniformed policeman chases after him. Finally, Father Christmas rushes back on stage and leaps at Elizabeth Green, causing her to fall backwards. Only then do the police catch up with Father Christmas and cuff him, his sack half empty beside him on the stage floor.

*

"I'm fine, really. But I won't be able to deliver my keynote now," Elizabeth looks up, glaring at Michael, then back at Lemon, "Is this the same Father Christmas?"

"Yup. Small children somewhere will be crying," Lemon replies, then he shouts to the audience, "don't touch the parcels. They're evidence," clearly seeing that some have already been opened and people start hurriedly attempting to rewrap the paper. The Master swans in, with the Porter, still wearing his bowler hat, following behind.

"Everything under control here? Nothing to see. Right ho." And with that, the Master leaves.

"We've been keeping tabs on him, his coming and going," the Porter offers to Elizabeth by way of explanation for the abrupt intrusion, "not just at Catte College, but a number of colleges. He's been all over this morning. Only, he's robbing the presents, or swapping them. That's what Sid and Eric said too. All over the Colleges of Oxford. Swapping parcels. What's that about?" the Porter asks Sergeant Lemon.

"We have a real Robin Hood here. This here Santa has been robbing the rich to give to the poor. Isn't that right?" Sergeant Lemon tells Father Christmas, who bends his head. He'd really rather not give any explanation. But has the grim realisation that he's been finally caught. His wife had found out a few nights ago and told him to stop. He should have listened to her.

"You should see their faces. Families, relying on food banks," Father Christmas says under his breath, "Over a million you know, in this country. And people here, in these Colleges, they don't notice their missing presents. They don't even collect them half the time."

"This one of yours?" Lemon asks, pulling out a present from the sack. Father Christmas nods. Lemon opens it. It's an ice scraper for a car windscreen.

"Bought that in a charity shop. Ten pence," Father Christmas replies.

"That's a jolly good present," Elizabeth says, picking up another present and unwrapping it. This time it is an expensive pair of cufflinks with a diamond on each one. "Now what use is that to anyone?" Elizabeth adds, throwing it back down.

"That's a robbed one," Lemon explains.

"So, you have nothing to do with the murder of Dr

Starborneck, do you?" Elizabeth asks the man dressed as Father Christmas. Father Christmas shakes his head.

"Is that the lady who died? I saw it in the paper. I feel awful. I don't know her. She grabbed me. I didn't push her. I struggled to get out of her grip; that's all. She must have slipped backwards."

"Why did you run?" Elizabeth asks him.

"I didn't look. I was just keen to get away. Her breath smelt of whisky." It is clear to Elizabeth that Father Christmas wouldn't harm a fly.

"What's your name?" Elizabeth asks.

"Fred," the man replies, "I work backstage at the Arts and Stage Theatre most of the year, down the Cowley Road, just building sets and that. We got the idea from a play we were watching. About robbing the rich, no offence," Fred replies, flinching a bit from his cuffs.

"I'll do the questioning." Lemon glares at Elizabeth.

"I wasn't stealing anything that mattered. I was swapping nice presents for bargains. That's all. The nice ones I was sending to the orphanage. Got them a lovely blender and a few electric toothbrushes. A beautiful bracelet, it's been good. It's gonna go to this little girl who just lost her parents in a terrible accident. Or was. They can't afford this stuff. It's your luxuries, isn't it?" he says, before being led away to the police car waiting outside.

"Everyone, please remain in your seats!" Lemon shouts at the audience, "We'd like to question you about what you saw. Then, you'll be free to go."

"Swapping presents. Hardly the crime of the century," Elizabeth offers, watching Fred hang his head.

"Only Dr Starborneck interrupted him," Lemon says, "or else, he probably would have continued right under the College noses. He's been spotted in almost all the Colleges," says Lemon, repeating what the Porter had said, realising how cunning this man had been.

"No one knew who had hired him, so no one said anything. Genius!" Elizabeth laughs, "He fooled everyone.

I like it."

"No, you don't," Lemon replies.

"You've got to give it to him. It's creative. Fooling the so-called most intelligent minds in the world, or so they think. And, not just some of them, all of them. If it hadn't been for a drunken woman who was already poisoned having grabbed him for her balance most probably, he would be a free Father Christmas now. He had a sack of presents he was stealing. He didn't push her at all. That's not what killed her."

29
NAME YOUR POISON

It is nearly lunchtime, and the conference has not long resumed after the eventful morning of Professor Elizabeth Green's interrupted keynote speech. Michael Pussett is working overtime to get everything back on track, picking up stray leaflets, pointing to the Catte College staff to bring in more refreshments, fussing after dirty cups and propping open doors to encourage fluid movement between the exhibit rooms. Elizabeth watches as Gabriel and Alexander stand at their personal exhibition displays, and one by one shake their heads at Michael, taking books from him that he has picked up, pointing in the direction of people Michael is looking for, and generally irritated by Michael's overly dramatic brow wiping and deep breathing.

The police are still milling. Even the Oxford Inspector has turned up; Lemon's Inspector Elizabeth met earlier up at Sandy and Haven's Summertown house. Elizabeth observes how he seems distinctly disinterested in the case, checking his phone and laughing with some of the caterers. She watches the Oxford Inspector walk over to speak to the Master, who has popped his head into the room for a short while, not entirely putting his feet over the threshold of the conference room, just checking to see what food is available. From a distance, Elizabeth can see that the Master doesn't like the Oxford Inspector and vice versa. There are a few scowls exchanged. No doubt, this Inspector shares the disdain Inspector Abley has for all academics. At least Bob hides it reasonably well most of the time she thinks, well, some of the time. Then, the Master disappears as quickly as he came.

Most conference attendees are now standing by their exhibits, with colleagues and peers reading materials on desks and studying each other's successes. Elizabeth notices Michael Pussett chase after the Oxford Inspector – who has walked to the Christmas cake stand to pick up a slice – only to be given the back of the hand as a signal not to interfere. She hears Michael ask, "When are you leaving? There's nothing more to investigate, is there?" but the Oxford Inspector doesn't reply. Elizabeth is just about to walk over to find out the latest when she is halted in her steps by Michael, who stands on a chair and taps his coffee cup with a spoon, to audible groans.

"Just a quick interruption. It's great to see so many of you here this morning. I wanted to take a moment to thank everyone for being so stoic and coming back to make this conference what it is, a great success in these troubling circumstances. These rooms of exhibits are, without a doubt the best we have had since I started organising this conference ten years ago. So thank you for helping make it so wonderful," Michael beams, then spots Elizabeth. "And, we're so sorry that we didn't get to hear from Professor Elizabeth Green. Perhaps she can send her talk to us, so we have it in writing and can distribute it to you all." Michael suggests but sees Elizabeth shaking her head, no way. "Or, invite her back next year?" Elizabeth continues to shake her head, so Michael quickly changes the subject. "We have a tasty luncheon in a while, followed by several lectures this afternoon. So, please do take a slice of Christmas cake to tide you over, from our lovely Linda." Michael looks at the chief caterer, Linda, whose face remains deadpan, so he continues, "and I hope we get to speak personally, as I come round the room. Thank you. Enjoy your time and come back next year!"

"We can't have a dead body interrupt proceedings, can we Michael?" Gabriel whispers to Elizabeth, adding, "If he comes over to my exhibit again I'll have to say something, He's completely making this the Michael show. Sandy will have had family and friends who will be missing her this Christmas. We can't brush over that like it's some small hiccup to the smooth running of today."

"A little insensitive," Elizabeth agrees, adding, "Apparently though, she had no family. Haven mentioned. So, at least there's that. You know, the Oxford Inspector over there says I should stay here while he investigates, but won't let me investigate. Where's the sense in that? I wasn't supposed to stay this long. Where's your home, Gabriel?"

"I told you already. It's here. And you should probably not get on his wrong side."

"Does he have a right side?" Elizabeth looks at the Oxford Inspector now stuffing his face with cake. "Are you not going home for Christmas?" Elizabeth asks.

"I shall be in College, as I said before," Gabriel replies flatly.

Elizabeth thinks about how she can't wait to get home. She thinks fondly of her favourite grandchild, Godric, who has travelled to be with her and make sure she's not lonely. Though goodness only knows what they are up to right now. Did she hear right? Did Godric tell her he was going to be in a pantomime? How is this coming over to see her?

"What about your family?" Elizabeth presses Gabriel.

"Alexander and I find that the College bar on Christmas Day is a very peaceful place." Elizabeth glances at Alexander, who is standing by the next exhibit and nods, silently. "Two bachelors, alone at Christmas." Gabriel finishes Elizabeth's thought.

At the other end of the room, Elizabeth watches the tea trolley come in, with a big tea urn on top and some coffee pots. The caterer, Linda, guides it into the corner next to the Christmas cake, then comes back moments later with another trolley, this time with cups. Finally, she returns once more with a trolley laden down with even more cakes and scones. Elizabeth decides to pour herself a cup of tea.

"Do you have any peppermint?" Elizabeth asks Linda.

"Oh, yes. We do. One moment." Linda bends down and picks out a pot of herbal teas from the bottom of the trolley, "Not many people ask for peppermint." Linda pours some hot water on the teabag, "Would you like a saucer, or will you leave the bag in?"

"Leave it in, that's fine. Some nice cakes." Elizabeth looks at the cakes.

"Would you like one?"

"I'm vegan."

"The carrot cake is vegan," Linda replies helpfully.

"What do you make of Dr Starborneck's death?" She asks Linda.

"She didn't eat much, but she did tuck them away."

"Was she often drunk?"

"I don't know. I only remember her because she came a lot to the drinks trolley. But I don't know her," Linda replies. At which point Haven joins Elizabeth at the trolley.

"Mmm, this looks delicious!" Haven smiles at Linda and the cakes then puts a watch beside the urn and looks at Linda to do something with it. They both spot the bruises on Haven's wrists. "Someone must have dropped this outside the restrooms. You might want to put it in lost property?" Haven tells Linda about the watch, who nods.

"You seem very chirpy this morning?" Elizabeth asks Haven, "especially for someone with such bruises?"

"I'm just in the moment, Professor Green. Just living in

the moment. Right now, I'm going to enjoy a sugar hit and the carrots from the earth. And I fully intend to stick it to the man, who is responsible for all my bruises. All of it."

Elizabeth watches Haven eat the cake, and from the corner of her eye, she spots the caterer, Linda, picking up the watch and trying it on. She watches as Linda heads out of the room, perhaps to the kitchens, and so decides to follow her, curious to see what she does with the watch. Elizabeth leaves Haven dancing around the tea urn, and thinks she'll come back to Haven later.

As Elizabeth follows Linda along the corridor into the kitchen, and from behind can see that Linda has definitely put the watch on her wrist, it makes Elizabeth think is there another Robin Hood in the fold, only this time female? She looks at the profile of Linda's mischievous face as Linda turns into the kitchen. Quite the pixie, Elizabeth thinks, for a woman who looks like she's touching her fifties. Then Linda turns and smiles.

"Can I help you?"

"Are you keeping that?" Elizabeth looks at the watch on Linda's wrist.

"Perhaps. It fits. Look," and Linda smiles then waits for Elizabeth to answer.

"I wanted to come back to the kitchens, as the woman who died was poisoned."

"Don't look at me," Linda replies, "been making cakes here for over a year. No one has complained yet."

"Can anyone come back here?"

"Well, you have." Linda lights up a cigarette on the stove.

"Aren't you supposed to smoke outside?" Elizabeth raises her eyebrows.

"Yes, but I've no lighter," Linda replies, walking to the backdoor.

"You'll get cold. I've never understood smoking," Elizabeth says. Linda opens the door, and a cold burst of air shoots through, making them both shudder. A female undergraduate walks past Linda along by the bicycles parked up at the back of the kitchens and asks her for some cake. Linda pops into the kitchen then brings her out a piece of chocolate cake. Linda the walks over to a bicycle and wipes snow off the seat then finds a cardboard box and puts it over the seat.

"You cycle in this weather?" Elizabeth asks.

"I cycle everywhere. It's the only way to travel," Linda replies.

"How did Dr Starborneck have poison in her veins? Elizabeth asks. "We were all eating Christmas dinner, but she ate what Dr Gabriel Deersman ate, and he was fine."

"I don't know." Linda looks shocked to be asked, then says, "But I do know that he's the loveliest man. Glad it wasn't him who copped for it. Such a shame."

"What's a shame?" Elizabeth shakes her head.

"About his wife," Linda replies, but Elizabeth draws a blank, so Linda continues, "dying like that, so suddenly. He had the dream. You know. Perfect life."

Elizabeth did not know this about Gabriel.

"What did she die of?" Elizabeth asks, still holding her tea.

"Apparently, she just died in her sleep. That's what the College grapevine said."

"And what about Dr Starborneck. Did you notice anything strange about her?"

"Like I've told you. Couldn't hold her drink. Don't know what she saw in him. That other American, not sure her name. She puts crystals on the tables. I keep having to move them, as they're not sanitary. They have mud all over them? She's as bad." Linda walks in with her cigarette and opens a kitchen drawer. Behind Linda, a young female student walks into the kitchen and opens the fridge.

"Hey, help yourself, why don't you!" Linda smiles at the student, who steals a fizzy drink out of the fridge and grabs some cake then leaves. Linda looks back at the kitchen drawer, stuffed with what looks like lost property, and she rakes about in it with one hand until she finds what she's looking for and pulls out a rather large violet-looking crystal. Elizabeth notices Linda's fingers adorned with rings and wonders if she has also stolen those too.

"Are you not going to give it back to Dr Usrey?"

"She chose to leave it on the table. I left it there for a day. S'not my job to go chasing after people, reuniting them with their cast-off crystals. Finders keepers."

"Or watches?"

"God, you've got it in for me and this watch. Here, take it. I wasn't going to keep it."

"I don't want it, but I will give it to the Sergeant outside. It might be related to the case."

"Case?" Linda asks.

"This is a murder case."

"Murder?" Linda looks shocked.

"What do you think I was asking you about the food for?"

"D'you think it was that bloke dressed up as Father Christmas? The police were chasing him earlier. Didn't he disturb your talk?" Linda asks.

"No. I don't. Please give in any other items you find. They might be evidence."

"Of course." Linda looks worried now, aware that she has been playing with fire.

*

Elizabeth walks back out of the kitchens, hoping to find Sergeant Lemon still in the exhibition hall. When she enters it is busier, stragglers having come in just in time for the lunch gong and free food, but she spots the back of Sergeant Lemon's head and ploughs her way through the crowds. Elizabeth also notices the Oxford Inspector again, who seems to still be hovering just for the cake and is standing very close to the tea urn trolley.

"Hello Sergeant," Elizabeth says to Lemon as she walks

up behind him.

"Professor Green." Lemon turns.

"What's happening?" Elizabeth hands Lemon the watch.

"We're just gathering a bit more evidence, from the conference organisers, you know, since the autopsy threw up poison in her system. What's this?"

"I found the other glove of the pair. At Sandy's home, there was the other one of these in the wastebasket. Remember? I'm sure they match. This one was on Broad Street. They have a little green clip. Look. The brawl you mentioned? Someone who has been to Dr Sandy Starborneck's must have dropped it there. It was right there. It looks like a man's glove. There's traces of paint on it? Worth testing when you get more DNA samples, to find out whose it is."

"There are a lot of black gloves. Everyone has black gloves. And anyway, I can't use this as evidence now you've touched it," Lemon replies.

"I used a bag."

"You know how this works." He shrugs.

"Take it anyway, and this watch. Haven found it, gave it to lost property. That's me. I'm also good on poisons. If you let me speak to the pathologist on the case?" Elizabeth hands the bag to Lemon.

"Okay," Lemon puts them in his coat pocket.

"You should be shutting the kitchens for starters," Elizabeth adds bossily.

"There's nothing to suggest she was actually poisoned here though."

"You saw her home. There was blood. Whose blood was it?" Elizabeth asks, staring at Lemon.

"We know it wasn't Dr Starborneck's. Dr Haven Usrey has agreed to give a sample, but without a suspect, we can't start asking conference participants for their blood," he tells her, trailing off, aware he's saying too much.

"It has to be Michael Pussett's. He was seen arguing

with them on Broad Street. It has to be his glove too. I saw him comforting Dr Starborneck outside the St Giles' Hotel, and we've all seen him kiss her in the quad here. It has to be his. It could have been a lover's tiff."

"We have no evidence."

"Can you introduce me to the pathologist, please?"

"This isn't Cambridge, Professor. You don't work for the police here."

"There has been a murder. And, I'm the best chance you have of solving it. The murderer could be anywhere."

Sergeant Lemon raises his eyebrows but says nothing.

"Together, we can solve it together," Elizabeth continues, irritated she has to go through this charade every time. "Dr Starborneck was poisoned. Your Oxford Inspector said it himself that there was poison in her body. This is murder." Elizabeth repeats quietly to Lemon.

"Are you intent on ruining this conference?" From across the hubbub, everyone hears a man scream. It is Michael, the conference organiser and he's screaming at the Oxford Inspector, who is tucking away another mince pie. "What are you even doing here? You're just harassing us now, as far as I can see. Didn't the Master tell you to be discreet, for chrissakes?"

"Sir, we are investigating a suspicious death. And, if it hasn't escaped your notice, the deceased died while at your conference. So, we would ask you not to obstruct our investigation."

"All I can see is you eating mince pies! On your Christmas holidays already?"

"And what harm is that doing, apart perhaps from to my cholesterol, hmm?" the Oxford Inspector replies.

"You've got everything you need, just clear off."

"If you have time now, Sir, then it would be good to speak to you down the station," the Oxford Inspector insists.

"I've already spoken to your Sergeant!"

"Then you won't mind going over your statement one

more time with me, will you," the Inspector says calmly, popping in a large mouthful of mince pie.

"Are you happy?" Michael turns on Haven. "You've ruined everything! This is all your fault."

"What? What have I done? They're asking you to the station, Michael. Not me. What does that tell you? Look what he did!" And Haven shows the police her bruises.

"You're toxic, woman. Toxic! If it weren't for you, Sandy would still be alive." Michael leaps at Haven and tries to grab Haven by the throat. Lemon jumps on him and starts to pull him back just in time, as Haven now watches on, holding herself and recoiling. There is a commotion in the room, as the crowd parts and people gasp. Lemon hands Michael to a Constable, and the Oxford Inspector points to the Constable to usher Michael out, handcuffing Michael as he goes.

"The lady might like to file for assault. You're in big trouble, son." The Oxford Inspector turns and looks at Linda, who has returned to the cake trolley.

"Is it okay if I take a piece of the Christmas cake? It's been one of those mornings," the Oxford Inspector asks her, then smiles at Linda as she places a large slice of Christmas cake onto a linen napkin and hands it to the Inspector. "I'll bring the serviette back," he says.

"Keep it," Linda replies and heads back to the kitchen. The Oxford Inspector nods, some way behind Michael, who can still be heard shouting as he is led to the squad car.

*

When the Oxford Inspector has left, Elizabeth eyes Haven carefully. Haven looks at Elizabeth guiltily.

"This is all too much. I feel dizzy, I'm going to get some water," Haven says, holding her neck and heading out to the kitchens.

"You don't know it's murder. You need to stick to the

facts," Lemon raises his voice a little at Elizabeth. Lemon left Cambridge for several reasons, asserting his authority and finding his own voice being a large one of them. As he turns, however, he feels like he's just seen the ghost from Inspector past. "Inspector Abley?" Lemon says, dumbfounded, wondering if he is hallucinating after a week of long shifts.

"Ah, Bob. Did you bring it?" Elizabeth asks nonchalantly.

"Hello to you too." Inspector Bob Abley arrives with a parcel in his hands. "Here you go," he says, handing her the box. "Hello, Sergeant."

"What are you doing here?" Lemon is stunned, "This is ridiculous. Are you both following me?"

"A Constable outside just tried to ask me the same thing, wanted to take my statement. No, I've just come to see if everyone's all right over here. You see, I know the both of you very well. And when I get multiple calls from Professor Green telling me there's been a murder, that Father Christmas is a suspect—"

"Oh, he didn't do it," Elizabeth corrects Inspector Bob Abley. "That's old news. The little children can relax. But I need to speak to the Oxford pathologist. Would you have any sway with Thames Valley?" Elizabeth asks Bob.

"Excuse me!" Sergeant Lemon interrupts.

"That's when I said to myself 'When Professor Elizabeth Green gets a bee in her bonnet…' So, I've come to try to make this as easy as possible for you." Inspector Abley looks at Sergeant Lemon. "I have a few days off—"

"Great, this is just great." Sergeant Lemon walks out of the room, then walks in again. "You have to leave," he says to Inspector Abley.

"Aren't you going to introduce me to this handsome man?" Haven asks Elizabeth, as Haven enters with a glass of water.

"Really?" Sergeant Lemon shakes his head and sighs.

"I am getting sensations." Haven shuts her eyes.

"Well, stop those immediately," Elizabeth says, frowning.

"Inspector Abley, Bob Abley." Inspector Abley shakes Haven's hand.

"I've been through a lot in the past two days, Bob. But I can tell, you are a man who wears a white hat," Haven says, smiling at Inspector Abley.

"Excuse me?" Lemon is incredulous.

"Why thank you Ma'am." Abley flicks his imaginary wild-west Stetson. "We just have to catch the men in the black hats, and we'll be on our way," he says and blows the smoke from an imaginary fired gun. Haven giggles coyly.

"I'll leave you playing cowboys and bad cowboys then, shall I?" Elizabeth asks. Abley shakes himself out of the fantasy and smiles again at Haven.

"Excuse me, little lady, I have to—"

"Don't let Michael see you if you haven't registered." Haven tips off Inspector Abley, her eyes darting around to see if Michael has really gone.

"Michael?" Inspector Abley asks.

"Conference organiser," Haven explains.

"I repeat, what are you doing here? And you need to go!" Lemon raises his voice, frustrated.

"I'm on an ordered three-day leave. Just had to get something over for Elizabeth, thought I'd take a drive. She said there was no snow here. Thought I could find a golf course. Bloody snow everywhere?" Abley looks out the window, then beams another smile at Haven. She is quite taken by the tall, tanned man standing in his leather jacket, now practising his imaginary golf swing.

"I'd like you to let me know what the pathologist finds," Elizabeth says to Lemon, trying to ignore the chemistry between Haven and Bob Abley.

"I can't do that," Lemon replies.

"Well, then, perhaps you can pass this on." Elizabeth hands Lemon the cardboard box Inspector Abley has brought with him to Oxford. "I asked Inspector Abley to bring this over for me from my lab as soon as I knew the results; it was precious cargo." Elizabeth's eyes pierce Lemon's. "I picked up Dr Sandy Starborneck's glass, the night she died. From the conference Christmas supper. It has her lipstick on it and everything, DNA. Look, a tiny bit of nail varnish. So you will be able to verify. I couldn't do the tests here, so I sent it express post to my lab, and they ran them for me. All bagged and kept tamper-free. They found traces of *Taxus baccata*, or better known to you as yew. Dr Sandy Starborneck was poisoned by yew. Probably pine needles. Very effective."

"What have you done?" Lemon's eyes are now wide open.

"Your Oxford Inspector said that your pathologist was struggling to find the poison, didn't he? Seemed obvious to me – a Christmas poison. Nice touch. So this is murder, Sergeant, whether you'd like to listen to me or not. Murder."

"Sandy was poisoned. Poisoned with yew?" Haven asks.

"That's right. It's a very clever poison. Unlike your rat poison or hemlock, there are often no seeming symptoms. Yew can do that. Just make you a bit off colour and then, bam."

"Did she suffer?" Haven asks Inspector Bob Abley, "So you're an Inspector too?"

"Sometimes those who ingest it suffer an accelerated heart rate or convulsions," Elizabeth says – irked that Haven asks Bob and not her – adding, "They might have problems breathing or have a heart attack. But sometimes there are no outward symptoms. They just collapse, and it can be swift, within hours of it entering the body. That's what made me look for it. Dr Starborneck seemed to give up the ghost, just like that. Almost as if the drink killed her. But drink very rarely kills. So when we found Father Christmas to be innocent, it only convinced me more."

"Thank you, Inspector Abley, for bringing this and

solving the case," Haven smiles again, as beguiling a smile as she can, to Inspector Bob Abley.

"No problem," Bob Abley replies, quite taken with this kooky woman.

"So you didn't do this?" Elizabeth stares at Haven, waiting for a reply, more frustrated by the fact that Bob is getting all the credit for her hard work.

"I'm sorry?" Haven turns, frowning.

"You didn't poison your friend? You were seen shouting at her on more than one occasion." Elizabeth's beady eyes glare at Haven.

"Professor Green." Lemon tries to stop Elizabeth, then turns to Haven. "I have to stress that Professor Green is not working for us," Lemon interrupts, explaining to Haven.

"Do you work for the F.B.I.?" Haven asks Elizabeth. "They are trying to knock me down all the time. I've phoned them many times. I am not working for the Cuban resistance. I just spent a nice two weeks on holiday there. Ah, the salsa, the moonlight. But that is a different day and none of your business."

"I am not working for the F.B.I. But I do want to find out who murdered your friend."

"Professor Green. You don't work for Oxford Police, Thames Valley," Lemon adds sternly, but quietly, now carrying the box. They both know full well that if the pathologist finds traces of yew on the glass, Lemon will find a way to get Dr Starborneck's remains tested. "We still have the body. We can do our own forensics."

Elizabeth raises her eyebrows at Lemon's seeming lack of thanks for her findings.

"The glass has a very distinctive lipstick colour on it," she reminds him, "that might help with your enquiries. I found this one back at the house in Summertown. It might match. Haven doesn't look like the kind of person who washes up every day, you might find some more clues."

"Hey! It's not good for the environment," Haven

replies, then smiles at Inspector Abley.

"Don't wash any glasses and give Sergeant Lemon here your keys, if you want to help with his enquiries," Elizabeth says matter of factly. Haven looks at Lemon who nods. She hands over her keys.

"You've already been in. I know these things. I left tape over the door. F.B.I." Haven touches her nose. "That was you."

"Oxford Police have been calling you, Dr Usrey. We came to see you, but the door was open. So we entered to check everything was okay. There was a call from a neighbour that they were concerned by a loud noise. You left windows open at the back of the property. We have left messages since we paid a visit," Lemon explains. Then Lemon's phone starts to ring, and he picks it up, putting a thumb to his other ear to try to block out all the noise from the room.

"Oh, I'm always losing my phone," Haven explains. "I have this one now. Or, I had it with Sandy. It's a walkie talkie. Much better than a mobile phone as you don't get any interruptions," Haven explains to Inspector Abley.

"You were seen attacking Michael Pussett, on Broad Street a few nights ago," Elizabeth tells Haven. "The police stopped you and cautioned Dr Starborneck."

"They picked on the wrong person. He laid into us. I had to restrain him on the ground, with my trustee Mr Mugway. He was shouting at Sandy. Telling her she was an embarrassment, that she was coming on too strong to him. That's rich. He's as sleazy as they come."

"Hmm, but that's not what others saw. What were you doing with Dr Starborneck exactly? Will your joint research now all be included in your own references? You'll do well out of her death?"

"As you already know, we were working on the effects of biodegradable plastics. Plastic doesn't biodegrade. It's always there. If it ends up in a landfill, it just stays there, mummified. It doesn't biodegrade. And we are looking at what impact it has on plants. It's not good. They are also releasing greenhouse gases if they do biodegrade. Does the public know this? Of course not." Haven smiles. "You think I care about taking the credit for Sandy's work—" Haven is interrupted by the lunch gong.

"Elizabeth." Gabriel pats her on the shoulder. "I wondered where you'd gone. Lunch? And, we could have afternoon tea back at our favourite place on the corner of Little Clarendon? The one we went to the other day. Why don't we sneak over at four in the break, hope to see you there. We can easily make it back here for lectures." Gabriel smiles and is about to talk about the menu when he is interrupted by Lemon, who has just hung up his phone.

"Actually," Lemon interrupts Gabriel, "my Oxford Inspector, as you call him, would like to see you, Professor Green, at the station. He asked me to find you," he says, raising his eyebrows, "he'd like to know why you wanted to go to Summertown and to Dr Sandy Starborneck's home. He found it odd," Lemon adds, feeling a little guilty himself, having enabled her. "And, we won't be able to use this as evidence." Lemon lifts the box with the glass.

"Good. I would like to see your Oxford Inspector, and perhaps I will get a chance to talk to the pathologist direct, once they've heard my evidence," Elizabeth replies, adding, "and I know you can't use it directly now, but you could test for the same poison in the body."

"My Oxford Inspector is not asking you for help. He actually hasn't ruled you out as a suspect." Lemon bows his head, looking up at Elizabeth from under his brow. Both Haven and Bob Abley stare at Elizabeth.

"A suspect?" Haven is taken aback at the news.

"What have you done, Elizabeth?" Bob asks.

"Nothing, other than providing the strongest evidence that this is murder and no accident. For which you will thank me later," Elizabeth replies to Lemon matter of factly, "and you should know better." She turns to Lemon and glares for the trace of guilt on his face, then gathers her jacket and goes to walk towards her boots, ready to attend the station for questioning. Bob Abley looks at his friend, a little worried about how events are unfolding.

30
PROFESSOR GREEN QUESTIONS

"Can you stop!" The Oxford Inspector shouts at Professor Elizabeth Green.

"I'm just trying to find out what you know," she replies.

"We're supposed to be asking the questions." He is losing his temper with Elizabeth.

"If I might say, the horse has bolted. You failed to treat the banqueting hall as a crime scene two nights ago, and you're playing catch up. At this rate, you're never going to solve anything," she reprimands him.

"I'll be the one who gets cross with you. You're really pushing my buttons." The Oxford Inspector tries to calm himself.

"I am trying to do more than that. Let's get a rocket under there. The murderer could be getting away," Elizabeth replies, frustrated.

"The murderer could be closer than we think, being questioned even."

"Oh, don't talk nonsense." Elizabeth frowns then shuts her eyes.

"You're the common denominator at every crime

scene. You were there the night of the murder. What was to stop you putting something in Dr Starborneck's food?" the Oxford Inspector leans back and puts his arms behind his head.

"Pish. Is this the best you've got, when I've given you evidence of yew poisoning?"

"You could have done that yourself, tampered with the evidence. Put the poison in her glass before giving it to us. Very clever. But you'll have to stay more than two steps ahead to convince us."

"Oh deary no, this is bad." Elizabeth shakes her head.

"Yes, yes it is." The Oxford Inspector raises his eyebrows at Elizabeth and glares.

"No, I mean, for you. You're so far off," Elizabeth says, unperturbed.

"And I mean for you. You turn up at the victim's home. Perhaps trying to remove evidence before it incriminates you."

"I helped you find evidence. I have given you the glass, the glove with paint on. And I'm still waiting for a thank you."

"Well, you know everything there is to know about poison, so you would know how to poison Sandy Starborneck without it showing."

"Which is why I've just told you it was yew," Elizabeth rolls her eyes.

"Precisely," the Oxford Inspector replies.

"Precisely," Elizabeth says in return.

"Precisely," the Oxford Inspector won't back down.

"Why would I tell you if I was guilty? That's insane? Look, I don't have time for this," Elizabeth gives the Oxford Inspector her hardest glare. "I've never met Dr Sandy Starborneck in my life before. I've no motive whatsoever."

"Maybe you were jealous. I understand she was having a relationship with Michael Pussett?"

"Are you mad?"

"I beg your pardon?"

"Michael is the most weaselly, slimy, ignorant, narcissistic, awful excuse for a man. Present company excluded."

"Exactly, jealousy. Eh?" The Inspector is slow but realises her insult. He pushes back his chair and leaves. Elizabeth waits for a moment, then starts to speak to the Constable still in the corner of the room.

"Can I go now? I'm going to go," and she gets up and walks towards the door, but the Constable stands in her way. She then starts to pace the room instead. "Oh my, what's this? Look. I've never seen anything like it." Elizabeth looks at the floor. "I think that's a false widow spider". She looks up at the open window. "Are there gardens outside?"

"Yes," the Constable says, not moving.

"You have to catch this. They deliver a poisonous bite."

"I'm not catching a poisonous spider." The Constable clearly has spider issues.

"Then you need to get help. This is serious." Elizabeth warns. "Stand back from it. It's moving!"

The Constable runs out of the room, and Elizabeth catches the door and leaves in the other direction.

*

Sometime later the Oxford Inspector walks back into the room. He can't see a spider and looks at the Constable.

"The only false widow you saw was the one with two legs that has now got away."

"Shall we put out an APB?"

"For a spider? No, and leave the Professor as well. Our pathologist just ran the test on the body. Came up positive. She was right about the poison. Bloody woman."

31
HAVEN

Not long after Elizabeth left with Sergeant Lemon for the Oxford Police Station did Inspector Abley decide to follow Haven out of Catte College. They were both now making their way in the snow to the Carfax Tower.

There was something unusual about Haven. Normally, Bob Abley didn't make kindred friendships with new-age hippies who hold up their fingers to make the peace sign to people they pass on their way down the street. And as he walks beside her, her clothes chime and clink, which he knows would drive him bonkers after time, and her talk about crystals more so. But Inspector Abley likes that she must be rubbing all those traditionalists here in academia up the wrong way. He also likes her sense of humour and the sparkle in her eyes – although he is less sure about the pink in her hair.

"I just need to be up high, to lift my mood. Will you join me?" Haven asks.

"Sure. Let's take a trip to the top of the world. It can't be any whiter up there," he replies. But as they pay, and walk up the narrow and winding steps, Abley has to stop to catch his breath.

"Do you think the plastics industry murdered Sandy?"

Haven asks, staring back down the steps at Abley.

"It's almost always someone close to the victim."

"I hope you're not accusing me?"

"Thankfully, I'm not accusing anyone. I don't work here."

"But you're an Inspector, aren't you?"

"My recent endeavours to find missing cats and stolen clocks don't say much for my credentials, so I'm grateful to be leaving it to the Oxford Police."

All kinds of odd things happen at winter solstice you know," Haven says, changing the subject. "We're entering the winter solstice. A time we still don't understand, where many things die. But there's always rejuvenation."

"Not for this Dr Starborneck," Abley replies. They reach the top of the steps and climb out to view Oxford.

"Everything is so white." Haven looks out across Oxford and the dome of the Radcliffe Camera, as well as the surrounding Colleges and spires, covered in snow.

"Nothing compared to Cambridge, where I've come from."

"I was hoping to celebrate the winter solstice up on Boars Hill. I've been told it has the best views. There are so many ways to enjoy this special time. The conference has a celebration in the College Chapel later but I can't go to it."

"Why?"

"Because I'm a big fat atheist, that's why. I'm with the spirits, man," Haven holds up two fingers in the peace sign.

"Your friend Sandy liked a drink, didn't she? She was drunk the night she died?" Abley asks.

"She's been drinking like it was going out of fashion. We met when she had given up drink. And I've known her for a long time. This was new, her falling off the wagon."

"I'll come up to Boars Hill with you. I can check out any golf clubs on the way. So long as we can find something to eat."

"What, to bomb them," Haven says, with a twinkle in her eye, "for all the environmental destruction they bring? Pesticides, herbicides, water they take from around the area. Do you know there are over eight-hundred golf courses where I'm from, and each one uses millions of gallons of water every year?"

"Is that all?" Inspector Abley says, genuinely thinking they use more.

"Stop jesting." Haven thinks he's joking and smiles.

"D'you think Professor Green is right? D'you think there has been a murder?" Bob Abley asks.

"I thought it was Santa but turns out he was a good guy. It must be the plastics evil empire," Haven says, reiterating her point.

"Is there any evidence they have ever caused you malice?"

"Oh, definitely. They hack our computers, have spied on us by pretending to be volunteers in our office. Yes, yes. Our joint project, Sandy's and mine, was on the impact of biodegradable plastics – biopolymers. We were looking at cress actually, on how they impact plant growth."

"I like a bit of cress in my sandwiches," Abley replies.

"We have our enemies in the plastics industry."

"What if it wasn't them?" Abley asks.

"Michael. He was always sniffing around her. Wouldn't leave her alone. Maybe she told him to get lost, and he lost his rag. He's odious," Haven says, trying to convince Bob Abley.

"Michael?"

"They were in a relationship. She met him when she came over. They'd been seeing each other for a few weeks I suppose."

"How do you know Dr Starborneck?" he asks as he looks out on the Oxford skyline.

"We're colleagues. You heard me tell your friend."

"Yes, but how well do you know her?"

"We work in the same department, have done for years. We have this project together. Thankfully, we future-proofed it so that if anything happened to either of us, the other could continue. Well, we aren't getting any younger. But I didn't expect this. She came over earlier than me, to Oxford, to fulfil some of the prerequisites to get her prize." Haven holds up her hand and gives the peace sign to a younger couple who have just climbed the winding steps up to the top of Carfax and look like they are in love. Haven smiles at Inspector Abley. "You have a lovely craggy face."

"Thank you," Abley replies, not sure that was a compliment.

"I sense you have had a lot of pain recently." Haven clinks some bells on her skirt and pulls out som herbs from her coat to smell.

"Yes, you could say that."

"You will come through this, stronger. Or, it will kill you."

"Good to know, good to know."

"Ahh." Haven breathes in the cold air and herbs. "Are you feeling Christmassy?" Haven shoves the herbs under Abley's nose and he recoils.

"A dear friend just bought me some Christmas lights, but apart from that…"

"This isn't the trip I was expecting. This place, it's so beautiful. And now, the snow has turned red." Haven raises her eyebrows. "Winter solstice will sort us out. With death comes rebirth."

Inspector Abley feels a little numb. He certainly doesn't believe in the spirits and rebirth. Haven's mumbo jumbo makes him feel a bit queasy. But, he's curious as to whether this woman could have killed her friend, and a trip to a hill to check out the golf courses on the way sounds just the ticket. He knows he's stepping on Lemon's toes, but how can he avoid it if he's to protect Elizabeth?

32
BUTTONS

Liz finds Godric in Jericho Community Hall in Oxford, up on Walton Street. When she arrives, a full dress rehearsal is taking place, with Godric on stage in pantaloons. The dogs are asleep by the side, but when they see her their tails wag, and she crouches down to say hello as they jump off the stage to greet her.

"Buttons, what am I going to do? I can only dream in a million years of meeting Prince Charming," Cinderella sighs and throws herself to the floor by a prop fireplace, fake flames flickering.

"Don't be sad Cinderella, you shall go to the ball, we will find a way," Godric replies to Cinderella, with all his acting passion to the fore, he opens a cupboard to reveal the most sparkly gown. "See? You will look beautiful in this," he says and lifts Cinderella up from her knees and holds the gown to her body, the two of them cooing over the pretty frock. From stage right in walks a man dressed up as the Wicked Step-Mother — a few backstage boos at his entrance. Elizabeth joins in with a 'boo' and chuckles a little.

"Clean those steps. I can't see my beautiful face in them," the Wicked Step-Mother scolds Cinderella then looks into a mirror. Backstage, for effect, we hear the sound of glass smashing. Godric spots his Nanna and gives her a thumbs up. Elizabeth opens her eyes wide. From stage left, the Director rushes on.

"Take five everyone," he says and grabs the Wicked Step-Mother to give him floor directions. "We need to see your face, Luv."

Elizabeth thinks of Dave Brubeck and starts to hum as she watches Godric walk towards her in full costume.

"This is a little surreal. Why don't you dress like that all the time? You look very smart. What are you doing?" Elizabeth gives Godric a drink of water. "Don't dehydrate."

"It's Christmas. I'm having fun. Yay. Someone dropped out who was playing this part, and they said I looked like a Buttons. They were right. Would you like some of my falafels? There's a lovely deli around the corner. Soup in the flask too. Bet you've not had lunch." Godric points to his little picnic, resting on a chair, then kisses his Nanna.

"In between the fun, I have a request." Elizabeth pops a falafel in her mouth and nods thanks.

"Name it."

"I need you to do some research for me."

Godric pulls out his smartphone from his codpiece.

"These are useful, aren't they? I can put my loose change in it and everything," Godric says, jangling his coins.

"You can't do it on that. You need a computer."

"Bunny, this is a computer," he strokes his Nanna's arm affectionately.

"I need you to investigate the plastics industry. Inspector Abley thinks it might be a lead. He left me a message at the hotel just now. I'm not so sure."

"Inspector Abley?"

"It seems you're not the only one who can't keep away. We have a full house."

"More to come and see our show. I'll get some tickets!"

"I think we'll be a bit too busy to watch pantomimes, Goddy."

"It's not the Oxford Playhouse, but no one is ever too busy to watch a pantomime. Especially as the dogs are in it now."

"No, Goddy. I said no."

"Just pulling Cinderella's carriage. I mean, they're not pulling it. They'll be on stage for five minutes."

"No."

"So why do you need me to look for plastics and what am I looking for?"

"Father Christmas didn't do it. So, if he's innocent, who did? It's a clever murder. Yew poisoning is subtle."

"So it was yew poisoning. How does someone die of that?" Godric stuffs two falafels in his mouth.

"It can be quite silent and then cardiac arrest. I suspect the Oxford Inspector, although he'd hate to admit it, is probably getting confirmation from the pathologist around about now. I got questioned at the station, so it must be irritating him that I'm right. You'd think he'd be grateful."

"Hang on. You've been questioned?"

"Yes, Lemon's Oxford Inspector thinks I did it. Planted the evidence. How stupid. He's building a case, but I ran away."

"You escaped from the police station?"

"Funny, isn't it?"

"Won't they be looking for you?"

"I expect so, but I'm hardly a fugitive on the run."

"They think you killed Sandy and you're now on the run?" Godric is aghast.

"Don't put it like that. It's insane. And that Oxford Inspector is an idiot. Dr Starborneck's work colleague, Dr Haven Usrey, they both worked on biodegradable plastics and their impact on plants. Haven has said she thinks the plastics industry could have killed Sandy."

"Oh?"

"Well, this is her card. See what you can find." Elizabeth hands Godric Haven's card.

"But you think it's a waste of time?"

"I do, but look in case. Haven could be the murderer. Please look into her as well. She could have killed her colleague. Wanted all the research for herself. It happens."

"Be careful, Bunny." Godric watches as the costume and makeup team fuss over them, putting bows in the Afghan's hair.

"Can you look after the dogs here?"

"I thought you didn't approve of using them as entertainment."

"I don't. They have my permission to misbehave at all times and test the patience of the director."

"If Father Christmas is innocent, does that mean he's going to come down our chimney and bring me lots of nice presents?" Godric winks, pleased his Nanna is warming about the dogs taking part,

"He may not be a murderer, but he is a thief. He's being detained at her Majesty's pleasure. So, don't hold your breath." Elizabeth winks back at Godric then leaves.

Godric opens up his smartphone and looks at the business card Elizabeth gave him. He sees the photograph of Haven riding a camel and her name, Haven. Then he turns it over, expecting there to be email details, phone numbers. There is just another photograph of Haven, this time blowing a raspberry at the camera, with the word 'Seek and you shall find'. Godric smirks and says to himself, "That's right, crazy lady. Laugh it up now, while you can. Godric is on your case."

33
LUNCH WITH GABRIEL

"You came! Here, sit." Gabriel stands and removes his bag and coat from a very comfortable large armchair in the cafe, Kinder Habits, on the corner of Little Clarendon Street and St Giles'. Its windows are partly steamed up, small chatter coming from tables full of people drinking soup, hoping to stay in the warm for as long as possible. "I was hoping you'd make it. Saved a seat," he says. Elizabeth walks over to Gabriel and sits, her hood still up on her duffel coat. "You missed lunch?" Gabriel asks. She nods, chilled to the bone, having left Godric in the Community Hall in Jericho and walked here on the icy pavements. "Well, let's rectify that," Gabriel waves his hand in the air and calls over the maître d'.

Elizabeth spots the concierge assistant from the St Giles' Hotel in the corner, who waves and smiles at her.

"You've only been here five minutes, and already you have admirers," Gabriel says, noticing.

"I think he's more interested in my grandson." Elizabeth smiles back at the concierge assistant. Then she looks at Gabriel who seems happy. She remembers what Linda told her about Gabriel's dead wife, and wonders why Gabriel won't talk about it.

"Have you got any of that tomato soup you made me yesterday, Dave?" Gabriel asks the maître di', adding, "Dave, the maître d' here, shares my dread of Christmas. But I explained to him how I feel slightly better just by trying to be kind."

"Potato and leek today, Sir. Freshly made. Gabriel looks at Elizabeth, who nods.

"Any of those crispy kale chips and some of the ciabatta with olives?" Gabriel looks at Elizabeth again to check she is happy with his choice for her. She nods. Gabriel continues talking to Dave. "Thank you. If it can come now, that would be much appreciated. We need to stave off hypothermia. Otherwise, peppermint tea straight away, thank you."

"We can bring the soup, then the tea later, if that would suit?" The maître d' asks. Elizabeth nods and shuts her eyes until finally, after a while, she speaks.

"What happened to Michael?" Elizabeth asks.

"He was charged with assaulting Haven but is out on bail. So, he's prancing around like nothing's happened. The police are idiots. I heard they took you in?"

"More for questioning," Elizabeth replies, "I hope. They would be so off the mark for anything else. I grew tired and left."

"They've been back to the conference. They're looking for you." Gabriel smiles at Elizabeth, a little concerned. "Here, have some of my pastry, I can't eat it all. It's vegetable," he says. Gabriel uses a knife and fork to cut a section of his afternoon snack for Elizabeth, who remains in her duffel coat and munches on the pastry, crumbs falling down her front. Gabriel opens a clean serviette and places it on her lap and smiles again.

"Why did you want to meet me here? Do you know the maître d'?" Elizabeth asks.

"Only a bit, just chatting now. And…" Gabriel looks at Elizabeth intently, "I enjoyed our lunch before. I suppose

I wanted to get to know you better?" He looks down and fiddles with the rest of his pastry.

"Why?"

"You're an intriguing woman," Gabriel admits.

"You should be less intrigued about me, and more curious to find out who murdered Dr Sandy Starborneck in your College," Elizabeth thinks, wondering whether to question Gabriel about his wife.

"I've never been good at puzzles."

"What are you good at?"

"Tomatoes." Gabriel looks up. He can see the maître d' bringing over the soup who then puts it on the table in front of Elizabeth.

"Low on staff again?" Elizabeth asks as he places the tray, also with olives, ciabatta and kale crisps next to the soup, moving Gabriel's newspaper.

"You remembered? Yes, it may be the Christmas rush, but it's also the colds and coughs running through the staff. We can't have those in the cafe. I see you're keeping warm," Dave replies.

"Did you ever serve two Americans here?" Elizabeth asks.

"I beg your pardon?"

"Middle-aged. Loud. One is a hippy, loud clothes, has a distinctive elephant bag."

"I can't remember any two particular Americans. Though come to think of it, there was a rather eccentric one in the other day. Streak of pink hair. Came in a few days ago. I only remember because she was trying to get me to have a henna tattoo. She had a kit in her bag, was giving strangers tattoos of the sun. Why?" Dave asks, shaking his head at the memory.

"Because one of them is dead, and I don't know why."

"She gave me a drawing. She drew the cafe. But not two Americans no. I hope she's okay? She was lovely."

"It was her friend who died. I'd like to look at that now," Elizabeth says.

"I'll bring it down if you like. I have it in the flat upstairs. I was going to frame it. It's kooky," Dave replies.

"Show me now." Elizabeth gets up and pushes the maître d' towards a small flight of stairs. Gabriel, curious, also stands.

"I can bring it down."

"It's okay. I'll come with you." Elizabeth starts walking.

"No, you're all right," Dave doesn't like being told what to do.

"I'm investigating a murder."

"Are you the police?"

"I'm a police consultant, yes," Elizabeth replies. Gabriel tries not to show the shock on his face, knowing she is not working for the Oxford Police, but is interested to see where this goes. Elizabeth and Gabriel follow Dave upstairs.

When Elizabeth reaches the final step to the first floor, she can't believe her eyes. The flat is covered in art, and down one end an easel and a drawing desk with pots of brushes and paints.

"Oh, sorry, ignore the mess," Dave says, as he starts to search for the little sketch. Elizabeth's eyes run across his walls, squeezing past the two bicycles in the corridor.

"There must be a hundred paintings hung just in this room," Gabriel suggests, looking around.

"What can I say, I paint small." The maître d' rustles through some papers and finds it on his desk. "Here it is." Dave picks out the sketch and hands it to Elizabeth.

"Oh," Elizabeth says.

"Ha. Art is such a subjective form. I like it," he replies.

"Hmm." Elizabeth is not going to commit, and thinks the sketch very childlike, of people with googly eyes and is disappointed not to find anything in it.

Next to a small cluster of paintings of a woman laughing, Elizabeth observes a portrait of a goat, walking at night under a full blue moon. Small boats behind on a river, with trees and cattle in the far distance.

"Who did this painting?" She asks.

Dave studies the painting and pauses for a long time. He looks closer at it.

"Found it in a junk shop," Dave replies.

"That's Port Meadow, isn't it? Behind the goat in this painting at night?" Gabriel asks.

"Yes. It must be a local artist. I can't remember." Dave tries to walk away from the painting.

"Hmm. Or was. It looks old," Elizabeth says, still studying it as it looks familiar.

"Yes, it does, doesn't it," Gabriel replies. "Boats can't moor there anymore," he says and he points to a couple of boats in the top right of the painting moored near the cows. "There is a marina lower down that's much bigger now."

"Perhaps it is just an impression of how the artist wants to see it," Dave suggests.

"Or, perhaps it's old. Perhaps I'm not a real detective."

"What?"

"That was my alumni card I showed you. I am a detective, just not with the police."

"Then go and eat your soup before I push you down the stairs," Dave replies.

34
BOARS HILL

After they stopped at a local pub for a late lunch – having missed the one in College – Inspector Abley and Haven shut the doors to his warm cosy BMW, and start to set out on foot across the snow. They head towards the top of Boars Hill, for Haven's early winter solstice walk. Everything is quiet up here. While Haven laughs and starts to make a snowball, Inspector Abley is beginning to regret this trip. He was hoping to find at least one golf course that might be open nearby. But the journey made it clear that everywhere was white, and nothing was open for a round. Just as he is getting despondent at the lack of golf before Christmas he gets hit by a snowball, smack in the face.

"Haha, I caught you." Haven laughs. "Come on, let's go and toboggan. Weeeee. Look, a man is doing it over there." And Haven rushes off. Inspector Abley looks at his car and hopes that the wheels don't get stuck. He can't stay here forever.

"Okay, but we can't stay long, in case we get snowed in. It's icy up here." But Haven is not listening, she is already out of earshot and has run-up to a man who has a tin tray and is shooting down the hill, and borrows it and flies down herself, laughing all the way. Inspector Abley catches up with the man who has loaned his tray and nods hello. It is a while before Haven climbs back up the hill, as she falls a few times and laughs each time in a fit of giggles. Bob Abley finds this a little odd. Surely she should be more upset about her friend? When she finally says goodbye to the man and his tray, she sees more people on another hill with proper sledges and looks at Abley as if to say she wants to stay all afternoon. Inspector Abley, however, instead suggests they walk. They start to climb higher.

"You have no problem with the cold?" Abley asks, looking at Haven just in her multicoloured jacket.

"I'm naturally on fire." Haven smiles, pulling some clove boiled sweets out of her pocket and offering the Inspector one, then continuing, "have you been to see the Northern lights?"

"No, have you?" Abley pops a sweet in his mouth and after a few seconds screws his face up and spits it back out.

"Stayed in an ice hotel." Haven nods. "It was so spiritual. I want to go to Stonehenge next week, for the solstice itself, but I think I'll to stay here, while Sandy is still with the police. I can't let them mess with her body. I need to get Sandy home."

"Did she have family?"

"No, I told Professor Green. It's just me. She never married or had children. Not sure why. She never said. She said she never wanted kids. She'd never talk about it."

"You said she was seeing this Michael man," Abley asks.

"I don't trust him. Look, look what he did to me." Haven shows Abley the bruises Michael gave her, pulling up her sleeves.

"I saw them earlier, back at the College," Abley admits, shaking his head.

"Yes, and these," Haven pulls up her skirt and pulls up

her leggings to reveal more bruises.

"Oh, goodness," Abley is shocked.

"A regular charmer. But don't worry, I swiped him with my bag to get him off Sandy the other night. We'd been having such a nice time. I like your English pubs. So cosy. Then he came at us. Surely the cops would have found the bruises he left on her that night. They would surely have still been on her body? He really laid into her. That's the only reason I hit him. The bastard. I don't trust him."

"You think he could have killed Sandy?" Abley asks.

"I'm so sick of it. Sick of everything being about Sandy."

"But your friend just died."

"And don't we know it." Haven glares at Inspector Bob Abley.

"But you feel sad, don't you?"

"D'you know, I don't know what I feel. I've been carrying that woman every day since I got here. It's been exhausting." Haven sits in the snow and looks at the view.

"But you'll get all the credit now at least. I mean, if you were researching together. It all goes to you now, isn't that right? I've had a bit of experience of dealing with academics," Abley smiles wryly, thinking about home.

"Be able to dine out on it." Haven offers a hollow laugh. "Even when I quit."

"Quit?" Abley asks.

"I've had enough of this game."

"Thank you. Academia is a game, and we pay the price. All the silver spoons must choke you all."

"I was going to say chasing all the grants, competing with other teams, late-night writing up of reports, College administration, more and more teaching. It's a cut-throat world we work in. Sometimes shitty Heads of Departments breathing down our throats."

"Huh, shitty bosses." Abley thinks of Raynott.

"Word. And I like England, though you guys are

repressed. My massage therapist said we Americans have tight arms from all the hand gestures we make. Talk to the hand, high five, whoop whoop. You get it. And that the English have tight jaws and tight arses from all the shit you hold in. True dat."

"What can I say? We live on a packed island far too close together. We have to get along. Not speaking is how we do it. Or my job would be far busier."

"Are you on duty?"

"No."

"Well, Mr Cop, I'm going to start a commune in Santa Fe. Grow organic veggies and have pet goats."

"It's good to have dreams."

"What happened to yours?"

Abley smiles but says nothing.

"She's worth coming over from Cambridge for. She's crazier than me," Haven says, looking at Inspector Bob Abley, aware that he knows she is talking about Elizabeth.

"You have no idea. Come on, let's get a hot drink in us. Then we can try to solve who killed your friend."

35
YOU SAID YEW

As Elizabeth walks down St Giles' from the cafe, Kinder Habits, she is spotted by a police car which pulls up alongside.

"Can you tell me your name?" A police officer asks.

"Professor Green."

"Do we need to cuff you?" The police officer unhooks the cuffs from his belt and dangles them out the window.

"Most certainly not. I was about to return to the station as I need to speak with Sergeant Lemon. Will he be there?"

"No idea, Luv. Inspector told us to shove you in the cells until his return in the morning, make you sweat until you squeak," the Constable says, then laughs.

"Are you arresting me? Aren't you supposed to read me my rights?"

"We can do that at the station."

"No, Barry. You're doing it wrong!" The other police officer in the car shouts at his colleague, gets out and walks around the car, "So sorry, Professor. It's his first day on the beat. He's watched too many cop shows on the box. We're not arresting you, and Barry needs to go back to desk work or perhaps be shifted to a role in the canteen," the friendly Constable smiles. "But, the Inspector did ask if you'd be kind enough to come back in for more questions. He left a note with Sergeant Lemon, who is indeed at the station. Perhaps, you wouldn't mind speaking with him?"

"That's what I said?" Barry complains, huffing and putting his hands up in the air, then phones the station that they are coming in with 'Professor Elizabeth Greens'.

"It's Green, not Greens," she corrects him.

*

"You were right," Lemon greets Elizabeth at the door of the station, whispering to her. "I would have called you if you had a phone. I left a message at the hotel. Dr Sandy Starborneck was deliberately poisoned by yew. It's definitely murder. The pathologist thinks it was probably ingested over a period of days in small amounts, but that on the night she died she was given a larger dose. I have the pathology report. I can't show you it. But that is the gist of it."

"Can I speak with the pathologist?"

"No, in fact, come with me. Play along for a minute."

"Where are you taking me?"

"An interview room. That way we can get some peace in here." Lemon takes Elizabeth's arm. Elizabeth walks beside Sergeant Lemon along a corridor.

"Where is your lovely Oxford Inspector?"

"Half day, Christmas shopping with his Mrs. He won't be happy."

"Good."

Sergeant Lemon ushers Elizabeth into the interview room, and they are joined by a junior female Constable who stands in the corner.

"It's okay, Sara. It's not a formal. We've just come in here for a bit of quiet. Just chatting."

"Oh, okay. Didn't the Inspector—"

"Not anymore." Sergeant Lemon interrupts her. Sara

leaves, and they are on their own.

"You know the cafe on the end of Little Clarendon Street?" Elizabeth asks.

Sergeant Lemon shakes his head. His knowledge of Oxford is mainly of the clubs and rowdy pubs, the railway station and other hot spots with their possible altercations.

"You want to hear about the pathology report?" Lemon asks, ignoring her.

"This man calls himself the maître d'. But it's a cafe for goodness sake. He's the manager, I guess. Anyway, we go up to his flat."

"We?"

"Dr Gabriel Deersman and I. Stop interrupting. This completely random man, Dave, has a painting on his wall. Well, actually, he has dozens. Packed walls. It looks rather busy, as most were not masterpieces. But, one of them, one of them was by the same artist as a painting in Dr Starborneck's home. What are the chances of that? They had the same initials on them, the same signature. He said something about them being a local artist, and he picked it up in a junk shop or something. But he paused before he said anything about the painting. His pause felt too long. And Dr Haven Usrey paints too. Why do they have a local painting?"

"What?" Lemon wonders where this is going. "Perhaps it came with the property?"

"I checked. It was rented unfurnished. Why do Haven and Sandy have local art on the wall?"

"Inspector Abley texted me," Lemon replies, changing the subject, "Apparently, Haven's giving work up to go and live in Santa Fe. I thought that was a hippy mecca? And, doesn't that make you suspicious? That she's running away?"

"Quite the reverse. It gives her no motive. She doesn't want to piggyback on her colleague's research and use it for her own benefit," Elizabeth replies.

"That's what she tells us. But they had a fight with

Michael Pussett. The witness who phoned it in reported the women were attacking him."

"Hmm, nothing rings true about it. That was self-defence. Godric and I found some witnesses too. They saw something different. If anything, what they said pointed to Michael's guilt. But what is his motive?"

"So, it's the hippy. And, why didn't you tell us about the other witnesses?"

"Don't you love this? Bob texting you, me here."

"You should both go back to Cambridge. I'm going to get into more trouble."

"What, for not arresting me?" Elizabeth scoffs.

"He'll know you've been in. That I haven't questioned you."

"You have."

"Not formally, no tape, no witness."

"I'm not really a suspect, am I?" Elizabeth asks.

"I'm afraid in his eyes, yes. And, you ran away," Lemon replies.

"Excuse me, Sergeant?" says a voice as a head pops around the door. Lemon turns around and sees Inspector Bob Abley in the doorway.

"All I could see were the indents from the bunkers. Too much snow. What's that course called?" Abley walks into the interview room and sits down. "Up by Boars Hill?"

"No idea." Lemon looks at Inspector Bob Abley in despair. "You can't come in here."

"On an educational trip. Just seeing how a neighbouring force does things. Impromptu. Am on holiday, just popping in. Who's to care?"

"My Inspector. You're on his patch."

"On the way up to Boars Hill earlier, Haven tells me that Michael has this shed with a dartboard, and the people he hates he puts a picture up of them and throws darts on their face," Abley raises his eyebrows. "She said we should go and see what picture he has up. She bets it's Sandy. She said Michael tried it on with her, Haven, but she rejected him. That he was already with Sandy when she turned up, but that he was trying it on with her as well. That's what the fight was about, in the street. He was attacking her, she said, cross at her rejection and her trying to warn Sandy off him. It felt like she was telling the truth."

"Or, she's just jealous. It's classic. Haven wanted Michael so killed Sandy. And now, she's pinning it on Michael as he still doesn't want her. It's got to be her. We also found traces of yew in the laboratory, where Sandy and Haven were temporarily working together at the University," Lemon confirms.

"I bet you didn't find any in Summertown, at their home." Elizabeth looks at Lemon, her beady eyes waiting for his agreement.

"No, all right. But, if Haven wanted to kill Sandy, she's hardly going to do it at home, where she's most likely to be the suspect. She's cleverer than that, at least. Though how much more I don't know," Lemon replies.

"Where is she now?" Elizabeth asks Abley.

"I left her by a mobile drinks stand up at Boars Hill. We had hot chocolates. It's cold up there. But she wasn't ready to come back down to the city. She said she wanted to walk back through the snow. Because of what happened, to clear her head."

"Yeah, I bet she's trying to bury evidence up there," Lemon suggests.

"What evidence?"

"I don't know. But why walk back in the semi-darkness on a cold winter's night in the snow otherwise?" Lemon huffs.

"No idea, though she did say she likes the winter solstice. She said that already, to be fair," Abley offers. "We just don't know, so hard to reach conclusions."

"That told me then," Lemon looks at Abley, then sneers.

"No, I'm just saying. She seemed genuine about being

into celebrating the shortest day," Abley replies.

"Well, I've put tags on her for flights out of the country, and she's booked tickets to go home already. Bit odd, isn't it? When the remains of Dr Starborneck are not released yet. In fact, the more I think about this, the more I think we should bring her in." Lemon raises his eyebrows.

"I think that's a good idea. We can question her about her art," Elizabeth suggests.

"We? You two. You must get out and leave me to my job." Sergeant Lemon looks at them both.

"Your officers are the ones who brought me in here in the first place. I can think of nothing better." And Elizabeth deliberately whisks herself away, leaving Abley and Lemon to talk.

*

Inspector Abley shuffles in his seat, and looks around the room, then locks eyes with Sergeant Lemon.

"Let me start."

"I haven't got time for this. I have to go out and find Dr Haven Usrey for questioning," Lemon replies.

"But there are things to talk about."

"Talk's cheap. My Dad always says you can judge a person by their actions, not their words."

"I know, I know." Abley gestures his acceptance of the criticism.

"You nearly wrecked my career."

"And for that, I cannot tell you how sorry I am. I hate myself for it. I hated myself. Full stop. But, I'm out of that now."

"What, you love yourself, so everything's all right?"

"No. No, that's not what I'm saying," Abley replies. Lemon stands up, ready to leave.

"It's all hot air with you, isn't it? Until the next disaster in your life and then you'll reach for the bottle." Lemon throws his hands in the air.

"I haven't been drunk since... I can control it."

"I don't want to hear it. I don't care."

Lemon opens the door.

"Wait."

"What?"

"What is it like in Oxford?" Abley asks.

"There are hills. What do you want me to say?"

"Just tell me you're happy, and then I'll leave it," Abley replies.

"Why are you asking?" Lemon stands still, unable to leave the room, adding, "I hope you're not thinking of following me over here."

"I just want to hear that you're happy."

Lemon turns.

"Actually, no, not really. I've had to relocate. The girlfriend promised it would be lovely, but she's fallen out with her family here. The main reason we chose here when we wanted to leave. And I keep getting put on double shifts, night shifts. I'm the new boy. There are no favours. So…"

"I'm entirely responsible. I'm gutted. I'm so, so sorry."

"Don't be stupid. You didn't tell me to come here. You should have come here!" Lemon suggests crossly.

"Maybe we can arrange a swap?" Abley tries to be helpful. "You could come back to Cambridge, and I could work here."

"I don't think my Inspector would like you."

"Why?"

"He's not a people person," Lemon replies.

"I can try to win him over. Invite him along for a game of golf."

"I never hated your golf," Lemon laughs. "In fact, I found myself watching it on the box the other day. For no reason."

Bob Abley realises there is a chink of hope.

"I won't get in your way. I'll go tomorrow. I just want

to make sure Elizabeth is okay. It's Christmas, and she keeps sending me all these funny presents. I think it's because of Gerald," Abley says. Lemon slowly begins to defrost.

"I'm not saying I'm not mad. But I suppose you can stay with us if you have nowhere to go. The hotels are often full."

"It's okay. I'm sorted. I have a friend, a golf buddy actually, who lives near the Perch. He's got a country pile. Always got a room."

"All right, but if you get stuck. But stay out of this." Lemon looks at Abley. Abley smiles, then Lemon leaves. Abley isn't sure if he's just been offered a place out of pity, or if things are defrosting between them. He looks out of a tiny window in the room and sees more snow falling outside and has his doubts about any big thaw soon.

36
REINDEER AND SANDWICH BOARD

After Elizabeth leaves Inspector Abley with Sergeant Lemon in the Oxford Police Station, she tries to see if she can find the police pathology lab nearby, but somehow ends up on Pembroke Street still with no joy. She doesn't get very far when a police officer on a pavement beat asks if she is lost – as she noticeably keeps changing direction – then starts to look at her curiously. Elizabeth immediately recognises this officer as the Constable who is scared of spiders and is shocked when he doesn't twig it's her. Not exactly detective material, but she decides to cut her losses and leave in case he finds his memory, and so slips into a local art gallery for a while until he passes.

It isn't long before Elizabeth is popping her head back out onto the street to spy the all-clear. She says thank you to a tall, glamorous art gallery curator for speaking to her, a woman in her early thirties who clearly has a passion for art deco, her crisp, black bob, and black, flared trousers paying homage to the era. Elizabeth's shorter frame and unruly curls nevertheless are full of life as she steps out into the snow, her eyes determined, and her pace speedy.

As Elizabeth continues along the path, she breathes in

the fresh air. Her boots crunch on the grit on the pavements, cutting into the ice. She wishes she could bang Inspector Abley and Sergeant Lemon's heads together. Boy, has she had her run-ins with Bob in the past, but she knows they both care about each other. If only they could see it.

As she continues on her walk, with a growing thought to head back to Catte College to find Gabriel again, she heads along Bear Lane into Blue Boar Street, and spots Godric, outside The Bear Inn pub, wearing a sandwich board and standing in a crowd of young people while handing out leaflets. The dogs spot her and pull Godric's arms out of their sockets, and it is enough for him to keep upright.

"Bunny!"

"Godric."

Elizabeth fusses the dogs and then reads the sandwich board Godric is wearing. It is a poster of the pantomime, with all the drag queens he met now all dressed up in costume as wicked stepmothers and the handsome prince. She takes a flyer, a photo of the three dogs dressed in sparkly costumes and a sign in the corner of the image stating a pound off purchasing a ticket.

"They've exaggerated it for the advertisement. Those aren't actually their costumes," Godric says.

"What did I say? I don't agree with using animals as entertainment."

"They get paid," Godric replies.

"What?"

"They get paid for their performance. The Production Manager said they need contracts, so they get paid."

"No," Elizabeth shakes her head.

"I've already signed," Godric shrugs.

"You know, there are times when you remind me of your mother. They'd better not wear those hideous things."

"They won't, I promise. Au natural."

"What have you found out about the plastics industry and Dr Haven Usrey?"

"If they're being hounded by the plastics industry, then it's doing it very covertly. I found nothing, nada, nowt. The company that sponsored their research are full of good guys as far as I can see. They shout all over the net about their next steps to help the environment. Been very open. So no bad guys," Godric snatches back the leaflet from Elizabeth who is still frowning at the images of her dogs all dressed up on it.

"So we're back to square one. We have no motive from the plastics industry."

"Oh, there was one thing," Godric stands bolt upright to exaggerate the drama of his next point. "Hippy Haven used to be an alcoholic. Was on the Twelve Steps programme. That's how she met Dr Sandy Starborneck. So Sandy was an alcoholic, and Haven was too." Godric opens up his phone and shows Elizabeth the page of Haven giving a talk to an audience about how she gave up booze.

"Hmm, well, Sergeant Lemon suggested she's the murderer because she's jealous. It would explain her shouting so much at Dr Sandy Starborneck for being drunk. Somehow, I find it hard to believe that Haven killed her friend. No, this is someone clever, someone who knew her. We have to find out more about Michael Pussett."

As Elizabeth is talking a young woman comes up to Godric giggling and points at her friends who have already bought tickets to the pantomime. She hands over a ten-pound note to Godric.

"You've just bought my last ticket! I can now leave this cold place and retreat into the warm. I hope you enjoy the show this week." He smiles at the young girl and turns to Elizabeth. "You'd better come and watch me."

"Only if I'm still here. I want to get home tonight if I can solve this. In the meantime, I must find Gabriel."

Gabriel had taken a photograph of the painting on his phone and she wanted to send it to the art gallery and the lady she'd just spoken with.

"I am looking forward to a nice cup of tea." Godric shuts his eyes.

"Don't forget water for these lovelies," she says, pointing at the three huffing dogs at their feet.

"I'm not going to forget." Godric smiles. His Nanna would always remind him of the most obvious tasks with the dogs. But then he had left them at the airport that time, and he does have a tendency to fall straight asleep on bourbon when his head hits a pillow. So, he forgives her and ushers the dogs in the direction of the warm comforts of the hotel. Perhaps he will see that concierge again.

Elizabeth marches off towards Catte College. She must get that photograph Gabriel took, and there are other things she needs to ask.

37
WINTER TOMATOES

Gabriel sits at the Steinway, playing Mel Tormé and Bob Well's *'The Christmas Song'* in the Master's Lounge. Linda, the caterer, comes in with a tray of tea and cake for him.

"Oh, thank you, Linda. Will the Master be joining me?" Gabriel asks.

"No, he's reading in his rooms."

Gabriel touches his nose and winks at Linda, and then mimics the Master sleeping and snoring.

"Oh, Dr Deersman, you're so funny," Linda laughs.

"Do you have any requests?" Gabriel asks.

"D'you know any that have been in the charts that aren't posh?"

"D'you know, I don't believe I do? Can you sing one?"

"Behave, everyone knows something," she says and starts to sing a popular song.

"That's fabulous! Why is that not in my repertoire?" Gabriel smiles

"You make the whole place feel Christmassy," Linda tells Gabriel.

"Do I? That's nice."

"Perhaps this year, with the snow and everything," Linda says. She pours a cup of tea and puts a coaster on top of the piano, then places a cup and saucer there. She knows how Gabriel drinks his tea. He nods thank you as he continues to tickle the ivories. "Sorry."

"What?" Gabriel looks at Linda.

"I don't know. Must be hard," Linda says. Gabriel knows she is talking about his lost wife.

"Don't be silly," Gabriel replies, watching Linda looking out of the window at the snow. He spots her bicycle, "You're brave getting about on that in this icy weather. Brave or a little mad."

"Oh, I'm used to it. Had that bicycle for twenty-two years now."

"I love my bicycle too. Good to see you have a crash helmet. D'you know what they call cyclists up at the hospital who don't wear crash helmets?"

"Donors." Linda raises her eyebrows. Gabriel raises his finger at her and points a 'well done'. "I must admit, I don't like cycling home in the dark. I can bring some Christmas cake over from the tray if you like?"

"How can I say no to you, Linda, you spoil me. Conferences must be tough,"

Gabriel rolls his eyes. "How do you work for that man?"

"He's a bit of a plonker," she says as she cuts the cake, "but I don't take any of his bullshit."

"Quite. You think he's a violent man, Linda? D'you think he could have hurt Dr Starborneck?" Gabriel stops playing the piano.

"It makes me wonder if I'm safe. Nothing like this has happened before," Linda replies. Gabriel leans down into a briefcase and pulls out a brown paper bag.

"Here, would you like these?"

Linda looks into the bag.

"Tomatoes?"

"From my laboratory," he replies.

"I'm not going to turn into something if I eat them, am I?"

"No," Gabriel laughs, "they have vitamins and minerals in them. Don't take your normal vitamin pill. All you need is a tomato. Hey, presto!"

"One tomato?"

"Well, a few, but not all of them. Just a few."

Linda is unsure but tries not to show it. Gabriel can see.

"They won't hurt you. They're good for you," he says trying to reassure.

"Thanks." Linda holds up the bag, not sure about taking them but doesn't want to hurt his feelings. He can tell.

"They really are safe to eat."

*

Elizabeth pops her head around the door of a very quiet Porters Lodge.

"Anyone know where I can find Dr Gabriel Deersman?"

"You'll hear him before you see him. He's in the Master's Lounge on the Steinway," the Porter replies. Elizabeth passes Linda in the corridor, as Linda carries a teapot somewhere. They exchange a nod. Then Elizabeth opens the Master's Lounge door.

"Hello!" Gabriel is so pleased to see Elizabeth, "Long time no see," he adds cheerily, aware they've just met for late lunch in the cafe not long before.

"I wondered if you might be able to email me the photograph you took of that painting?"

"What? Oh, yes, yes. What, now?" He asks.

"Yes, please."

Gabriel fumbles in his pocket and laughs nervously. Then he gets out his phone.

"What's your email?"

"Just use the one you have from the conference. It's on the welcome pack. It's my university one."

"Oh, right you are," and Gabriel searches for that, a little disappointed that Elizabeth hasn't given him her private email.

"What are you doing here?" She asks.

"Playing the piano. I tend to prefer the organ, but they don't have one in College. Rather disappointing."

"Don't let me stop you. The piano would make anything sound nice."

"Oh, thanks." Gabriel finds Elizabeth's email and sends the photograph he took of the picture in the cafe flat. "Done. Why are you so hung up about a painting?"

"It links Sandy and Haven to Oxford. There are no clues, nothing concrete in this case. As far as I know, the police have turned up nothing with the poison, apart from the fact that they think I might have done it. Sergeant Lemon is a little suspicious of Haven. Are you?" Elizabeth asks.

"I don't think Haven could kill a fly if it were masticating on her three-bean salad," Gabriel replies.

"Will you play something?" Elizabeth asks.

"Thought you'd never ask. Why don't we play something."

Elizabeth doesn't need any convincing. There is nothing better than a duet on a Steinway. She smiles as Gabriel starts to play Astor Piazzolla's '*Libertango*', then shuffles across the piano stool to start playing the lower notes, so she has to quickly pick up the treble clef.

The two play through almost all of the tune without speaking a word, then Elizabeth breaks the silence.

"You didn't do it, did you?"

"What?"

"Did you kill Sandy?" She presses him.

"Excuse me, are you joking?" Gabriel looks affronted.

"I have to ask everyone."

"Oh, you had me there. You look so serious."

"I am serious." Elizabeth raises her eyebrows.

Gabriel abruptly stops playing and stands back aghast. "What? I'm most certainly not a murderer. What on earth has given you that opinion?"

"I don't know. They always say don't trust the nice ones," Elizabeth's eyes lock on Gabriel. "I heard you were married. What happened to your wife? Linda said she died. How did she die?"

"This isn't funny." Gabriel clears his throat and has gone bright red. "You've just accused me of doing something unforgivable, and you expect me to remain calm?"

"I'm not laughing. Why are you so defensive? Your reaction is a bit over the top if you're innocent."

"Are you the murderer?" Gabriel throws it back at Elizabeth, "I mean poor woman, but perhaps you were jealous of her. Maybe you like tall conference organisers yourself."

"Now you're being ridiculous. I only asked you of your guilt. You should consider yourself in a lower category than the other suspects. To be honest, if I thought you were really guilty, I would never just come out with it. I'd spend hours, days sometimes weeks watching you, watching your moves. So you should take it as a compliment. Yes. But why are you acting all hurt?"

"Because, well because I like, liked you." Gabriel finds the words incredibly hard to utter and then turns his back on Elizabeth, who is still sitting at the piano. He looks out at the snow in the quad. "My wife passed away last year. I walk past the house every day. I can't stop. I want to stop. I think about her every day, every hour, every minute. You, I don't know. You're so different, different to her. You helped me forget. I am – until you accused me of being a murderer – was able to be in the moment. No matter."

"Now you say," Elizabeth says, passive to Gabriel's emotions.

"And there I was developing a soft spot for you. But

you're right. It's too soon. I'm not thinking."

"No one has ever had a soft spot for me. Now I can't trust you again."

But Gabriel just shrugs his shoulders.

"I love your dogs by the way," he breaks his silence, "My wife, she was allergic. She loved dogs. But she couldn't touch them. It was heartbreaking. Imagine not being able to have a hug from a dog. You should probably go," he says. Elizabeth can tell that Gabriel is tired.

Just as the two are trying to reset the clock and calm the moment, Michael storms in, out of breath and covered in snow with a red mark on his cheek with a cluster of little circular indents. "On cue! Ready and waiting," Gabriel hits a few bottom notes on the piano.

"Oh," is all Michael Pussett says at first, when he stumbles into the Master's Lounge, expecting it to be empty, as it usually is at this time. "I thought? Oh, never mind what I thought. Professor Green, I implore you to reschedule your keynote."

"Please don't bring this up again. I'm not in the mood," Elizabeth shakes her head at him, noticing the strange shape on his cheek like he's been hit with something knobbly.

"You just can't do anything to help me out, can you?" Michael Pussett is angry now with Elizabeth, knowing there is not a chance she will do her keynote. "Why, if not for a few loyal returners each year this whole thing wouldn't hang together. It's to help further your careers, you know — not mine. I really don't know sometimes why you lot even come? You're just showing off, aren't you?"

"Hey!" Gabriel is angry now, "Don't talk to Professor Green like that."

"Did you kill Sandy? I mean, you've already been charged for assault on Dr Haven Usrey, what else are you capable of?" Elizabeth asks Michael, then turns to Gabriel. "See, I'm asking everyone." Then she turns back to Michael. "We know it was murder by poison, by yew."

"Oh, for god's sake. You're not a detective in Oxford." Michael sneers at Elizabeth. "I'm very sad about Sandy passing away, and I will mourn. And I'm mad that Haven is all but accusing me of Sandy's murder. But I've got to get this conference over the line. I can't think about it now, or I won't be able to think about anything else." Michael storms out.

"Perhaps you should go too," Gabriel adds, before sighing and sitting back down at the piano, waiting for her to leave. Elizabeth rolls her eyes at Gabriel and then leaves the Master's Lounge.

38
GONE TO HIPPY HEAVEN

Elizabeth leaves Catte College, having tested the waters with Gabriel and been surprised by his reaction. She decides to make her way back to the hotel to check up on Godric and the dogs. On the way, Inspector Bob Abley's car screeches towards her and stops suddenly.

"Get in!"

"Hello, pleased to see you too, I think?" Elizabeth replies, surprised by his abrupt greeting.

"Now!" He shouts. Elizabeth reluctantly gets in. As Inspector Bob Abley's car speeds away down Broad Street to join Abingdon road he explains, "Lemon called me. Dr Haven Usrey is dead. She was found by two dog walkers just half an hour ago up on Boars Hill."

"But you'd just left her?" Elizabeth replies, her manner changing to one of shock.

"I know. Apparently, you and I are on the Oxford Inspector's most wanted list right now. Lemon told me better to be up there than doing anything suspicious down here. It's ridiculous."

"I wasn't doing anything suspicious," Elizabeth replies, affronted.

"Neither was I." Abley thinks of the indoor driving range he'd sneaked off to when he'd received Lemon's call.

"Right. How did she die?"

"They don't know. Found with a bottle and a note."

"Surely, not suicide."

"No, indeed. She was a woman sounding like she was off on a new adventure. She was happy. It was the only thing that made her a little suspicious. Her laugh. You know, her friend dead. Still happy. No, this is fishy," Abley replies firmly.

*

Inspector Abley's car pulls into a lay-by near where the police have already parked up, yards from Boars Hill. Dog walkers local to this spot, and on their usual walks at dusk, are now huddled in a little gathering, clearly talking about Haven's death. Inspector Abley and Elizabeth Green march through them, the snow beneath their feet quite trampled, from all the SOCOs. As they reach the clearing and can see the view back down across all of Oxford, they spot the police tape, one-hundred foot square, around a park bench. On the bench, still sitting, is Haven's body. The police photographer is snapping away from every angle, as two other SOCOs start to hurriedly erect a tent around her.

Elizabeth Green is used to a crime scene but can't help but feel sick at the sight, as she catches a glimpse of Haven's face in the dying sun, already looking stiff, her eyes still open, staring out across the snow as the light fades.

"She wanted to watch the sunset. Winter solstice coming. That's what she said." Abley's voice breaks a little as he explains his last conversation. Elizabeth looks away. She can't imagine how much pain Haven must have been in if she took pills in this cold. But as Elizabeth is clocking all the numbers the SOCOs are marking out on the ground, close to the body, to signify items or scuffs spots which might be relevant, the Oxford Inspector walks up to both Elizabeth and Inspector Bob Abley.

"Sergeant Lemon mentioned you drove the deceased up to this spot not two hours ago."

"Yes, that's right," Inspector Abley replies.

"Returning to the scene of the crime?"

"Oh come off it. I don't know this woman,"

"Then what the hell are you doing leaving your scent all over my patch?"

Inspector Abley turns away and walks down the hill, doing his best to diffuse the situation for Lemon's sake, as the Oxford Inspector shouts after him, "you shouldn't be here. And as for you…" The Oxford Inspector turns to Elizabeth. "I told you not to leave Oxford, but I didn't tell you to follow us around like some creepy groupie. Are you guilty of this?"

"Don't be ridiculous," Elizabeth grumbles.

"Then bugger off. In fact, don't come within a mile of any of my investigations."

"That might be hard, as I'm staying in the centre, which is very convenient for all the Colleges and this is an academic crime. You told me to remain in Oxford. And you have already had one murder in a College. I'm presuming the murderer won't stop here," she says, glaring at the Oxford Inspector.

"If I find you at the crime scene again, then I shall arrest you and throw away the key. Now take your Cambridge Inspector and bugger off."

"Are you expecting more murders before you catch this criminal? That's not a good strategy, is it?" she says cleverly.

"Get out of my sight."

Elizabeth walks down to join Bob Abley on the edge of the hill in the snow.

"He's got ants in his pants." Bob Abley raises his eyebrows at Elizabeth.

"And on a charm offensive." Elizabeth pulls shut her beady eyes. Abley's mobile rings and he answers.

"Yes, where are you?" Abley turns and sees Lemon waving a hundred yards away. "Why can't you come over?" Abley covers the phone and explains to Elizabeth. Abley puts his phone on mute. "It's Lemon. He can't be seen in cahoots with us."

"Put it on speaker then, quickly," Elizabeth says, leaning in. Abley rolls his eyes and puts his phone on speaker, turning down the sound. Lemon's voice comes over the phone in a whisper, while they both watch him in the distance up the hill. Elizabeth pulls the phone to her ear, and Abley leans in.

"She died from hypothermia the pathologist suspects," Lemon says, "though can't confirm until he takes her back," They all watch as Haven's body is now covered and finally taken off the bench and placed on a stretcher in a body bag. Lemon continues in a whisper, "She had some gin as well, and I mentioned before when I rang earlier, she left the note. It just said, 'I'm sorry. I couldn't help it. I can't stand for everything to be raked up again.' And that was it. My Oxford Inspector thinks Haven must have killed Sandy and says it's all wrapped up now. But, I'm not so sure. What didn't she want raked up?" Lemon asked them both. Elizabeth turned and shook her head at Lemon and shrugged a little. She had no idea — two dead and still no firm suspect.

"Where's her elephant bag?" Elizabeth asks.

"What?" Abley looks at Elizabeth. "Ask Lemon," he encourages.

Elizabeth leans into the phone to ask Lemon, shouting, "Where's her elephant bag?" A few SOCOs look around at Elizabeth. Why is she shouting? Lemon raises his eyebrows.

"He's trying to talk to us quietly, Liz." Abley grabs hold of Elizabeth's arm.

"I've never seen her without it. Did she have it with her

when you drove her up here?" Elizabeth impatiently waits for Abley to think. "Well?"

"I don't remember."

"Ugh. It was only two hours ago."

"Yes, but her clothes match her bag. They're all really loud."

"Did she put anything in the footwell of your car?"

"I don't know."

"Think." Elizabeth stares at him. Lemon is still on the phone the other end, listening.

"There was no bag with her here. Nothing."

"Disgusting sweets." Elizabeth looks nonplussed, so Abley continues. "She had these sweets which tasted of cloves. Thcy were dreadful. She took them out of her bag, maybe."

"Could she have left it where you got a drink?"

"No. I must have left her with it. You can check in the pub. It was The Putter. She may have left it there? I made a point of stopping as it had so much—" But as Abley is about to start to pontificate on all the golf trophies and memorabilia in the pub, Elizabeth spots something on the ground in the snow.

"Look," they both look as it glints.

"Hedgehog," Abley suggests.

"Porcupine." Elizabeth picks it up.

"Don't touch it." Lemon says down the phone, cuts the call, then rushes over. They all peer at the ring in the palm of Elizabeth's hand.

"It matches the injury on Michael Pussett's cheek," Elizabeth says. Lemon gets an evidence bag.

"He'll say you placed it there," Lemon says, looking at his Oxford Inspector, now curious as to why Lemon has joined his nemesis.

"Oh, for goodness sake, I just picked up a ring that was already there. I thought he thinks Haven did it. Just say you found it," Elizabeth replies. They both know what the other is thinking. Elizabeth and Abley briskly move away from the spot, as Lemon beckons a SOCO over to put a number to mark the spot.

"Lift back?" Abley asks Elizabeth.

"Yes, please. If we can take a detour to Summertown, there must be a clue we missed there. There has to be."

39
THE HAT AND CUFFS

Inspector Abley pulls up outside Haven's house she was renting with Dr Sandy Starborneck.

"This breaks all the rules."

"Are you coming?"

Elizabeth walks around the back and sees the window is still open. Inspector Abley follows her.

"Bend down."

Unsure of her plan but suspicious of her intentions nevertheless, after shaking his head, Abley bends down so that Elizabeth can climb onto his shoulders and squeeze through the window. Once inside, she opens the front door for Abley.

"This is the painting I was talking about," Elizabeth points up at the wall in the living room. Inspector Abley looks at the painting in blue and green of a woman holding a chicken, floating in the dark starry sky.

"Right. Different." He looks around the place and is a little jealous, comparing it to his small flat, "It's all right for some, isn't it?"

"You do realise that both inhabitants are dead, suspected murdered. I would say that living here is most definitely not all right for some. And look at that, Michael Pussett's hat. That wasn't here last time. He must have a key. But why would he be visiting his girlfriend who is already dead."

"Maybe he wanted his CD collection back."

"Has Maureen got yours?"

"My Pink Floyd, Zeppelin, Hendrix. She doesn't even like them."

"They were visiting. There is hardly anything here. Well, the only new thing is the hat. We have to go to Michael Pussett's."

"You realise we are leaving a trail of DNA that plants you more and more into the frame for both murders in the ridiculous mind of a certain Inspector," Abley says to Elizabeth,

"If I go down, I guess you're coming with me. Who will believe that you drove all this way just to help me if it wasn't to commit a double murder? You were with Haven Usrey last. So you have to hope that we are one step ahead of the Oxford Inspector, and solve this before he pins it on us." Elizabeth allows herself a small smirk.

"He does have a name, you know."

"Most people do. But I don't see the point for him. My brain is too full of important things to remember everybody's name."

"You know it was the last part of the brain to develop, the part that remembers names. That's why it is the first to go," Abley replies.

"Very scientific explanation," Elizabeth uses her gloves to open the front door as they both sneak out of the house. Standing outside, waiting for them with two squad cars with silent flashing lights is the Oxford Inspector, his Constables, and Sergeant Lemon.

"Elizabeth Green, I'm arresting you on suspicion of the murder of Dr Starborneck and Dr Haven Usrey. You do not have to say anything, but it may harm your defence if you do not mention when questioned something that you later rely on in court. Anything you do say may be given in evidence." The Oxford Inspector holds up the ring. "We'll run some tests, and if your DNA is on this ring, then we have enough evidence to charge you. You have been in the location of all the murders and are an expert on poisons. And we know this to be Dr Haven Usrey's ring."

"For goodness sake, I picked it out of the snow."

"Elizabeth!" Abley shouts, "Don't panic. We'll get you out of this mess!" Bob Abley looks at Lemon standing behind the Oxford Inspector, shaking his head very subtly.

Elizabeth watches the faces of both her friends. She can't believe what is happening. She thinks about Godric and the dogs back at the hotel. "Tell Godric everything's okay." Then she looks at Lemon's face again. It is unreadable. Surely he doesn't think she did it? She holds his eyes until he looks away. That's all she needs, Lemon thinking she's guilty. Now, who is going to solve the case?

40
CELL MATE

"Don't tell me to calm down. Do something. This is just staggering. What does the man think he's doing? I was trying to solve the case for him. Does he not know I help the police? I've never been arrested in my life." Elizabeth stands in a corridor speaking on the telephone to Inspector Abley, not twenty feet from a custody suite, where she is being held. "I can't find out anything, you heard them. I'm perfectly aware they can hold me for up to ninety-six hours without charge if it's two murders they think I've done. Which I hasten to add, I haven't."

Elizabeth looks around at the Constable behind her and glares at him. "Don't tell me to calm down, Bob. What's Lemon doing? Did you find Gabriel? I was with him, in the Master's Lounge. He'll vouch for me, give me an alibi. Although he is cross at me." Elizabeth pauses to listen to Bob Abley on the other end ask why, then replies, "Because I asked him if he'd murdered the Americans…." Elizabeth lets the irony sink in. "Yes, I know. But he will know that I couldn't have killed Haven. Anyway, why haven't they arrested you? You could've been one of the last people to see her?" Elizabeth listens again as Bob

Abley most probably explains that he is a police officer and beyond reproach. "Yes, it could never be one of their own. You have to get me out of here before the murderer strikes again." Elizabeth listens to Bob. "I'm fully aware of that, but I don't want someone to die to prove my innocence. I'm not having that on my conscience. You need to go to Michael's house." Elizabeth listens. "You can't leave it. I don't care what Lemon's said." Elizabeth is told by the police officer on duty to wrap up the call as he makes a circle in the air with his finger, so she places the receiver very gently on the hook.

The police Constable ushers Elizabeth back to her cell, a grey brick-lined room with one small window high up on a wall. It is dark outside now, and as Elizabeth enters, she sees that another woman, dressed as an elf in green and red with a bright green hat with a bell on top, is leaning over the toilet in the corner, throwing up. She looks back at the Constable wondering where this woman has come from, and he explains, "It's a very busy night. We don't normally do this but it looks like you'll be sharing. Budget cuts. Happy Christmas." Then shuts the door behind Elizabeth.

Elizabeth moves to the lower bunk and sits, observing the thin mattress and the one blanket which has most definitely seen better days and been through a washing machine hundreds of times. The room smells of bleach and cleaning fluid, which is no relief given now it is mixed with the smell of sick from the woman's retching.

"Perhaps you might like to flush that away," Elizabeth suggests. But the woman continues to lean against the toilet. So Elizabeth grabs some toilet roll from the side and holds a piece as she pushes down the flush. This causes the women to rail back, splashed by the force of the toilet flush.

"Don't do that again if you know what's good for you!" The drunken woman shouts and stands up, swaying and threatening to punch Elizabeth. Elizabeth can tell that this woman is sailing three sheets to the wind and that there is no reasoning with her.

"I wouldn't threaten me if I were you. I've been arrested for double murder, and I won't think twice about making it a third. Do I make myself clear?" Elizabeth uses her coldest, hardest voice and glares at the woman who temporarily stops swaying and starts to blink, trying to eye up Elizabeth to see how much of a threat she is. Elizabeth holds her hands up to her face and makes them into the shape of two claws. "These hands. Just don't tempt me."

The drunk woman slides down a wall onto the stone floor and tries to keep her eyes open but looks very pale.

"I don't want no trouble. It's his fault! The bastard. It's him I want to skin alive." The woman shuts her eyes.

"What's your name?" Elizabeth figures it is going to be a very long night and she would like to try to get some sleep, so if she is going to be able to do that safely, she had better try to make a friend rather than an enemy.

"Sharon," the woman slurs.

"Mine's Liz. My friends call me Curls, but we're not there yet." Elizabeth puts a hand in her curly hair, making up her nickname to try to bond with this drunken woman.

"Is that because of your curly hair?"

"It's because I have a grip like a python," Elizabeth replies.

Sharon frowns.

"I'm not feeling so great. I'm—"

"Missing your family, no doubt."

"Yeah, my little'uns are with their gran. It's his fault. You got a fella? I'm telling you, they're no good. Always causing trouble." Sharon looks at Elizabeth, waiting for her to agree. But Elizabeth doesn't.

. "What are you doing here?" Elizabeth asks instead.

"I stole a train. The one in the shopping centre in the grotto. You know, that goes around the centre with the bell? Father Christmas's."

"No."

"You know."

"I haven't been to the shopping centre."

"Yeah. It shows." Sharon pulls at Elizabeth's trousers, "I don't know anywhere that sells stuff like this." Sharon is so drunk. Her polite button is turned off. "You don't look like a murderer," Sharon says very calmly.

"What do murderers look like?" Elizabeth asks.

"Not like you."

"Yes, well. In fact, I didn't do it," Elizabeth comes clean. Realising that this woman, Sharon, is no harm to man nor beast.

"That's because you don't have a bastard husband like mine who sleeps with Mrs Christmas."

"Mrs Christmas?"

"Found them in Santa's grotto! Having his end away. The bastard. Sorry, but he pushes all my buttons." Sharon can hardly speak; she is still seriously under the influence. "So I got him, didn't I. Pushed him into the wishing well. It's just the shopping centre fountain. They dress it up, but it's still a fountain. Wet, ain't it? Then I stole his train, you know, the one people ride on to take them to Santa."

"When was this?"

"Half an hour ago," Sharon says after reaching for her confiscated phone and then looking at where a watch might be on her wrist.

"Was anyone hurt? How big is the train?"

"I didn't run anyone over, nah it was empty. I was after him. He did look funny with his trousers around his ankles. Splash. Ha ha. Splash," Sharon then shakes her head and tries to look straight ahead, opening her eyes wide, "Did me for drunk driving."

"Drunk driving?"

"Stealing Santa's express. Wish it'd been ruddy murder. The bastard. When I catch him." Then Sharon looks more closely at Elizabeth, her eyes focusing. "You one of them, swings the other way?"

"Why d'you say that?"

"Dunno, what you're wearing. Who wears corduroy?"

"It's cold outside. And you can't talk. Elf?"

"Guess him indoors isn't fussy. He's probably playing away from home. With a bird who doesn't wear corduroys."

"If he is, she must be an angel, or perhaps a fairy," Elizabeth replies.

"Eh?"

But Elizabeth shakes her head.

"Never mind."

"Oh, you're one of them who defends her man. He hit you?"

"No."

"Mine does. Well, he ain't gonna no more. He's her problem. He's not coming back in the house. I reckon you should do the same. Lock him out." Sharon looks at Elizabeth, who remains quiet, so Sharon continues. "Look. You're an idiot if you forgive him. He'll only do it to you again. They're all rotten. Men."

"He passed."

"A test? So what."

"He's not here."

Sharon looks blank.

"He's not with us anymore," Elizabeth doesn't want to say the word. It finally sinks into Sharon's brain. There is silence for a while, as Sharon leans on her elbow stretching out on the cold stone floor. Elizabeth is thankful, but the silence is broken as Sharon stares at Elizabeth.

"Bet you were the right power couple, eh? Was he as annoying as you? Bet he was one of those businessmen who makes it difficult for the rest of us. Your get up, worth a bob. The rich always have it easy. Fly off to exotic islands over Christmas, don'tcha. While the rest of us, we have to scrimp and scrape. It ain't fair. You think you have everything. You think you're better than the rest of us." Something in Sharon's words makes Elizabeth's emotions bubble up too much.

"He was a doctor. All he did was make people better," Elizabeth says quietly, trying to shut down any conversation.

"They get paid a fortune. I only ever get ten minutes with them."

"A surgeon," Elizabeth replies.

"Loaded." Sharon nods. "Told ya."

Something in Elizabeth snaps. She can't let anyone think that Gerald was just a surgeon or doing it for the money, even though she was so proud of the work that he did. Yet, he was so much more.

"Funny thing is, he loved Christmas. We never flew off, as you say. He would have probably been Christmas shopping today. He did spoil me, you're right. Rose creams. You can't get them everywhere. He'd go searching for them long before you could order what you want with a click of your fingers. He crossed county borders. I'd tell him not to, but he would. He wanted it to be perfect," Elizabeth is exhausted and doesn't know why she's confiding with this woman and stops. Perhaps it is because she doesn't know her. Elizabeth looks around the room.

"Well, you're lucky. What you doing in here?"

"The police here are idiots."

"Ha! You're so right. You're just like the rest of us after all, eh?"

"I still have a box at the ballet, so I suppose... He booked it every year for twenty years. Because he took me once. To see The Nutcracker. And I loved it so much I cried. I don't cry. Ever. So he wanted to take me to see a ballet every year until our legs wouldn't carry us to London."

Sharon climbs up on her top bunk bed and crashes out, ready to sleep.

"My Karen's in the school ballet. Well, she's dancin'. I can't afford her new shoes. He drank all the money down the pub. But her Nan, she found some in the charity shop. And she's gonna be dancing in the school Christmas show.

I'm gonna miss it at this rate."

But Elizabeth is not listening; she is in her own world. Thinking of Gerald.

"I've never been since," she says quietly to herself. "A friend said it's just an empty box, that the staff sometimes sit in it. Some shows have mannequins they put in the boxes, so they look full."

"You should go. Or give it to someone else. That's just a waste." Sharon looks up at the ceiling, the quiet of the cell making it possible to hear every whisper.

"There is something about ballet. The synchronicity of the orchestra and musicality of the dance. It's magical, theatrical, transcendent." Elizabeth waves her hands about.

"You're nuts. At least you had a good bloke. If you're missing him, take mine."

"No, thank you." Elizabeth couldn't think of anything worse. Then realises perhaps that came out a little rude. But Sharon doesn't reply, so Elizabeth lets it pass, and the two sit in silence for a while.

Elizabeth watches a beetle crawl across the sheet. She can see there is no food for this animal, so catches it between her fingers. She opens her handbag and pulls out a paper bag. She pops the beetle in the folded bag then back into her purse.

"What you going to do with that? Eat it later?"

"Something like that," Elizabeth replies.

41
WOLVERCOTE

The next morning Elizabeth steps out of the cell and collects the rest of her belongings. Last night, she had persuaded the custody officer that she needed her bag for medical reasons. She was allowed to take in her inflatable pillow, eye mask and earplugs, items Elizabeth rarely leaves home without.

In fact, to say she had chewed his ear off until he capitulated wouldn't be far from the truth. Had Elizabeth not had the earplugs, she would have heard Sharon snoring all the long night but was consequently blissfully unaware. However, the lumps and bumps on the bed had caused her to toss and turn, so swings and roundabouts as far as she was concerned.

Elizabeth's wallet and other items had been removed from her bag, including her nail clippers and cat biscuits, although she wondered what the police thought she'd do with those. Poison someone? She gathers these items and sees some of the biscuits are missing. She opens her wallet and takes out a fifty-pound note, then hands it to the officer.

"Oh, I can't accept bribes."

"This isn't for you. Give this to that woman in there. Sharon. Tell her to buy her daughter some ballet shoes."

Having spent the night in the cells, Elizabeth leaves the police station, her eyes now acclimatising to the brightness of the snow on the buildings, streets and trees. To a passer-by, she looks frail, and her curls are all squished on one side where she's not had a comfortable night's sleep. However, Elizabeth is made of sterner stuff. With an iron rod up her spine, Elizabeth buttons up her duffel coat and shrinks a little from the cold. Outside, waiting for her is Godric with the dogs and Inspector Abley. Godric is holding a flask.

"Got the very cute concierge to make you up hot chocolate. Vegan." Godric labours the word 'concierge', then pulls out two huge biscuits from his pocket in a paper bag.

"You're the best," Elizabeths says and pinches one of Godric's cheeks and then runs her fingers through Hector's coat. She shuts her eyes to hide a spike of tears. She isn't upset about being arrested. She's feeling guilty for putting the dogs through their time in Oxford. Being away from home, being pulled up to be in god-knows-what on stage with Godric. "But you're not making these dogs do things they don't want to do in that play, are you," Elizabeth tells rather than asks Godric, and gives him a beady stare.

Godric smiles, happy that the police haven't broken Elizabeth, that she seems herself.

"I promise, Bunny. The first performance is tonight. I hope you can come and see it. I'm enjoying the whole thing. Well, apart from finding out my Bunny has been thrown in gaol!"

"Wouldn't miss it for the world now," she says, thinking of the little girl, Sharon and the ballet.

"Is it all okay now?" Godric says tentatively.

"I'm here, aren't I?" Elizabeth sees Bob Abley, having parked the car twenty yards away, walking towards them both. "Thank you, Bob. I know you don't like the dogs in the back." Elizabeth now scratches Clive and Monty at the same time, leaving no hands free for the flask or biscuit, so handing them back to Godric. Godric opens the flask, taking that as a hint that he can drink the hot chocolate himself, and opening the biscuit bag to dunk.

"I made an exception." Abley smiles, touching Elizabeth's arm.

"They're on a roll of bin bags on the back seat. Been sliding all over the place." Godric tries to make light of Elizabeth's situation while scoffing biscuits. "But we're very grateful Inspector," he adds when he senses Bob Abley feels he's not grateful enough.

"You'd have done the same for me, Liz," Abley says. "He was going to set bail higher than I can afford, so it's good that he hasn't charged you."

"I can't sit around waiting for him to work out who did it. I was questioned for twenty minutes last night. You're right, no charge yet. Probably because he got pulled away on another case, Constable handing me my personal items this morning said I was lucky. Something about a lorry carrying a load of mints crashed into a field."

"That doesn't sound that big a deal," Abley replies.

"Right next to some national dressage event with hundreds of horses."

"So they ate a few mints."

"Apparently more than a few. There was a rave in a field nearby, and the ravers thought they were hallucinating when they saw the horses high on mints dancing to the music, so they started to take off their clothes and run into the road, he said. In this snow."

"A minor disturbance, surely," Abley smirks.

"It caused lorries to build up into a huge traffic jam. One van with vet tranquiliser medicine in it was broken into by the ravers."

"Did they put the horses to sleep?"

"What do you think? The horses wore themselves out

naturally I'm told, unlike the extremely high ravers that the Oxford Inspector is apparently still trying to deal with."

"Right," Abley replies.

"I don't know. Maybe the Oxford Inspector thought I'd squeal if he made me stay in the cells and I didn't, and he had to leave and forgot to renew the time to keep me, or didn't have strong enough evidence? I'm sure he doesn't know I'm out," Elizabeth suggests.

"Lemon phoned Godric, said he'd told the Inspector he saw you pick up the hedgehog ring in the snow and that's why your DNA was on it," Bob Abley explains, Godric nodding.

"Porcupine. But he didn't see me do that, even though I did. So I guess he trusts me," Elizabeth sighs with relief, realising Lemon is the reason she is now free.

"It did belong to Haven, apparently," Abley continues, "Why take off a ring if you're going to kill yourself. The snow in the area where it dropped had evidence of a fight. And because the snow kept falling, they could point to it being at a time when you most probably had an alibi."

"When did they know this?" Elizabeth asks.

"Last night. Lemon's Inspector wouldn't release you," Abley says.

"We need to get to Wolvercote. But wait a minute," Elizabeth replies, then walks over to a thick bush in the police garden. Behind it are residential homes. She looks at the bush and then walks further over to a brick wall, with ivy and a cherry tree poking over from another garden. She pulls out a paper bag from her handbag and carefully opens it on the wall. "It might be colder out here, but it's much more beautiful," she tells the beetle, who scurries away to look for somewhere to keep warm.

"What are you doing?"

"Freeing a cell-mate." Elizabeth walks towards Bob Abley's car. "Ready now. Wolvercote."

*

Inspector Bob Abley puts the heaters on full in the car as they head up towards Walton Street.

"And that Oxford Inspector will get one of my stern dressing downs." Godric is making his point very forcefully after Elizabeth has suggested that he might like to go and relax back at the hotel. However, she is too tired to argue with him. "You're not going back to prison. I'll make sure of it. I'm not letting you out of my sight until we've cracked the case."

"That will only inflame everything, son. You should listen to your Nanna." Bob Abley tries to reason with Godric. Having three large dogs in the back of his car all day is also something he's not looking forward to and didn't sign up for.

"I'm coming with the both of you, and that's it," Godric insists.

"What about your rehearsals, Goddy?" Elizabeth has one last trump card.

"They will have to do without me this morning. I'm ready enough," he retorts.

This settles the matter, and the three of them drive for a while in silence towards Wolvercote. Elizabeth doesn't recognise some of the roads, as she sees new flats have been erected, with architecture increasingly crowding the trees. But, she can smell Port Meadow, and see the birds flying over the glass roof of Abley's car. Monty, Hector and Clive are all sitting well behaved in the back with Godric. She knows he must have some treats to keep them this quiet. Godric can't keep the silence any longer.

"You don't think he's going to charge Bunny, do you?" Godric asks Bob Abley.

"Of course not. Your Nanna's arrest was the act of a desperate man."

"I am sitting here, you know."

"Lemon told me that they are at a loss as to what might have caused Dr Haven Usrey's death. You were arrested because of the ring and the fact that you're at every crime scene. But, they do have the suicide note," Abley says.

"She didn't kill herself. Like you said, Haven wanted to live, had booked her ticket home. I was right about the Yew poisoning. I'm sure I will find the poison that killed Haven." Elizabeth looks pleased with herself, and also irritated by this Oxford Inspector. "I'm glad you're not as stupid as this Oxford Inspector."

"As stupid?" Bob looks at Elizabeth curiously.

Elizabeth papers over her Freudian slip, and bluffs it out, "He doesn't have half the wit of you. You're much smarter is what I mean. The fact of the matter is that this Michael Pussett, he knew both women. Yet, the police have not arrested him. Why? Surely, he has a motive? And, he rushed into the Master's Lounge out of breath, and he looked like he'd been rolling in the snow. Perhaps he'd been up at Boars Hill with Haven just before. It was, after all, just after she'd died up there that he burst in and we saw him. And why did he leave abruptly? He could have been looking for an alibi from the Master."

"What motive does Michael have?" Godric asks eagerly, but Elizabeth isn't sure. How could it be jealousy, as he was dating Dr Starborneck? She saw it with her own eyes at the conference Christmas dinner, snogging Sandy's face off. And they seemed on good terms. She even saw Michael walk over to Sandy in the snow, outside her hotel window, and tenderly pick her up from the kerb.

"Why are we going to Michael's home?" Godric asks, hoping his Nanna will have a clear reason.

"We are looking for something."

"What?" Godric asks.

"I don't know. But I'm confident we'll find it. There's something eerie about him." Elizabeth trails off, looking out of the window, leaving Godric and Bob Abley a little more anxious than they were earlier. If she has no strong idea, then how long can they keep her from the Oxford Inspector? "Did you ask Lemon if he could join us?"

Elizabeth asks Bob.

"I did," he replies but says nothing more. His answer says it all.

As they approach the home of Michael Pussett, Bob Abley decides to pull up a short way back from the front and on the other side of the road. Everything is quiet. Perhaps because of the snow, probably because it is still early morning and no one is rushing to get to work yet. A solitary cyclist cycles in a groove in the snow on the road past Abley, precariously near his wing mirror. Abley touches an electric button, and the wing mirror moves inwards until it is hugging the car.

"Come on. I don't want to stay here all day. Let's see if the bleeder is in," Abley says, getting out of the car. Godric follows with the dogs, then Elizabeth.

They look like they are headed towards an early Christmas party, as Elizabeth hadn't noticed earlier outside the police station that Godric has dressed the dogs' harnesses with tinsel. Inspector Abley knocks on the door, and they all wait.

The house looks unloved. It is surrounded by homes with Christmas trees lit up in the windows and snowmen built in the front gardens. In Michael Pussett's garden, Elizabeth observes garden pots, but even through the snow, it is possible to see that they have weeds in. The front window has a curtain half-open and partially coming away from its hooks. The front gate is hanging off its hinges. There is a typed note on the door. Elizabeth peers closer. It reads, 'This house is for sale. I don't want to waste your money or mine on estate agents. If you are interested in purchasing, please call. I am looking for a sensible offer. No time wasters.' Then Elizabeth can see Michael's phone number.

"Bit daft to leave your phone number on the front of your home. Data protection and all the rest of it," Godric comments, pulling off the note and pocketing the number in case it is useful later, worried for his Nanna.

"Quite."

As they continue to wait to see if anyone will open the front door, a police patrol car drives past. Godric's heart skips a beat.

"Perhaps we should see if anyone is in, let's go round the back?" Abley suggests. And they all traipse off down a narrow alley to the side of the property, the dogs rushing past Bob and nearly tripping him over.

When they emerge from the alley, they enter an overgrown garden. There are metal chairs around a semi-rusted garden table. Down a path at the bottom of the garden is a shed. Godric tries the backdoor, which isn't locked.

"People never lock their backdoors in the countryside," he suggests.

"We're still in Oxford," Elizabeth reminds him.

The kitchen is dark, but what strikes them more is the lack of any cabinets, a cooker or even a sink. There is one table in the corner, with every inch of it covered with appliances fighting for space. A kettle, toaster, microwave, coffee maker. Around them are spoons, a cup and a stack of paper plates.

"Redecorating?" Abley suggests. But they all wonder as the walls are covered in spiders' webs and dust. It looks like nothing has been done for months, likely much longer.

As they walk into the next room, the same situation confronts them. Empty walls, a lack of furniture. There is one room with a TV propped up on some wood. It is no way to live, no way to exist. Bob Abley looks around at the grey walls and dark blue ceilings.

"The only strange thing about this place is the place," Abley says.

"It's just a bit lonely old man. I mean, where's the Christmas tree?" Godric replies, looking at the dust on a mantelpiece. Godric's comment makes Abley make a mental note to get a big tree when he gets home.

Elizabeth walks out of the house and down the

snowy garden path towards the shed. She is followed by the dogs, who sniff and pee on the way. The shed is locked with a padlock. She peers into the window. On the walls are old photographs of Michael doing magic tricks. There is magic memorabilia, a black hat with a toy rabbit poking out of it. Handkerchiefs are hanging down, clearly all having been tied together. There is a dartboard on the wall, and the photograph pinned to it with three darts is that of the Master of Catte College. Then they hear the familiar sound of Michael's Ford Mustang approaching his home. Elizabeth tries the shed door again, but can't get in. They think about hiding, but there is nowhere to go. The noise of the car engine stops as Elizabeth continues to peer through the shed window.

"I want to confront him. There's bound to be something he's hiding in here. Let's have it out with him," she says to Bob and Godric who have followed her up the path by the shed and are now standing behind her. That's when she spots it. Haven's bag, on a chair. At that moment, she feels a hand on her shoulder.

"What are you doing?" Michael asks Elizabeth and grabs her arm.

"Get off her." Godric punches Michael, who falls back into the snow. Godric leaps on him, and the dogs start to bark.

"I'll have you for trespass and assault," Michael cries.

"What is Dr Haven Usrey's handbag doing in your shed?"

It is Elizabeth who hears the sirens in the distance first. She is in big trouble.

"Go." Abley orders Elizabeth.

"Why have you got Haven's handbag?" Elizabeth persists as the sirens grow louder. "Take the dogs over the road to Port Meadow, Goddy, now."

"Not without you."

"Go, we're coming," Abley tells Godric.

"You're in so much trouble!" Michael shouts.

"Now." Elizabeth urges Godric. For once, he does as he's told and grabs the dogs' leads and walks them down the alley.

"You killed her, didn't you?" Elizabeth looks at Michael, who is now sitting up, brushing snow off his coat.

"You can't come in here, accusing me of all sorts. Get out!" Michael screams at Elizabeth.

"Did you go out with Dr Sandy Starborneck to raise your credibility, to keep your stupid conference going? Dating an academic. What was your problem with Dr Haven Usrey? Too much of a hippy? Need to get her out of the way? Why was your hat in Summertown? Why have you been there recently? Was it to hurt Haven?"

"Get out!" Michael repeats.

"You going bankrupt? Selling your house now? People go to all kinds of extremes when they have no money. Why did you kill Dr Sandy Starborneck? Did she dump you? But why did you kill Haven too?" Elizabeth waits for Michael's reply. But it doesn't come. The sirens grow louder. Michael gets out his mobile phone and takes a photograph of Elizabeth standing in his garden. Then he walks back down the path. "Let yourself out. I will be reporting your breaking and entering." He looks back as he pockets his phone. "You took quite a bit, all my valuables. I'll be letting my insurance know after I've called the police. Though, sounds like they're on their way." He disappears down the alley, but then he rushes back. "Wait. Haven is dead?"

"Who do you think I was talking about?"

"Sandy. Haven is dead?" Michael looks genuinely shocked. He scratches his head. "She can't be dead?" Michael heads back out the front down the alley, not listening to anything else.

Elizabeth and Bob Abley rush through his house to watch Michael Pussett speed away in his noisy Ford Mustang. They also see the police squad car, with its sirens blaring, pull up outside.

The front door is locked. Elizabeth can see Godric standing with the dogs, watching from the other side of the road. She lifts the net curtains and waves him to go away. Godric begrudgingly turns to walk onto Port Meadow. Elizabeth and Abley start to walk towards the back door as Michael's car can still be heard along the street, going much too fast on the icy roads. Sergeant Lemon greets Elizabeth and Bob Abley as they enter the back garden.

"We got a report from a neighbour of a suspected burglary. A woman and two men with three dogs," Lemon says, adding, "I told you to stay away."

"He has Haven's handbag in his shed."

"Right, well, thank you. This is a police investigation. You're a suspect, Professor Green." Lemon opens his eyes wide, clearly signalling that his Constable is outside in the car. "What am I going to do now? Finding you here?"

"Thank you. The ring. You didn't have to—" Elizabeth says.

"I did," Lemon replies, "to get you out. And now look at you."

"We have just been speaking to Michael Pussett. You might want to find him. He seemed very angry. Let me look at Michael's shed," Elizabeth pleads.

"I don't know how you're going to get out of here without my Constable seeing you. You're asking—" Lemon struggles with finding the words. Elizabeth has put him in an impossible position. "This is my job. My livelihood." Lemon shakes his head. "You need to leave. If I'd been my Inspector, you'd be heading back to custody. Don't you know how serious this is?"

"Let us just see the bag, and then we'll go. We can go over the back wall through the fields out there," Abley chips in. "Your Constable will never know."

"Don't tell me what you can or can't do. Not here." Lemon looks at Bob Abley, disappointed, then to Elizabeth,"One peek, then you're gone."

But Elizabeth has already grabbed a rock. She starts to hit the shed bolt. Lemon pushes her out of the way and uses a universal key from his pocket to open the lock. Lemon then turns to Elizabeth, "You have two minutes. Don't go in. Just look. Then, you're gone." He knows she might spot something he misses, and despite his Inspector's hunch she's involved, he believes Elizabeth is just trying to solve the crimes. It's in her veins. If he can solve them too, his job might be safer than it is at present. Lemon looks around, then calls up his Constable. "Constable, I need you to stay there and keep an eye out for Michael Pussett in case he comes back. Let me know, okay? Don't leave the car."

As Lemon is on the phone, Elizabeth rummages through Haven's bag. It is like a bottomless pit, but she quickly reaches in and finds Haven's water bottle and hides it in her coat. Abley hears the excuse Lemon is spinning to his Constable and looks at him gratefully. Lemon replies to Abley, covering his phone, "Don't. Just get her out safely."

Elizabeth nods and continues to peer around the shed. It looks orderly, but nothing like the rest of the house. Almost as if Michael lives here. There is a bed and wood burner. There is a small kitchen. This isn't a shed. It's more like a holiday home. It feels cosy. There is all sorts of memorabilia from the forties, fifties, but mainly from the sixties. Lemon now turns his attention to the shed, as Elizabeth stands now by the door. On the chair in the office space he spots Haven's elephant bag. Lemon puts on evidence gloves and opens it. All the usual paraphernalia, as well as Haven's passport.

"Look," Elizabeth points on a wall of this rather homely shed. Lemon looks up and sees a painting on the wall, similar to the one in Sandy's room. It is of a dog on a bicycle, only it's painted all melty and in blues and dark crimsons. Inspector Abley's phone rings.

"Hello? Superintendent. How lovely to hear from you. Yes, I'm not working today. That's correct, as you advised.

What?" Abley mutes his phone and looks at Elizabeth. "He knows I'm here." Abley puts Superintendent Raynott on speakerphone so that Lemon and Elizabeth can hear the conversation.

"While it is none of my business where you decide to vacation, it becomes my business when the Chief Inspector of Thames Valley Police, Oxford branch, calls me up to say that one of my Inspectors is barging in on a case of one of his Inspectors and should he set the dogs on you."

"Are you sure that's not someone else he's thinking of? I've gone looking for somewhere to play golf as there was so much snow in Cambridge, I couldn't even practice on the grass range," Abley replies.

"And is that place you've found to play your game with little balls, is that place perchance Oxford?"

"It's true that I just popped over to see how Lemon was doing," Abley looks at Lemon who rolls his eyes and says silently 'no', so Abley tries to backtrack, "but he was too busy to talk. So I hope to see him over Christmas." Abley shrugs. Lemon can't believe that Abley is now lying, as his Oxford Inspector saw them together.

"Don't forget you are covering for me over Christmas. I don't think you'll have time for much visiting old colleagues, Inspector," Superintendent Raynott replies.

"How could I forget? Was there something you wanted to talk about?"

"Yes, please stop interfering in other police business out of your jurisdiction. I'd just started to give you a second chance. Please don't make me have to call you back and ask you what the hell you're doing in Oxford, ruining your ex-Sergeant's career prospects and getting right up the nose of his boss. And please don't make me ask you if Professor Green is there with you, as she is one of our best consultants. I'd hate to have to have words with you for leading her astray as well." Superintendent Raynott hangs up, and Abley looks at Elizabeth.

"I just want to play golf," he says.

"This is bigger than I thought, Bob," Elizabeth replies, holding a small tree and willing her brain to think, to find some breakthrough. "We have to solve this before we take the rap. I think you're right, Lemon. I think we're in deep."

42
NO NEW CONTRACT

Michael Pussett's car hurtles down Parks Road, turning onto Catte Street. He has raced straight from his home to Catte College. He leaves it outside, knowing full well the Porters will have something to say about that. But he doesn't care. He rushes through the arch and runs towards the Master's Lounge. He can hear Gabriel playing the piano and bursts through the door, causing Gabriel to jump in his seat and stop playing.

"What have you done to me, eh? Why? Just tell me why?" Michael charges over, so angry with Gabriel that he starts to poke his chest violently. "It was you, wasn't it? Cancelled my contract. Spoke to the Master. Pretend to be all butter wouldn't melt – you backstabber. I've always given you the best slots for your talks, best locations for your stands. Always."

"You again. Huh, making a habit. Do you honestly think I care one hoot about your silly little event? People worth their salt are too busy to come, others are strong-armed to take one for the team, to pretend their departments care. You don't bring grants. You're obsolete dear boy. Just a chancer in a silly hat, which by the way makes you look like a bookie." Gabriel brushes the cuffs of his jacket down where Michael has been holding onto them, but before he gets the chance to look up, Michael has thwacked him across the cheek with such force it knocks him off his seat.

Michael stands over Gabriel, about to kick him, when Linda, the caterer, walks in and is aghast. She rushes over to Gabriel to help him up, then scowls at Michael.

"I should kick this bastard to Timbuktu. He's ruined my life!" Michael shouts.

"Leave him alone!"

"I did advise the Master not to rehire you. It's true, because of your violence to Haven," Gabriel says from the floor.

"Haven's dead!" Michael spits.

"What?"

"She's dead!"

"Oh, dear," Gabriel says.

"Oh, dear? Oh dear? You stuck-up academics. Do you have emotions? They're not like us, Linda. Not real people with real struggles. Up in their ivory towers. You want a lift?" Michael asks Linda.

"No, thank you. I'm good."

"You are on borrowed time here. I suggest you call it a day now and leave." Gabriel says quietly to Michael, clutching his cheek. "Don't frighten the staff. You're in no fit state to drive anywhere."

Michael storms out of College, and races away in his car. The quiet snowy street temporarily broken with exhaust fumes and engine revving.

43
KISS OF DEATH

After their time in Wolvercote and Lemon letting them sneak away, Elizabeth knows that Godric has walked across Port Meadow with the dogs, as he just called Inspector Abley's mobile to say as much, also recounting the quality of the sticky toffee pudding in the cafe he is currently sitting in over in Jericho and informing them that he'd take the dogs to pantomime rehearsal.

Inspector Abley now drives Elizabeth back to the centre. There are so many ideas swirling around her head about who poisoned Sandy. She needs to follow up on a few things. Having just left Michael's house, he seems like the culprit for nefarious activity.

"Perhaps he killed Sandy and Haven found out, which is why he left his hat at her home," Elizabeth suggests, still in the passenger seat of Bob's car. "He had gone to have it out with her. Maybe he followed you up to Boars Hill and watched until Haven was alone."

"Maybe," Abley replies.

"There are a lot of maybes. It doesn't add up, does it?" Elizabeth admits. "How can Michael have known he would have a moment to kill Haven on Boars Hill? And was he carrying around the poison and the suicide note? What if he'd been caught? Could Haven have killed Sandy, and perhaps killed herself? Was it a suicide after all?"

"She was going to live in Santa Fe. Not give everything up," Abley says firmly.

"Perhaps she was hoping to run away with Michael, and he said he wasn't interested now she'd killed Sandy. No, none of it makes sense."

Inspector Bob Abley pulls over to let Elizabeth out on St Giles', thinking she will go back to the hotel for a rest.

"Where are you going?" she asks Bob.

"Unlike you, I'm allowed to leave Oxford. I'm supposed to be on holiday you know. Have a rest and we can come back to this later." Inspector Abley pulls shut Elizabeth's passenger door before she can argue and waves from inside, driving away quickly.

*

As Elizabeth trudges through the snow, she turns away from the hotel, imagining the peace of her suite and longing to put up her feet. It is cold outside, but there are already many Christmas shoppers on the streets, and she has a suspicion that the day will only build with noise and people loaded with purchases. She can do without the reminder and starts to worry about the lack of shopping she has done, but knows she wants to spend her money at home to help build her local community.

Elizabeth watches a man carry a giant Christmas tree along the Lamb and Flag Passage, with a little girl skipping behind, holding a twig in her hand from the tree as if it is her new best friend. She wonders how the little girl will feel come New Year's, watching that tree die and be put out with the rubbish, as she did herself when very young too and vowed from that day never to kill a tree. She pictures the large pine tree in her garden that she decorates instead, and how every year she has to get a gardener from

Granta College to help her put up the lights with his tall ladder. She's proud that the tree is now almost fifty-feet tall, and how it was a tree that someone bought her in a pot one year, which she rescued.

It is not long before Elizabeth is back at the Department of Plant Sciences at Oxford. With her temporary pass, she is able to sneak in. Then a kindly post-doctoral student who remembers her from before lets her back in the laboratory. She finds a quiet bench to herself in the corner, tucked out of the way. She knows she will only need a short time to confirm her suspicions. Elizabeth removes Haven's water bottle from her bag and takes swabs from around the drinking spout. She thinks she knows what she is going to find and, if she's right, things just got a whole lot worse for peace in Oxford.

44
KINDER HABITS

It is some time before Elizabeth finds herself back on St Giles'. She is pleased her suspicions are right but also sad, as now she is pretty sure it is a double murder. Elizabeth feels most frustrated by the Oxford Inspector's unwillingness to let her help.

It is as Elizabeth is thinking about what she can do next that she notices Linda walking towards the Kinder Habits cafe on the corner of Little Clarendon Street. It comes as a momentary surprise to see the caterer looking for sustenance herself. Surely, she could get all the food she needs in College? Perhaps Linda just wants to escape. Maybe she is going to sell the things she's stolen from tables. Again, there are too many perhapses swirling around Elizabeth's head, so she decides to follow Linda inside.

When Elizabeth walks into the cafe, a wave of warmth hits her. Shoppers she has been hoping to avoid, with their excitement about Christmas, pack the chairs. The cafe is also tiny enough for Linda to see Elizabeth immediately.

"Professor Green."

"Oh, hello. This is a surprise." Elizabeth pretends.

"Really? I thought you saw me from outside?" Linda laughs,"I come here to get away from academics. The bells."

"Bells?"

"Kitchen service. Bit of peace."

"I know the feeling," Elizabeth says. Dave, the maître d' comes over and spots Elizabeth.

"Are you together? Are you going to rifle through my personal effects again?"

"No, and no," Elizabeth replies. "You mind if I join you? Not much space." Elizabeth looks at all the full tables. Linda shrugs then nods, and Elizabeth perches on a chair opposite. After they have both ordered drinks from the maître d', Linda comes straight out with her first thought.

"I hear you got arrested, for murder."

"Not stealing at least," Elizabeth replies.

"I don't steal," Linda grumbles.

"I don't kill. As a matter of fact, I've been trying to find the killer."

"It's terrible news about Dr Usrey."

"Have the police spoken to you?"

"Yes, they spoke to us all. Funny that they left Michael alone." Linda raises her eyebrows.

"They interviewed him?"

"Yeah, but did they go into everything?" Linda replies. Elizabeth shakes her head, needing Linda to explain, so she continues. "You know he's making a loss at these conferences? And now, he's lost the gig. He had a row with Gabriel about it. Think Gabriel suggested he lose it because of his violence towards Haven."

"Really?" Elizabeth leans in, focused on Linda's words.

"Don't you think he's such a cliché, going for women wealthier than himself? He does it every year. They lavish money on him, and they go home at the end of the conference. He's had a series of goodtime girlfriends. He lives alone in his sad little home, spending hours in his shed."

"You've been to his home?" Elizabeth asks.

"Yes, when he first started. I thought he was fun, but soon realised he was a narcissist. Creepy," Linda replies. The maître d' comes back over as Linda stands up with a packet of cigarettes. "I'll have the pizza, Dave." She nods to him as she walks out. Elizabeth is left sitting alone, not having looked at the menu.

"What's the special?"

"A three-bean risotto in vine tomato sauce with spinach parcels," Dave replies.

"I'll have that, please." Elizabeth hands him the menu and looks at Linda's little bag on her chair. It is silver with a small bunny on a keyring hanging off it.

Elizabeth can see Linda standing outside in the cold, smoking her cigarette. She is talking to another smoker. Elizabeth has been told often that she would find out more clues if she smoked, as smokers always have the best gossip, but Elizabeth doesn't think emphysema is worth any amount of clues. Linda finally comes back in as the food arrives, having been called back by the maître d'. Elizabeth thinks how Linda spent a long time outside chatting. Linda shivers and sits.

"Do you like working in College?"

"It suits me. I heard the other day that I'm getting a promotion, which is nice. Gabriel put in a good word for me. Said I'm a hard worker. Nice to be appreciated, Now there's a charming man. But I think he may only have eyes for you."

"Don't be ridiculous. Do you know the maître d'?"

"Been coming here for decades. Dave's been here as long. Started off making tea. Now, I think it's his place."

"It's very arty." Elizabeth looks at the paintings on the cafe walls.

"I guess. It used to have more paintings," Linda muses.

The maître d', walks up with some of their order.

"Do you know Michael Pussett?" Elizabeth asks him.

"He's not going to know him," Linda offers.

"Is that the tall guy from your College? Flashy, bit of a spiv. Why?" Dave replies, looking at Linda.

"Because she thinks he killed this academic and she's trying to find a motive," Linda looks at Elizabeth and raises her eyebrows as if to ask if she's wrong.

"He loves art, and you seem to. I wondered if you shared the same passion for it."

"I like art, but I don't go killing people. I don't reckon I have anything in common with him."

"It seems to me you still have quite a passion for art," Elizabeth says, looking around the little cafe with walls of art. "Last time we spoke about art, you threatened to throw mc down the stairs."

45
SUSPENDED CONFERENCE

As they step back out into the snow, Linda reminds Elizabeth that it is the last afternoon of the conference. So, despite being cold and tired, Elizabeth decides she can't miss it, given that there might be news about Haven she can glean from guests. So Elizabeth and Linda walk back together to College, and Elizabeth finds herself chatting to Linda about the beauty of bicycles. Linda pushes hers beside her, and Elizabeth appreciates that, like her own in Cambridge, it is a thing of wonder.

"I bought it off an old Don for a pound. He was leaving for Harvard. It's a bit big for me, but the basket comes in handy. For all the things I steal." Linda looks at Elizabeth, waiting for a response.

"I presume that's what the saddlebags are for?"

*

When the two women enter the conference rooms, they are confronted by a wall of screaming. Michael is shouting at Professor Alexander Resander, and Gabriel has hold of Michael's shoulders, keeping him away from the

Professor.

"Pick on someone your own size. This should not have come as a surprise. We've already spoken, if you can call it that. Blame me," Gabriel says as he struggles with Michael.

"He pulled the plug too. He stuck the knife in with you," Michael says, pointing at Alexander, who is cowering a little, waiting for the first fist to land on his face.

"We both recommended we take a different direction," Gabriel says firmly.

"Then I shall speak to the Master!" Michael shouts.

"The Master has already left for his Christmas holidays. Why don't you calm down and leave Professor Resander alone. Speak to the Master on his return."

"It will be too late by then."

"Well I'm very sorry, but if you carry on like this, I'm going to have to suspend this conference," Professor Alexander Resander warns from under his breath. Gabriel points to Linda to pass Alexander some water, but instead she pours Gabriel a cup of tea.

"Are you okay, Dr Deersman?" Linda asks, completely ignoring Michael and Alexander.

At this very moment, in walks Sergeant Lemon and a couple of Constables from the Oxford Police.

"We need to put a halt to proceedings for the foreseeable future." Lemon addresses the room. "We need to speak to every one of you. We ask that nobody leave. We are conducting further investigations now that another woman, Dr Haven Usrey, has died in suspicious circumstances." Lemon pauses when there is a gasp from the attendees, many of whom were still unaware of Dr Haven Usrey's death. "Everyone remain calm, and we promise to come round to you all as soon as possible."

Elizabeth walks over to Gabriel, not sure of the reception she will get after their last encounter.

"You going to blame me for this too, I suppose," he comments flatly, watching the Constables try to usher people into some form of queues for more questioning.

Gabriel then turns his back on Elizabeth. So Elizabeth heads for Lemon instead, as she has something to give him.

"Mistletoe," Elizabeth tells Lemon, handing him the water bottle, which she took from Haven's bag. "Haven was poisoned with Mistletoe." Linda gasps and looks up at a bunch hanging over the door, as Lemon gets out an evidence bag.

"Where did you get this?"

"Her bag," Elizabeth shrugs, "I'm running out of time on this."

"So again, we can't use as evidence," Lemon sighs.

"But if it's in Haven's body, then you will find it in more than her water bottle."

"Will we?" Lemon looks straight at Elizabeth, who knows she shouldn't have done it, but couldn't stop herself.

"Mistletoe?" Linda asks, "how?"

"Yes, it depends on what species. This was from the Phoradendron. It has a toxin called phoratoxin. It can cause death. Starts with blood pressure mainly, nausea. She was probably unable to see after a while. Ironic, as the killer left her looking at the sunset. This type of poison blurs your vision. That's what made me think it had to be murder, not accidental."

"Looks like I'm going to need to bring out the strong tea for this!" Linda leaves Elizabeth to head to the kitchens.

"We could all do with some comfort food too I think Linda," Gabriel shouts, but before he can say anything else, Michael comes out of nowhere and his fist swings for Gabriel's head and connects with such force that Gabriel falls to the floor. Elizabeth spots Lemon dash for Michael, to stop any more violence, but he gets caught in the second swing and a punch lands right on Lemon's nose. Two Constables rush to grab Michael's hands, and Elizabeth hears Michael having his rights read to him as he is frog-marched for the second time out of the conference room.

"Déjà vu?" Elizabeth says to herself about Michael being taken away by police, Lemon following, holding his injured nose, with the bottle now bagged.

46
IN FOR QUESTIONING

Elizabeth is standing outside the Oxford Police Station, waiting for Sergeant Lemon to come outside and update her on proceedings. Inspector Abley pulls up in his car, winds down the window and leans out a little. He is wearing a golfing glove and hat.

"When you said you were at the station and to come quickly, I thought you'd been arrested again? What are you doing outside?"

"Go inside and tell Lemon to come out. I bet he knows what's going on, and he's just keeping me hanging. You can get in there. Park up and go inside."

"What are you talking about?" Abley asks.

"They've arrested Michael Pussett."

"Again?"

"Don't just sit there," Elizabeth orders Abley to help, and he rolls his eyes.

"Sometimes, woman, you test the patience—" Abley starts to shake his head.

"Pot, kettle, come on. You're here now."

*

Michael sits opposite Sergeant Lemon – with his bruised nose – and the Oxford Inspector. He is quiet and has one arm resting on the interview table. His cufflinks are little skulls, and his watch has a Salvador Dali image of a clock inside the face. Lemon is immediately reminded why he doesn't like this man, and why Michael is now his biggest suspect.

"Why did you kill both these women?" the Oxford Inspector asks.

"I haven't hurt anyone, let alone kill them. You've already brought me in once, and I didn't even do anything."

"We charged you earlier for assault on one Dr Haven Usrey. Now you will be charged for assault on Dr Gabriel Deersman. And you wonder why you're back here?" Lemon asks.

"Have you seen the size of Gabriel? He's bigger than me. He's just ruined my life. He's fair game. And that Haven, she's crazy. She drove me to it."

"And yet now Dr Haven Usrey is dead, not long after you assaulted her. You say you haven't harmed either woman, so why was your hat found recently in their Summertown home after the death of Dr Haven Usrey? And more importantly, why was her bag found at the bottom of your garden in your shed?" Lemon asks.

"She left it behind."

"What was she doing at your home before she died?" the Oxford Inspector asks.

"We knew each other. I don't know. She came over."

"I want to suggest to you, Mr Pussett, that keeping secrets is not a good idea," the Oxford Inspector says.

There is a pause, and Michael winds his neck around and then tips his head.

"Because she was in love with me. Hard to believe I know. I didn't say anything before, well, to be honest I wanted the whole thing to go away. What if you'd thought

I'd killed Sandy just to get with Haven, which I didn't. And, I've been too busy with the flipping conference!"

"You would say all this, to prove you didn't murder Haven. To make her look like the jealous one, to shift things onto her. But, who would believe you?" Lemon asks. Michael gets out his phone and scrolls through messages. He gets to the messages that Haven sent him. And they all reveal her love for him. "How could you see her? We are meant to be together. Our passion was unstoppable." And, "I am speaking my truth when I say that my bosom is heaving for you." And, "Leave her and come back to me." Lemon and the Oxford Inspector squirm.

"Listen, I'd only just met Sandy," Michael adds, "she's not wanted to travel to England. So, this was her first time at the conference. And, I don't mind saying she was, well, wow." Michael raises his eyebrows.

"We took your DNA last time we arrested you. It was your blood found on the corner of their coffee table in Summertown, and your glove discovered near the site where a witness reported Dr Sandy Starborneck and Dr Haven Usrey were fighting with you. Did they hurt you, or was it the other way around?" Lemon asks.

"I hit my head while canoodling with Sandy."

"All right, all right. Put him in the line-up," the Oxford Inspector instructs Lemon.

"What for?" Michael throws up his hands.

"Because you're a violent man, and we have witnesses who say you were hurting both of the deceased. The original witness has disappeared into thin air. It was just a phone call. It was you, wasn't it?" The Oxford Inspector bangs the table.

*

There is a line-up. Michael stands in a row of tall men with bald heads and thinning hair. Behind the glass are four of Godric's new pantomime friends who he'd met dressed as drag queens the other night when talking about the Broad Street brawl, now all dressed up in their pantomime costumes having come straight over from rehearsals on request of Lemon.

"Yes, that's him. He was on the floor rolling about. I didn't realise he was so tall."

"Yes, I would recognise that face anywhere. It's very pointy, pointy nose, pointy chin. That's him. And, he was hurting those women." One of the drag queens says, "He was fighting them."

"Yes, funny that they all have those trousers. Where would you get that much paisley? Couldn't they have put them all in jeans?"

"It looked like he was teaching them a lesson. One of the women was trying to get him off. That's what we saw," an ugly sister suggests.

"If you're sure, then we would appreciate your statements."

"No problem. Can I write it in glitter pen?" the other ugly sister asks.

*

Lemon comes out and sneaks around the front of the police station through some bushes, where Elizabeth and Inspector Abley stand near the wall where she earlier released the beetle she had rescued from the custody cells. They are doing their best to blend in with a couple of possible criminals who are having a quick cigarette before they go back into the police station.

"You're still a suspect, I guess. Now that ironically you proved Haven was poisoned with mistletoe, and her death wasn't a suicide."

"Oh, for god's sake." Elizabeth shuts her eyes.

"Didn't he confess?" Abley asks.

"No. And he showed us these texts of Haven sent him

professing her love, so for now, he's been charged with assaulting Dr Gabriel Deersman, but not the murders yet. There is not enough evidence."

"What? She liked him? I don't believe it," Abley scoffs. Having seen Michael, and having spent time with Haven, he couldn't think of anything less likely.

"It takes all sorts," Lemon replies.

"He didn't do it," Elizabeth says matter of factly.

Lemon's phone rings. He answers.

"All right, I'll be right there."

"And?" Abley asks.

"There's been a break-in at the house in Summertown. My Inspector's just ordered me to investigate."

47
SUMMERTOWN BURGLAR

Lemon – the bruise on his nose from Michael's earlier punch now even more prominent – has raced to Summertown with a Constable in a squad car. Inspector Abley has followed behind with Elizabeth in his BMW and now parks up outside in the leafy avenue, still heavy with snow. As he parks behind Lemon's car, he finishes a call with his Superintendent.

"Yes, I'm on holiday. I have just been to the indoor driving range." Abley has Superintendent Raynott on the speaker on his dashboard.

"Why am I led to believe that you have just been spotted outside the city centre Oxford Police Station?" Raynott asks.

"BMWs are not that rare," Abley replies. Elizabeth's eyes widen but she keeps very quiet.

"Are you with Professor Green? How on earth has she been arrested? You said you hadn't spoken. I will hold you accountable, if one of our most esteemed academics is finding herself in trouble, no doubt the result of hanging about with you," Raynott finishes, waiting for Abley to reply. Elizabeth smiles at Bob, then shrugs. Raynott continues, "Are you there? Abley?"

"I… It. ..But…" Abley feigns a poor line on his mobile.

"You're breaking up. What did you say?" Raynott asks.

"It… You… Sausages…" Then Abley cuts the call.

"Thank you." Elizabeth looks at Bob, grateful he is with her now. Looking at his golf outfit and feeling ever so guilty, he has had little chance to relax.

"Are you coming?" Abley gets out of the car, fed up with not being able to help his friend. "I'm damned if I'm going to let Lemon's man here pin this on you – if he's failing to pin it on anyone else that's not your fault."

"Thank you for your help. It must be my Christmas biscuits that swung it." Elizabeth gets out of the car and follows Abley up the drive. Abley remembers nearly breaking his tooth on those biscuits the other day.

Lemon's Constable has gone around the back and doesn't notice either of them. When Elizabeth enters the house, she is confronted immediately with Lemon who beat them inside and is already talking to Professor Alexander Resander and Dr Gabriel Deersman. Elizabeth notices a cut on Gabriel's cheek from Michael's earlier punch. Professor Resander is holding his whippet's lead as the dog sits at his feet.

Elizabeth is surprised, as neither has a reason to break in, no motive. Lemon and Abley both wait for Elizabeth to ask questions to Professor Alexander Resander, but she is momentarily thrown. What is Gabriel doing here?

"Professor Alexander Resander," Lemon says.

"Professor Green, come to tread on my feet?" Alexander looks at Elizabeth. But Elizabeth stands, waiting for Lemon to do his job and not able to make eye contact with Gabriel.

"Professor Resander. You're aware that it is a crime to break and enter?" Sergeant Lemon asks.

"I just came to retrieve something. It has nothing to do with the case," Alexander replies, defensively.

"What?" Abley asks.

Alexander leans over to pick up a bowl.

"A bowl," Alexander replies. "I lent it to them when Dr Starborneck was in the department, with some of Gabriel's tomatoes in it. They didn't give it back. It happens to be sentimental. Isn't that right?" Alexander looks at Gabriel, who at this point is standing very still beside him and seems to have a tightly closed jacket. Gabriel nods.

"You both risk breaking into a crime scene – I want to know why it's sentimental," Lemon says, staring at Alexander.

"Just is. I didn't think you'd come rushing up here. I've not touched anything else. I'm sure if you hadn't stormed in you'd be none the wiser."

"And we're supposed to believe you?" Lemon asks. Elizabeth finally finds her voice.

"Where's the bowl from?" She takes the bowl from Alexander's hands before he can stop her.

"Er, I don't know. I didn't buy it. It was a present," Alexander sighs.

"Are you telling us that you came back for a bowl you know so little about? You must know who made it?"

"As it happens, no. I don't. It means a lot to me," he replies unconvincingly.

"Even though it is from 'Cheapy Cheaps?" Elizabeth asks, looking at the base.

"They're on the High Street. A bargain basement of odds and sods," Lemon adds helpfully.

"Means a lot," Alexander replies, snatching it back. "Yes, well. I have it now. So, I think I'll be going. Come on Gabriel."

Elizabeth watches them leave the house and rushes to follow, along with Lemon. When they are outside, Gabriel opens his jacket and hands Alexander a small brown package. He pats Alexander on the arm and walks in the other direction. Alexander heads towards his car and is about to start the engine when Lemon grabs his keys and asks him to accompany him to the station for questioning.

After Lemon drives away with Alexander, Elizabeth chases after Gabriel, who has grabbed Alexander's whippet and is briskly walking away along the snowy avenue. She has to run along the icy pavement to try to catch him, holding onto hedgerows and fences.

"Hey!" she shouts to try and stop Gabriel. But he doesn't look behind and keeps on marching. "Stop! Gabriel, stop!"

"Stop!!" Inspector Bob Abley screams at the top of his throat, rushing up behind Elizabeth. Finally, Gabriel looks behind, pretending he didn't initially hear.

"What? What do you want?" He asks acerbically.

"What was that?" Elizabeth asks out of breath, with Inspector Abley a few feet behind.

"Are you following me?" Gabriel's tone is colder than usual. Elizabeth thinks this is undoubtedly his anger at being asked if he was a murderer.

"What did you give him? Oh, and are you okay after Michael's punch?"

"I'm sorry? What are you talking about?" Gabriel shrugs.

"Don't play games. What did you give him? I saw you. From the window."

Gabriel pauses for the longest time and then says, "Oh, that. Just some papers from the department, why?" Then strokes Alexander's whippet.

"I don't believe you."

But Gabriel shrugs again and makes his apologies.

"I have to get to the laboratory. I haven't got time for your nonsense."

"With a dog?"

"Sure." Gabriel turns and walks down the road until he disappears around a corner. Elizabeth thinks how bizarre this is. One minute he is all overly friendly. And now. Now he is acting most peculiarly.

48
JERICHO

While Sergeant Lemon goes back to the station, taking Professor Alexander Resander in for questioning, Elizabeth has other ideas. After Superintendent Raynott has come down heavy on Inspector Bob Abley, he needs no convincing either.

Professor Alexander Resander made the mistake of leaving his home address on the conference contacts. So, the two, in cahoots, now decide to shoot over to Alexander's home, in Jericho, before the police likely arrive to have a poke about themselves now they've caught Alexander breaking into Summertown. And, maybe Gabriel will deliver whatever it is he is keeping for Alexander from Sandy and Haven's home. Gabriel's unlikely, Elizabeth thinks, to leave it at the laboratory, and it's so hard to gain access to private rooms at College. Jericho also feels further away from the police station and the Oxford Inspector right now. They also know Alexander will not be here.

"I like the road system up here. It's so easy to get about." Abley has come down the Banbury Road, along Beaumont Street and is now on Walton Street. "Cars can get about."

"Oxford is bigger. It's different," Elizabeth replies.

"I don't know why they shut St Andrew's Street. They could at least have left us that."

"We're not in Cambridge now, Bob. Can you drive any faster?"

"I don't want to get a ticket. Raynott'd be photocopying it and taping it up in the canteen, as a 'lesson to his men'." Abley does an impression of Raynott's voice.

"It's as if he's in the car," Elizabeth replies sarcastically. "We have to get there before the police do." She looks out the window at the quiet neighbourhood in Oxford that feels like its own small village within a city.

"Before Lemon, you mean."

"Let's solve this for Lemon."

As they continue up Walton Street, Elizabeth watches mothers walking their children, elderly men with their dogs, couples hand-in-hand, and a young man carrying a loaf of bread from the corner shop.

"Are you all right?" Bob Abley can tell that Elizabeth is not herself.

"Jericho feels like a happy place—" Elizabeth's thoughts are interrupted by Inspector Abley's phone, ringing from the car's dashboard. As Bob accepts the call, she hears Godric's voice.

"Is that the handsome Cambridge Inspector's telephone? Grandson to genius technophobe Professor Elizabeth Green here." Godric puts on a funny impression of his Nanna. "Might I ask if you know her whereabouts? She's gone off wandering again, into her own world, where she is safe. They know her there."

"Congratulations, you've found me," Elizabeth says, feigning surprise. "I'm on that dashboard thing in Bob's car. And I'm not a technophobe," she replies, as she adjusts the air conditioning to turn Godric up. "Yes, where are you?" Elizabeth speaks into Bob Abley's door speaker until Bob points her to the speaker in front of her.

"If I were you, I'd get off the dashboard and put your seatbelt on." Godric is pleased with his joke and laughs, then the wind blows into his phone, and it crackles in Elizabeth's ears. "I'm on the Meadow."

"We're so close. Are the dogs okay?"

"Yes, I'm okay too by the way. We've all been for food. They've had their usual. We're heading back to the panto rehearsals shortly. You are coming to see it, aren't you?"

"Yes, but only to check the dogs are not being mistreated," Elizabeth half-jokes.

"They're the most pampered cast members. I don't even have a dressing room," Godric objects.

"Keep it that way," Elizabeth tells him.

"Are you free of this case yet? Has that nutty Inspector seen your brilliance?" Godric asks.

"Which nutty Inspector?" Elizabeth smirks, "the one I'm with right now at least knows I'm brilliant."

"We're working on it," Abley chips in, shaking his head, still worried about the Oxford Inspector's intentions.

"Have you found who poisoned Sandy and Haven yet?" Godric asks.

"No, but I think we're getting close," Elizabeth says.

"Of course you are. Shout if you need me to do anything. Otherwise, see you back at the hotel or the panto later! Bye, bye." And with that, Godric hangs up.

Inspector Abley drives down a pretty street with small terraced houses and pulls up outside a home on Great Clarendon Street. It is painted pastel green and is the only home without a Christmas tree in the window.

"This is it," Bob says, and they both get out of the car.

"Is Scrooge sending us on his goose chase? Another absence of Christmas cheer here. We don't have a key," Elizabeth observes.

"We could try round the back? It worked last time," Bob replies.

Elizabeth pushes a gate, and it opens. As they walk

along a very narrow alley, they come to a row of back gardens, some more loved than others, each sharing the same street entrance.

They approach Alexander's back garden, which is entirely paved, with one chair and a table with an ashtray spilling over with half smoked cigarettes. The little garden reveals a backdoor and two downstairs windows, one of which Elizabeth peers into, through which she can see a settee, table and chairs, and the other which has frosted glass. Above those is what must be a bedroom window, which is ajar. They look at one another. Abley looks around the gardens and spots a ladder three gardens down.

"You'll have to get that then," she says.

"Or I could use this," Inspector Abley pulls out his universal key and opens the backdoor with it.

"Ugh, why didn't you do that in the front door?"

"Twitching curtains," he replies.

Both of them walk in, past Alexander's friendly whippet, which Elizabeth has to spend five minutes saying hello to and giving countless treats from her pocket.

"How on earth did Gabriel beat us here to drop off this gorgeous creature?"

"Traffic," Bob says bluntly, "even in Oxford. He's cut across, hasn't he."

Elizabeth immediately starts to examine everything, followed behind by a very friendly whippet.

"What made this man go to the dead womens' home and lie about what he was doing?" Elizabeth asks herself, "Lie about picking up a bowl?" Elizabeth can't see anything downstairs. "I can't see a package anywhere?" she adds, thinking of the mysterious item Alexander gave Gabriel outside Sandy and Haven's home just half an hour ago. She starts to walk up the stairs.

"There's something he's not telling us," Abley replies, still in the kitchen "Men who live alone can't be trusted," he suggests ironically, aware he is also a bachelor now living alone, then looks up at Elizabeth pointedly.

"I've told you. You should talk to that nice secretary at the station on the front desk. She likes you!" Elizabeth shouts down the stairs.

"Behave, she's sixty."

"Oh, and that's old, is it?" Elizabeth huffs then walks into a room and stands still. She says nothing.

"Well, no. I didn't mean that," Abley says, then listens out for Elizabeth's retort but doesn't get one, so shouts up the stairs, "Elizabeth? Hey, sixty is the new fifty. Liz? You're not there yet, anyway." When he hears nothing, he runs up the stairs until he is standing beside a mute Elizabeth.

In front of them both is a bedroom, a teenager's room. A poster of a huge yellow smiley face on the wall jumps out at them, beside it some paintings, tinsel around photographs, and a hook with scarves falling like a waterfall. A duvet with bold stars covers a double bed, while magazines on the bedside table fight for space with an old-fashioned portable CD player, cups and make-up. On a chair beside the bed a backpack in the shape of a sheep hangs half-open, with a brush and some textbooks inside. Like an exhibition from the late 1990s, a layer of dust everywhere coats even the carpet.

Inspector Abley walks backwards on the small landing and pushes open the door to the other bedroom, which appears normal, as does the bathroom he checks next.

"Maureen used to shout at our two to clean their rooms. But—"

"As you say—"

Elizabeth walks into Alexander's bedroom.

"It would appear that the wife blamed him for it," Elizabeth suggests.

"How so?"

"Pillow in the middle. One bedside table empty," she observes.

"Another single man who lives on his own. Blamed for everything." Abley looks around Alexander's bedroom.

"Come to think of it, Professor Alexander Resander has always seemed neutral about Sandy Starborneck's death." Elizabeth looks at Bob, having just realised this fact.

"Maybe he is. Maybe he shows it differently. This man is stuck. I recognise that."

"I saw him mixing something in the laboratory. Seeds. He was very cagey about it." Elizabeth looks at the wallpaper peeling a little in the hallway. The two of them walk downstairs.

"You think it was to poison Sandy?" Bob asks.

"It's unclear what he was doing. It could have been for Haven. But why? They're not even working in the same area of Plant Sciences." Elizabeth shakes her head as she walks towards the back garden.

"He's just a sad man, I think, Liz. Probably has to work the Christmas holidays, while all the happy families up and down the country get to celebrate," Abley suggests.

"You have policeman fairy lights. What more do you want?" Elizabeth tries to stop Abley feeling sorry for himself.

"Come on, let's get out of here before the police try to arrest me, and you. But, mostly me. But, also you," Elizabeth says as she pats the whippet on the head, gives him a final treat, empties some dried food from a sack into his bowl and fills up his water from the tap in the kitchen.

"Are we going to visit Dr Gabriel Deersman now? He was at Summertown."

"Leave him to me."

49
BODLEIAN LIBRARY

Elizabeth is buried behind a pile of books. She can smell their pages. She is sat at a library table alone in an almost empty section of the Bodleian, in front of stacks of first editions tucked back under arches and a staircase, taking scholars up to more books on a mezzanine above. Small lamps emit a warm glow on her face as she pours over a large tome on modern art. But this isn't helping her, and she frowns a little while watching through the windows yet more snowfall coming down outside. People are rushing to and fro, carrying shopping, with scarves tight around their necks and bobble hats and hoods up to protect their ears.

Elizabeth walks through the library to a section where there is a librarian behind a desk and several computers. She whispers a request to the librarian, who then picks up a key behind the help desk and takes Elizabeth to a laptop, unlocks it with a code, and then calls up some material, not directly from the internet, but which has been catalogued in the library's archives. Elizabeth clicks to the *Oxford Urban* newspaper; pages of countryside flick across the screen, including Wolvercote. Then, she continues to scroll. But, she can't find what she is looking for.

"Is this all you have?" Elizabeth asks the librarian.

"Shush," the librarian replies back from behind her desk a few feet away. Elizabeth looks around. There is no one apart from the librarian and herself.

"I'm disturbing no one. I'm just asking if you have any other archives of local art?

"Shush." The librarian puts her finger to her lips. Just as Elizabeth is about to go over to the librarian and give her a piece of her mind, she is interrupted. Gabriel puts his hand on Elizabeth's shoulder, making her jump.

"You were acting very strangely up at Sandy and Haven's house, and now you're here? Saves me coming to look for you, which I was just about to. What are you doing here?" Elizabeth asks.

"I'm a Don. Does a Don need to explain why he's in a library? Lord. You're a suspicious woman." Gabriel shakes his head then adds, "Saw your boy this morning." Elizabeth is unsure of Gabriel's meaning, so he continues, "at rehearsals." Elizabeth is still nonplussed. "The pantomime," Gabriel says flatly. "I wondered if you could give him this, on loan from the College. You'll see him before I do, no doubt. I won't be up until last thing. Too busy." And it becomes clear why Gabriel tapped Elizabeth on the shoulder, as he hands over a fairy wand.

"You're in the pantomime?" Elizabeth asks.

"Playing the organ, electric, that's all," he says matter of factly and is about to leave when Elizabeth holds him in conversation.

"Ah, well, I hope it's not too loud. The dogs won't like that." Elizabeth is surprised that Gabriel would want to be in a local pantomime. He reads Elizabeth's thoughts.

"Blame Alex. He suggested I play—"

"Alexander is in the pantomime?" Elizabeth interrupts.

"He's not in this one, but it's his local community theatre. He does everything he can to support it."

Elizabeth knows that it is close to his home, but she

doesn't want to admit to Gabriel that she knows that. Instead, tries to eke out some more information.

"Really? He lives up there?"

"For the past thirty years or more. Do you always ask so many questions?" Gabriel is now irritated by Elizabeth.

"What did you take from Summertown?"

"I heard you were arrested?" Gabriel says, smirking, and changing the subject.

"A misunderstanding. I hear your tone. Yes, touché. Well, you'll be glad to know that I'm getting closer. Do you have time for a cup of tea?" Elizabeth suggests.

"I'd rather enjoy the peace of the library." Gabriel declines.

"I believe I have unearthed something significant, but if you don't have time?" Elizabeth asks again.

"Nope," Gabriel replies coldly.

"Right ho. I will come and support the pantomime anyway." Elizabeth sighs.

"Whatever. I presume you've come to realise that I'm not the murderer, so if you can leave me out of things, I'd be most grateful, Professor," Gabriel says without a smile, walking off with several books under his arm.

"Did I come to realise that?" Elizabeth says to herself, growing more frustrated with her research, until she looks back on the computer and finds a photograph of Michael Pussett, wearing some dubious 1990s garb and holding a paintbrush in his hand. Behind him is a mess of paint on the floor in a building. The headline in the local newspaper reads: "Art Teacher Paints His Own Home."

50
A RIDE IN THE TALBOT

The Talbot glides out of the St Giles' Hotel car park, and it is not long before Elizabeth is driving up Woodstock Road towards Wolvercote. She is wearing gloves, a scarf, has her hood up, and has the heater going full pelt.

It isn't long before she is parking up in the parade of houses which back onto Port Meadow. She spots Michael's home again, this time the light is on. Elizabeth walks through the broken gate and notices the neighbours' curtains twitch as they admire her car. Most probably the same neighbours who reported her for breaking and entering on her last visit. She doesn't need to knock at the door, as it would appear that Michael has also spotted the car, and opened the door. It is only then that he notices the driver.

"Oh, don't tell me that's yours?"

"May I come in?"

'No."

"I need to speak to you," she replies.

Michael walks out of his home, as Elizabeth watches him pass her on the path. He tries the car door. But it is locked. Elizabeth realises what he wants, so walks back around the car and unlocks the door. They both get in.

"I've always wanted to sit in one of these." Michael brushes the dashboard.

"So you're an artist?"

"This is a work of art. Compared to this, I would never be able to design something so beautiful. Like a teardrop." But Elizabeth is stony-faced.

"I found your glove. It's a black leather glove. But, under the microscope, it's covered in speckles of paint. You dropped it on Broad Street when you had a brawl with Haven and Sandy. The other was at their home. I gave it to the police. I think they have spoken to you about it. About the blood on the coffee table, your fight on Broad Street, but I'm not interested in that. What is this art connection all about? Tell me."

"I might be able to answer if this were to move," Michael suggests. Elizabeth rolls her eyes but doesn't feel frightened of Michael Pussett.

"If you promise to answer my questions."

Michael nods, so Elizabeth starts the engine. They begin to drive around the small lanes near Michael's house, but soon he becomes irritated.

"Take it out onto the open road," he says bossily.

"If you think I'm leaving a built-up environment to drive off into the middle of nowhere with you, you're naive. It's time to spill it." Elizabeth is rapidly losing her temper, well aware of miscarriages of justice and doesn't want to end up as one herself.

"Spill what, exactly?" Michael rubs the dashboard again with his hand.

"For a start, why do you seem to live in your shed?"

"What's that got to do with anything?"

"There are paint splashes all over the floorboards in both your living rooms. You used to hold art classes at your home."

"Oh that, it's nothing. Many moons ago."

"What, and so you live in your shed?"

"It's cheaper to heat. It's tucked out of the way. No one bothers me, apart from you. Why not? I like my shed. Is that a crime?"

"What is it about art?"

"I don't know what you're talking about?"

"You have the same art on your walls as in Sandy's home, and Alexander's too."

"Is that so?"

"Yes, are they valuable? Even the cafe maître d', Dave, had one. I can't find the artist anywhere. I've looked, who is this artist?"

"I don't know what paintings you're talking about."

"You have one with a dog on a bicycle. Only it's painted all melty and in blues and dark crimsons."

"Ah, yes. That one. It was previously in a corridor outside the art department which was going to be redecorated. I thought they might throw it away and I rather liked it. So I took it. Nothing else to tell."

Elizabeth has had enough of Michael and pulls over.

"I'd like you to get out now. Thank you."

"No, I won't."

"I understand you've already been charged for assaulting Haven and Gabriel. I'd like you to get out," Elizabeth starts screaming at Michael, in earshot of the passers-by.

"Help me! Get him away!"

Michael looks at the large man who is now staring at Michael in the car. Michael decides to get out and walk rapidly back to his home.

"That's all you're getting from me!" He shouts back.

"That's more than enough," Elizabeth looks wounded and puts on her most frail face to the couple who have come to see if she's okay. When they finally leave, Elizabeth's face changes to one of anger.

51
CATTE COLLEGE

After Elizabeth drives away from Michael, she heads straight to Catte College and in a hurry, leaves the Talbot Lago parked outside. The Porter in the Lodge smiles and tells her he'll watch the car for her, then heads out to stroke the bonnet. Elizabeth wanders in and through to the administrative buildings. She arrives at a door which says 'Alumni' and knocks before she goes in. A kind-looking woman welcomes her in with a handshake. Elizabeth shuts the door behind her.

52
IT'S BEHIND YOU

Early evening and Professor Elizabeth Green enters the small Community Hall in Jericho. She knows she is going to have to suspend disbelief as the person at the door says 'Welcome to Oldenday land,' and a tannoy system hisses and spits as an elderly man informs the near-packed audience they have five minutes to be seated.

Elizabeth is given a programme and ushered into the hall. She walks through an entrance full of black and white photographs. She spots that one of the photographs is of Professor Alexander Resander dressed up as Father Christmas. He looks so young. Sitting at his feet is a small girl, dressed as a dormouse.

Elizabeth continues to her seat. Godric has placed a piece of paper with the word 'reserved' on a school chair in the front row for his favourite Nanna. Already sitting on one side is the concierge from the St Giles' Hotel, who awkwardly smiles and then pretends to read his programme. Elizabeth smirks to herself at the forward nature of her grandson inviting this man who no doubt either has a long hotel shift after, or has had one before. Elizabeth knew men would follow Godric to the ends of the earth.

There is an awkward moment when she sees Gabriel walking towards the organ. He clocks her and nods, but there is no warm smile. She feels a little sad that she feels something, but puts it out of her mind. Then Godric comes bounding over, wearing the best Buttons costume Elizabeth has ever seen.

"Bunny! You made it."

"Wow. They haven't scraped on the outfits then," Elizabeth beams.

"Oh, well. I might have found this online. I wanted to look my best," Godric brushes imaginary fluff off his shoulder.

"I thought you were hard-up? Did the costume come with the role?"

"Nah. Interest-free credit," he explains. Elizabeth despairs of Godric's finances. "I'm getting paid for this, as well as the dogs. I mean, the dogs are getting paid more than me, but tickets sales are really strong. And hopefully, help me with my debts to get rid of Reggie," Godric says quietly to himself.

"Debts? Break a leg." Elizabeth shakes her head, worrying about Godric, but also learning a long time ago not to get involved. Godric hugs Elizabeth, as Alexander walks up to his seat further along the line from Elizabeth and the member of the hotel concierge team.

"Right, well. That's good. Where are the dogs?" she asks Godric.

"Backstage. Getting ready."

"Oh, Goddy, no. You said there were no dog costumes."

"Just small ones, nothing that will annoy them. They like them. They're less intrusive than the harnesses you got them." Godric pays no attention to Elizabeth's complaint and looks at the man from the hotel and grins. He continues, "You know I found out that Dr Starborneck was making money for her art. More than I'm making, but

I think it was a hobby. I read in one article I found her talking about having attended a class here in Oxford."

"Gosh, Goddy, that is so useful to know. I wonder if she ever attended Michael's classes? D'you know he used to be an art teacher?"

As Godric leaves, someone comes up to him and asks, "Can I get a photo of the dogs dressed up when they come out?" Godric looks back at Elizabeth in case she hears, and quietly indicates maybe later.

*

Still seated next to Elizabeth, the concierge from the St Giles' spots that she is staring at Alexander.

"D'you know him?" he asks.

"Yes, from a conference. I wonder why he comes to see a pantomime. Not an obvious member of the audience."

"I come every year."

"Really?" Elizabeth replies, disinterested.

"I like to watch the actors," the hotel concierge grins. "I've been told that he used to come into the bar with a young woman, before my time. Huh, young enough to be his daughter apparently, if you know what I mean." He wiggles his eyebrows. "I've recently seen him go into that cafe you like too."

"Are you spying on me?" Elizabeth says.

"I was in it the other day when you were. That's all," he smiles, adding, "Your grandson is very handsome, isn't he?"

The lights go out, the stage lights lift and a hush descends. There is a space next to her seat for Inspector Abley, who rushes to the front out of breath. As the curtain goes up and Godric, the dogs, and Cinderella are all by the fake stage fire, and the audience 'ahh' at the sight of the dogs.

"He's dead." Bob Abley informs Elizabeth quietly.

"What?"

"There's been a crash. Michael Pussett. He's dead," Abley hisses.

Elizabeth wastes no time, stands up to leave, then shrugs to Godric who is watching the commotion in the front row and seeing his Nanna turn then run to the hall exit before his performance has even started. The dogs spot her too and grow agitated until Godric takes out a few biscuits from his pocket and distributes them, pulling their focus back to Cinderella. As he wipes his fingers on his costume, Godric watches his Nanna disappear out the door.

53
AMERICAN CLASSIC

Inspector Abley shoots along Wolvercote Green.

"It's not far from here. Lemon says Pussett up-ended a car off the Godstow Road and fell through the windscreen."

"Not wearing a belt?"

"No, and it wasn't his car. It was an MGB Roadster, strange. If you got yourself a mobile, Lemon could have called you direct. He didn't want me, actually," Abley replies wryly, now driving fast in the dark with the snow glowing against the night stars.

"It will take time." Elizabeth looks at Abley. "But you came through for me. Thank you," Elizabeth smiles, aware that her friend has stayed around on his holiday. Abley looks at her, knowing she would have done the same.

As they approach a bend, they can see the flashing police lights, but no sirens. Abley's car pulls up to a scene of eerie silence. The MGB Roadster is on its roof twenty yards ahead in a field, the hedge completely smashed through, and there is still smoke floating out from the engine. The wheels have stopped spinning, but Elizabeth can hear the music still blaring from the car radio. About twenty feet further up in the field is the body of Michael Pussett. Lemon spots them.

"No seatbelt," Lemon says, walking over.

"He must have been going full pelt," Abley replies.

Elizabeth can't help herself glance at Michael. His tall figure twisted, and his arms above his head. A grimace stuck on his bloody face, perhaps revealing the pain of smashing through the windscreen and onto the ground, where it looks like he hit a nearby tree stump as one of his legs is slightly bent the wrong way.

Elizabeth looks away. The art teacher, conference organiser and main suspect is now dead. But it is only narrowing the field, and Elizabeth has an idea of her own. Though she's not ready to share it just yet with a police force that perhaps are now more convinced of her guilt than ever before. She needs to find more evidence first.

"You again," the Oxford Inspector spots Elizabeth. Lemon quickly walks away from Elizabeth not wanting to make things worse, as the Oxford Inspector continues, "Did you do this?" He asks Elizabeth.

"Whose car is that?" She retorts.

"I beg your pardon?"

"Michael, he drives that black Ford Mustang. Was he driving this car? This isn't his car," Elizabeth says.

"Can you leave immediately," the Oxford Inspector tells Elizabeth then glares at Inspector Abley. "And I have more than enough on my own team. Are you looking for a bloody transfer?"

Bob Abley knows better than to reply. He looks at Elizabeth and indicates she should follow him. They get in his car and start to drive back down the lane. The snow hangs in the trees, and Bob Abley puts on a jolly radio station with an overly excited presenter.

"I'm trying to think," Elizabeth says, frustrated.

Bob Abley turns off the radio and sighs.

"You know, Liz, I have one day left, and I have to work over the entire Christmas and New Year. In the remaining hours, it would be nice to listen to one Christmas song."

"You won't hear it on that." Elizabeth refuses to feel sorry for Bob. She has already expended too much pity. "Christmas working sounds better than spending it with my daughter."

"Are you offering to do some shifts with me?" Abley asks.

"I might be in an Oxford gaol doing time for crimes I didn't commit." Elizabeth is about to start on the differences between the two cities when she sees a flash of light behind the trees. "What was that?"

"What?" Abley slows the car.

"Didn't you see it? Stop. We need to stop."

Abley slows further and looks in his rearview mirror before pulling over. They park the car and walk back. It is a good hundred yards as it took him a while to stop, as the road is icy. Elizabeth finds a hole in the hedge and sees the Ford Mustang in a lay-by, hidden behind some bushes. But, with the headlights still on.

"Michael Pussett's car."

They walk up to it, and Elizabeth is about to try the door.

"Don't touch anything, whatever you do. We don't need any more fingerprints on crime scenes from you." Abley pushes Elizabeth back, and for once she does as she's told. Bob Abley puts SOCO gloves on and tries the car door, but it is locked. He gets out his universal keys and slides one down the window frame and pops the door open.

"I may play cheesy music, but I have some uses," he smirks to himself.

"Look in the glove compartment."

"I hadn't thought of that." Bob turns around and gives Elizabeth a look.

On the floor of the car, they both see a few papers. Bob Abley puts evidence gloves on then flicks through them. He spots a cheque for five thousand dollars from Haven Usrey, made out to Michael. Bob Abley gets out his phone and takes a photograph, then dials Lemon.

"I think you're going to want to come here. Only, I'm not sure where here is?" Abley looks around.

54
THE FINAL CURTAIN

Elizabeth and Inspector Abley slip back into the back of the Jericho Community Hall, in time for the end of the interval drinks at the pantomime. Godric rushes over.

"Where have you been?" he asks his Nanna.

"There's been another murder," Elizabeth replies, taking her seat. "Michael Pussett."

"Wasn't he the chief suspect? Who's left?" Godric replies.

"Me," Elizabeth scoffs, knowing it won't be long before the Oxford Inspector makes the same deduction.

"Well, I hope you can stay at least for the second interval," Godric replies, trying to remain light, "a lot of my good stuff has already happened. But the dogs are on again," Godric says, not thinking about the pantomime anymore, more about whether his Nanna is sinking deeper into this mess. "I think you shouldn't move from there for a whole forty-five minutes," Godric suggests, looking at Elizabeth in her chair. "You're safe here. I have to go back, but I'll see you immediately after." Godric squeezes his Nanna in a big hug and then rushes backstage.

Elizabeth sees Linda and Dave, the maître d' from Kinder Habits, sitting with Alexander. Gabriel gets up from sitting with them too, and walks past Elizabeth. He nods a little frostily, trying to make his way back to the organ for the second half without having to engage in conversation.

"Everyone from College is here? I didn't see them before?" Elizabeth asks Gabriel, grabbing his arm for an answer.

"I had some complimentary tickets," Gabriel says matter of factly. "Thought it would be nice to see friendly faces in the audience. Some at least." Gabriel leaves and walks behind the curtain to the organ. The lights dim in the audience and brighten on the stage. Gabriel starts to play the organ as the curtain begins to lift. Elizabeth spots her grandson on stage and is so proud, but she can't shake the image of Michael's dead face from her mind.

55
WOODSTOCK

The next morning, the snow has stopped falling, and the blue sky stretches out above the Talbot Lago, which purrs its way to Woodstock. Elizabeth is glad of the fresh air and time to herself on the short journey out of Oxford. With the top off, Elizabeth, in a hat and driving goggles, can enjoy the sunshine streaming across the road. This is most definitely the coldest day yet, and it is helping to clear her head. Despite concerns over her own carbon footprint, she has avoided the passenger seat in Inspector Abley's car, which is in clear view ahead of her on the road. Some lines had to be drawn, and one was listening to any more of the chirpy Christmas music he plays on his radio.

Inspector Abley has been most helpful, however, in the past twenty-four hours. Especially when it became undeniable that they were running out of suspects after the pantomime and Michael's death. They stayed up late last night in the St Giles' Hotel bar, talking through the state of play – Lemon, with his slightly bruised nose, also joining them for a nightcap. There was something reckless about the evening, especially when singing broke out amongst the pantomime cast and crew who had also decided to crash the party. Elizabeth, in the end, remembers agreeing to drink one shot, in between her halves of stout, something she never does and never will again, something only Inspector Abley and Godric can persuade her to do when a possible looming arrest is on the cards.

But at least by speaking about the paintings and possible art connection into the small hours, it now makes her certain she is on to something. She feels terrible for not sharing everything with Bob Abley, but she doesn't want Lemon in on this as, if she is wrong, she needs to know for herself first. And, if she is right, she will have to move quickly, before the murderer does something stupid.

Elizabeth is pleased that Inspector Bob Abley took it upon himself last night to declare he was speaking to his Sergeant Goodey. Something Elizabeth knew nothing about, at least not until 2 am when Bob was knocking on her door having had one too many, then falling asleep on the foldable sofa with Godric and the dogs. Before snoring, Bob Abley had declared, with much finger pointing and tears in his eyes, that Goodey knew all the antique and art collectors. He was a bit of a swot on it, and that he would help them solve the case.

So, with less than a few hours sleep, both of them are now following Goodey's lead. Goodey informed Inspector Abley that he knows an art dealer, who is "One of the best in the country", and according to his new and slightly nerdy Sergeant, "if anyone knows anything about the paintings, it is this guy."

*

The two cars enter the picturesque village of Woodstock, with its stone cottages hundreds of years old, window boxes with deer fern and colourful heathers and gritted pavements. Inspector Bob Abley parks up his car outside an antique shop on Market Place. Elizabeth pulls in behind. A traffic warden is just walking towards them on the pavement, but the warden starts to look carefully at Inspector Abley's car, sizing him up for a ticket, so Abley pulls out his badge. The warden starts to walk on.

"Aren't you going to look at this?" Abley asks, pointing at the Talbot, affronted the warden is walking right past.

"I couldn't give such a beautiful thing a ticket. I'd be fearful of the ticket glue ruining perfection," the traffic warden smirks, as he ambles by. Elizabeth smirks to herself, hiding it from Bob as they walk towards the shop.

"How could you use your badge out of vicinity?" Elizabeth reprimands her friend, half-jokingly, "and when can you get me one?"

"When have you ever needed one?" Abley scoffs.

Inside the shop, Elizabeth is surprised by how far it reaches back from the street, just like a tardis. Almost one-hundred-and fifty-feet to the rear wall and packed with paintings, silverware, old army helmets, union jack bunting, jackets, old fireplaces and more. The shop is empty of people, however, save for an elderly gentleman sitting in the far corner at a desk.

"Hello?" he rumbles, as Bob and Elizabeth walk towards him.

"Hello, we've come about a painting."

"Hasn't everyone?" The man laughs with a wet cough and picks up a cigar from a saucer. "How much you got to play with? I mean, what vicinity are we talking? It can save you a lot of time, and me." The man looks up at Abley, eyeing his clothes to see what he's worth. Inspector Abley gets out his badge, flashes it at the man.

"We need to enlist your help," Abley replies, dryly.

"We're trying to track down this artist." Elizabeth grabs Bob's phone and scrolls through the photos. He snatches it back and shakes his head, finds the right photograph of the painting Lemon shared with him at Sandy's house in Summertown. Elizabeth continues impatiently, "You see, this artist links some murders that have just taken place in

Oxford. This one is of a woman holding a chicken. But we've seen two others. A goat walking at night on Port Meadow, and a dog on a bicycle."

"Oh yeah, those academics from America. I've just read about that in the local paper. Where is it?" The man starts to fumble about on his desk, which is deep in old papers.

"It's okay, we know about it," Elizabeth says brusquely. Bob Abley can see that Elizabeth's impatience is alienating this antiques man.

"What my friend here is trying to say – sorry, we have had little sleep – is that this painting might have some weight on finding out who is responsible. And, knowing that you are an expert in the field—"

"Oh, truly. Flattery will get you everywhere, as the vicar said." The antiques man coughs another wet cough and stands up. Elizabeth wonders what vicar the man is talking about, but nods, mildly irritated at Bob for undermining her.

"Yes, we want to find the artist so that we can find the link between the paintings. It might have a bearing on the case. I believe it will lead us to the door of the murderer," she says.

"Oh, well. I don't want any aggro. I'm keen on living," the antiques man replies.

"You won't be in any danger," Bob Abley reassures the man.

"Well, as it happens. I do keep quite a bit of art out the back. And, I like a puzzle." The dealer's head wobbles. "Let me just get the door." He walks to the front door and locks up. "Wow. What a car. I have never seen one in real life. Only this," he says and walks over to a book and opens it, and there is a photograph of a Talbot Lago. "It's so special," he says, looking at Abley, "they are paying Inspectors well these days."

"Yes, she's a good drive," Elizabeth replies, correcting his assumption.

"Let me show you the paintings." The antiques dealer's manner changes towards Elizabeth, "You know, I saw you and thought, here's a feisty woman, perhaps a little uppity. But, I must apologise. Women are hard to judge. They're not like they used to be. Anyone who can drive such a beautiful car must be a beautiful person in my book. A proper filly."

Elizabeth is entirely bored with this man, as either he is trying to be subtly sarcastic, or is shallow and Neanderthal. Either way, she has had enough.

"The paintings?" she says, trying to lead the way quicker.

"Right."

The three of them walk out the back of the antiques shop and down a cobbled path towards what can only be described as a large barn — perhaps one-hundred feet long.

"I have mostly local art. A huge archive of student stuff, which is what this looks like if you don't mind me saying. I hope you didn't pay much for it. Some of the art these days is crap."

"This is huge," Abley replies, walking into the barn.

"I make all my money from this. The antiques business just about breaks even, but art. The rich will buy anything. They don't know what to do with their money, you see. And I have a nose for relieving them of it. And I'm very good at it."

"You think this is student art?" Elizabeth looks around once they are inside the barn. It has proper insulation and a good roof. She notices the warmth when they enter.

"I keep a dry seventeen degrees. Don't want any cracks or anything to melt. Dehumidifiers, air con, the lot," he smiles at Elizabeth, "Yes, it doesn't seem to have a style of its own yet. It is derivative of too many other well-known artists. A hole many young artists fall into. Some climb out. Some disappear." He looks more closely at the photograph of the painting. "May I?" And takes hold of Bob Abley's phone and enlarges the image. "As I say, I never throw any art away, as you never know which one of these buggers will be the new Van Gogh. I found some Ricky Groat in a local charity shop. Kept it here for ten years before he took off. Made me a bundle. Paid off the mortgage."

Elizabeth and Inspector Abley follow the antique shop owner further into the barn, and down an avenue of catalogued art. Elizabeth surmises this man has spent many hours labelling each piece and putting it in tissue paper and is most clearly the tidiest hoarder she has ever seen.

"How many paintings do you have in here?" Abley asks, "and, what does the wife think of this?"

"The wife left me years ago. Said I was spending too much time with my paintings. I have ten thousand, one hundred and twenty-six. All catalogued, colour coded and with provenance. But, don't tell my competitors," and he touches his nose. "Follow me. The colours in this painting are very of their time, so it is easier to date this. They are nineteen-nineties yellow ochre. The fashions change, ever so slightly in the oils world. They use different brands, and then there are trends for using particular shades. Yes, yes. I think I have a couple of this artist. Are they still painting? What happened to them?"

"If you could show us the art, that would be very helpful," says Elizabeth, eager to find out the artist.

"Only, if they're doing well," he replies. "I might like to get these pieces valued. Here." The antiques shop owner starts to flick through a stand which next to each painting has a tiny red dot indicating 'Student Art'. "Here you are." And he lifts out two pieces. One is a drawing of a butterfly on a buddleia, and the other is a self-portrait. "This is kitsch and would have less value. But this," and he looks at the self-portrait, "a self-portrait of the artist, and she's a beauty." Both have the same initials on the front.

"How can you tell it's a self-portrait?" Elizabeth asks, leaning in. "It's got the same initials. I P."

"No, not I P, that's I R," he says.

"How can you tell?" Abley asks.

"Because it says on the back, look," the antiques shop owner replies and turns over the painting and it reads 'Isla Resander, Self Portrait, August 1995'.

"Isla Resander?"

"I feel like I've seen that face before," Bob says.

"Yes, she does have one of those faces," the dealer agrees.

"Professor Alexander Resander's daughter," Elizabeth looks at Bob Abley, "the girl from the dusty bedroom, the girl's painting in the Kinder Habits cafe upstairs. She painted the painting in Sandy Starborneck's home. And, I expect the little dormouse sitting below her father in the photograph from the Jericho Hall Community Centre. Maybe that's why he still goes to the pantomimes? She's the missing link."

Inspector Bob Abley's face takes a moment to understand and then Elizabeth watches as the realisation of what this meant spreads across his face.

"So Alexander's the killer!" Bob replies.

56
THE PERCH

On the way back from Woodstock, Professor Elizabeth Green and Inspector Bob Abley stop off at The Perch, a pretty public house adjacent to Port Meadow, to meet Godric after he has walked the dogs. Godric has another new outfit for this evening's performance and wants to run it past his Nanna. Though Elizabeth has little interest in pantomime, she always has time for her favourite grandson. And she is excited to tell him the news about the paintings. It is one step closer to solving these terrible crimes and clearing any suspicion from her door. One step closer to home.

As Professor Elizabeth Green and Inspector Bob Abley enter the main bar, a roaring fire provides a warm glow. A large Christmas tree makes the room smell of pine needles and lots of twinkling lights can be seen through the windows into the pub garden. Outside, in the snow, stands Godric half in costume, having walked from Jericho dressed as Buttons in his red velvet jacket. Elizabeth is cross because she can see him quite clearly smoking a cigarette. She charges through the bar and out into the cold.

Bob Abley watches Elizabeth through the window, as she snatches the cigarette from Godric and throws it into the cigarette bin. The dogs now jumping at her. Godric puts his arms around his Nanna and Bob Abley watches as Godric then stands back and does a twirl for Elizabeth.

Bob is pleased to see Elizabeth so happy with her grandson. Yet at the same time, it brings it home that Bob has no family now. His children are all grown up and moved away, and both have said that they are spending Christmas Day and Boxing Day with their mother. Bob smiles to himself as Elizabeth takes off her scarf and wraps it around Godric and then points for him to go inside. They both step into the warm, the dogs wagging their tails and sniffing under tables for dropped crisps.

"Howdy son, nifty jacket. I'll get them in." Bob Abley walks to the bar as Godric and Elizabeth find a cosy corner.

"This one wants a whisky. Just a juice for me please, and perhaps for you?" Elizabeth shouts across to Abley.

"I was only on the shandy last night, and I thought I'd try lime and soda actually," Abley replies, trying to make light of last night's alcohol consumption, clearly in denial.

"Good."

"Where have you been?" Godric asks his Nanna, "I've been worried about you," Godric says, stroking Hector.

"Woodstock. Alexander's teenage child did Sandy Starborneck's painting. Looks like she was quite prolific, his daughter. This art dealer had some of hers in his warehouse in Woodstock. That's where we've been this morning. Left you sleeping like a baby."

Inspector Abley walks over with the drinks, just as Sergeant Lemon comes into the pub.

"Oh, can I get you one?" Abley offers.

"No, thanks." On seeing Inspector Abley, Lemon is reminded how much alcohol Bob consumed last night. Having let Bob back in a little, it felt like a slap in the face.

"What did you want?" Lemon looks at Godric. "Calling

me over here like this. I have a terrible headache, about to start another double shift." Lemon nurses his hangover from the hotel bar last night, half blaming Godric for plying him with so many shots.

"He told me to call you," Godric points at Inspector Abley. Inspector Abley shrugs and orders Lemon a drink anyway.

"I thought you'd want to hear this. We went to investigate a link with art," Abley explains.

"I know I can't get you to stop investigating, no matter how hard I try, so go on then, tell me," Lemon replies.

"Paintings. Artists. Sandy Starborneck had a painting done by the missing daughter of Professor Alexander Resander," Elizabeth says, waiting for this information to sink in for Lemon.

"What?" Lemon temporarily perches on a stool opposite Elizabeth to hear more.

"Oh, so he could be involved in some way?" Godric asks his Nanna. "Professor Alexander Resander? He's so slight. He couldn't say boo to a goose."

"It's poison. The deaths are by poison." Elizabeth is firm. "You don't need muscles to administer them. And I'm sure that Michael's car crash was no accident either. I'm just not sure why that happened. Why murder Michael as well?"

"Let's stick to the facts," Lemon says, looking at Abley, who always repeats this mantra. "We know that two women died from suspicious poisoning. There's no actual proof that this car crash is murder though."

"Well, when there is evidence that the car is tampered with then you'll see that there is something iffy about Alexander visiting Sandy Starborneck's home," Elizabeth says.

"And Gabriel Deersman," Inspector Abley chips in, bringing over Elizabeth's juice and Godric's hair of the dog, and one for Lemon too.

"Ew, no thanks." Lemon looks at the whisky and

blackcurrant concoction put in front of him. "And should you be in a pub already this early?"

"This is lime and soda. And I was on shandy last night." Abley smiles to Lemon. Lemon knows Abley is fooling himself and can remember Abley drinking many pints and shots.

"Are you in denial?" Lemon replies to Abley.

"Maybe Professor Alexander Resander had an affair with this Sandy Starborneck years before," Godric suggests excitedly, also trying to get Lemon and Abley to stop niggling each other. "Maybe the missing daughter is in America and has been living with her American mother, Sandy, all these years. Maybe she went over there with her mother, and he isn't allowed to see her, so he killed her mother in spite or revenge,"

"The daughter was a prolific painter. There are even some in the cafe on Little Clarendon Street," Elizabeth adds, "so it looks likely she grew up here, at least."

"Sergeant Lemon is right. We should stick to the facts. The facts are this could just be a coincidence," Abley replies, sipping his lime and soda and pulling a face at it.

"Well, if you want to talk to him you'd better be quick before Alexander leaves the country for his Christmas holiday," Godric offers, adding, "He came backstage last night and was talking about going to see the Northern Lights 'for the Yuletide' he said. He's a bit laconic, isn't he? I couldn't tell if he was excited or disappointed. Leaving today."

"Are you sure?" Lemon presses Godric, sliding the drink Abley bought him back under the Inspector's nose.

"I can get you a soft drink," Abley gets up and walks back to the bar.

"No. Just drink yours," Lemon says frustrated with his old Inspector, "I don't want a drink. Looks like I'm already on the clock with all this anyway." But Abley gets up for the bar. Lemon rolls his eyes as Godric takes his cue to answer Lemon's question.

"He was showing us the lights on his phone. Booked this ice hotel. He said something weird," Godric explains. "Something about the world already turning his heart cold, and that his extremities might as well join it. It was a bit dark. I mean, we'd just come off stage from the panto and were on cloud nine." Godric rubs Lemon's shoulder, then the buttons on his coat. "What do you think? Too much?" Godric then touches Lemon's arm. Lemon looks at Godric's new 'Buttons' costume jacket. Godric takes out a red velvet hat he has tucked in the breast pocket and puts it on. "It's magnificent, isn't it? I'm taking it for future performances when they come. I'll look amazing, won't I?"

"Yes, you will," Lemon replies.

"Why were Professor Alexander Resander and Dr Gabriel Deersman together at Sandy and Haven's home? That's what I don't understand. Gabriel has been acting strangely," Elizabeth says. "I have a feeling we're overlooking something. Something about him doesn't fit."

"Have some juice, Bunny. You look thirsty." Godric lifts up her drink and gives it to Elizabeth, who sips it involuntarily. He is worried that she still looks tired from this case. "Have you eaten?"

"What if Gabriel murdered the two Americans?" Inspector Abley suggests.

"What's his motive?" Lemon asks.

"Working backwards. He was attacked by Michael the other day. Why? Why would Michael punch him? Perhaps Michael knew what Gabriel had done," Abley replies.

"What, murder the Americans?" Elizabeth shakes her head.

"Yes, and then Gabriel had to kill Michael to keep him quiet," Godric chips in enthusiastically.

"But he has such puppy dog eyes." Abley teases Elizabeth about Gabriel. Abley walks back from the bar and puts a cola down for Lemon.

"I'm off sugar at the moment," Lemon replies. Abley

raises an eyebrow but tries not to rise to Lemon's response. Instead, he takes a long gulp of his drink, unsure how long he is going to get some peace on his very short holiday before his mega Christmas shifts.

"I'll have it for my whisky." Godric pours the cola into his double whisky. "Perfect." Godric smiles at Abley.

"This Gabriel fellow has been getting awfully friendly with you," Abley suggests to Elizabeth.

"Just because you don't like Gabriel, it doesn't make him guilty," she replies. "And anyway, I think he's cross at me now. No, Lemon is right. We all need to stick to the facts."

"You always have to watch the nice ones," Abley says.

Elizabeth watches a magpie outside, fly down into the snow and retrieve something shiny, a bauble from the tree outside. It hops about, then flies away with the sparkling object in its beak.

"I have to go," Elizabeth stands up suddenly.

"If we are talking facts, I suppose it's only right before you shoot off that I tell you the car Michael crashed in. It was Alexander's," Lemon says.

"He didn't do it," Elizabeth replies.

"There is mounting evidence," Abley suggests, "Sandy Starborneck had a painting from his daughter. He's about to leave the country. It was his car."

"That may be so," Elizabeth shrugs.

"The car hadn't been driven for twenty-two years, no MOT," Lemon adds.

"I have to go," Elizabeth repeats.

"Want me to come?" Abley asks.

"I'll meet you later," she replies, then turns to Godric. "Get something to eat. On me, and feed the dogs. There's something I want to check." Elizabeth leaves her credit card for Godric.

"Should I be coming with you?" Sergeant Lemon asks suspiciously.

"No, you stay here. Talk to each other." Elizabeth

looks at Bob Abley and tilts her head towards Lemon, raising her eyebrows. Lemon catches her do it, and she smiles back innocently, then disappears.

"Can I get you a water then? Coffee?" Abley asks Lemon, trying to fill the temporary silence between them.

"No, thank you," Lemon says, getting up and shaking his head. "You really should go back to Cambridge. You're in the wrong place." Lemon gets up and leaves. Abley puts down his drink, suddenly having lost his thirst. He sighs and follows Lemon out the door, but far enough behind that it is clear to Godric they are not leaving together.

"Dogs, settle yourself," The barman comes over with Christmas treats for the dogs and water and brings Godric a menu. "Yes, please can you bring me another double whisky? And a glass of champagne. Merry Christmas." Godric smiles to the barman. "Make it the special stuff. And, I might squeeze in a quick luncheon, thank you." But as Godric settles back to enjoy one of his favourite things, alcohol, a fleeting worry crosses his brow and unsettles him, about the safety of his Nanna.

57
BACK TO THE BODLEIAN

Professor Elizabeth Green is back in the library. She rushes in, her pace much quicker than before. Charging up to the desk out of breath.

"It's important. I need to see the local news archives from 1997."

"If you can wait your turn, I'm just serving this gentleman," the same librarian from Elizabeth's last visit is still behind the information desk.

"This is a matter of life and death."

"I very much doubt that, Madam. If you can wait your turn please."

Elizabeth bangs the counter.

"I'm a police consultant, and I need that archive now." Elizabeth raises her voice.

"Where's your badge?"

Elizabeth huffs and rustles around in her bag, looking for her purse. She pulls out her purse and opens it, showing the librarian her badge – which is from the last time she was hired.

"I'm afraid that's not valid here, it says Cambridge. I think you'll find we're in Oxford. So, you'll have to wait your turn." The librarian turns her back on Elizabeth. Elizabeth goes blue in the face and lifts the corner of the counter and walks through.

"Hey! You are not allowed around here," the librarian says.

"Oh, shush. This is a library," Elizabeth replies.

"Madam, I have to insist you leave."

Elizabeth looks through the catalogue system and finds a key for the computer she was using before.

"It's okay, I've got it. Thank you for nothing."

"You can't take that."

"I just did," and with that, Elizabeth rushes down the stacks of books towards the table of computers. She puts the USB key into the laptop and opens the security password. The librarian chases after her.

"Give me that."

"I'm in now, so thank you. I don't need it anymore. Don't you need to serve the gentleman?"

"I could ask you to leave."

"Shush, don't you know the rules?" Elizabeth says, then ignores the librarian's huffs and starts to search through the news archives from 1997. She scrolls through various dates, putting in Professor Alexander Resander's name, looking for missing children. But she gets nothing.

Elizabeth grows frustrated. She knows what she is looking for now but can't find it. Then, she starts to put Alexander's name in again, but this time alongside Dr Sandy Starborneck. And there it is, the face in the painting, the face in Alexander's photographs on the wall in his home, the face of the missing teenager. The title of the article is "Car Crash. Teen Killed." It is all Elizabeth needs. She attempts to print the article, but the printer is out of paper. Elizabeth realises that the fresh paper will be behind the desk along with the friendly librarian.

Elizabeth creeps back up towards the counter. She can see the librarian stamping some books, so ducks behind a stack, peeping out to watch the librarian's next move.

Elizabeth leans back to think what to do, but then as she is thinking, serendipity strikes, as the librarian glides past with a student, helping him find a book.

Elizabeth seizes the moment and rushes behind the desk to look for paper. But she can't see it anywhere. She pulls out drawers, lifts stationery to check underneath, opens a wardrobe-type dresser and finally, the last drawer in which she looks she finds a packet of paper. Grabbing some, she rushes out, only to pass the librarian on the way to the printer.

"Hey! Where did you get that?"

"Out of my way," Elizabeth brushes past her, briskly walking towards the communal printer. As she is filling the tray, the librarian goes to grab the paper.

"You have to pay for the paper," the librarian pulls. Elizabeth breaks free and runs over to the laptop, just as she sees the Oxford Inspector marching towards her with two Constables.

"You and your meddling. We were about to arrest Michael Pussett for murder last night, and you scuppered it," the Oxford Inspector says as he comes up to the table where Elizabeth is fussing over a computer.

"Officer, I'm so glad. Have you come to arrest this woman?" the librarian asks.

"Oh, shut up," Elizabeth tells the librarian, "I told you, I was working on solving a murder,"

"She stole from the library!"

"I took paper because I need to print this story, but now you're here I don't need to anymore," Elizabeth says, looking at the Oxford Inspector. The printer wakes up and starts to print. "It's here," Elizabeth points at the computer.

"Professor Green, we'd like a word please, about Michael Pussett. You were seen leaving the pantomime around the time of his death."

"What?"

"If you can tell us what time you left, please, and

make a statement. We want to interview you down at the station."

"Shut up a minute," Elizabeth replies.

"See. This is what she was like with me. So rude." The librarian chips in.

"Shush," Elizabeth directs at the librarian, then turns to the Oxford Inspector. "Dr Sandy Starborneck was a murderer. Well, perhaps, manslaughter. But she got away with it. Over twenty years ago."

"Dr Sandy Starborneck was murdered, Professor Green, she wasn't the murderer," the Oxford Inspector corrects Elizabeth.

"She was indeed murdered, but not by Michael. It's all here." Elizabeth looks at the computer screen, willing him to read.

"We're looking for Sandy Starborneck's murderer. Keep up for chrissake," the Oxford Inspector says, dismissively, "and you wrecked our plans for arresting Michael Pussett for the murder. Now he's dead, and you slipped out of a show around the same time. You're quite literally at the scene of every crime," the Oxford Inspector emphasizes the word, 'every'.

"I wouldn't put it past her," the librarian crosses her arms over her chest and tucks in her chin.

"Oh, please. I would have thought as a librarian you would know the correct usage of the word literally." Elizabeth rolls her eyes at the librarian and the Oxford Inspector. "Michael Pussett is not a murderer. He was an art teacher. He knew Sandy Starborneck many years ago. But he didn't realise it for a while when she returned many years later. The hands of time paint a different face."

"He was a conference organiser, as well you know," the Oxford Inspector corrects Elizabeth again.

"But to be seeing someone you'd met years before and not even realise it. That's crazy," Elizabeth almost says to herself, "until he did remember her. It just took him a while. Then when it all fell into place, that was his undoing. If you look at his body you will find an imprint of Dr Haven Usrey's ring where they must have argued before Haven died. Michael was certainly not squeaky clean. He was blackmailing Haven. That's probably why there was a cheque from Haven for a large sum, in the footwell of Michael's car the night he died. But no, he didn't kill Sandy, or Haven."

"Professor Green, you're rambling. I'm going to read you your rights."

Elizabeth can't be doing with this and walks over to the printer to get the article in black and white.

"Here," and she shoves it in the Oxford Inspector's hand. "Professor Alexander Resander has a daughter, *had* a daughter. And, she was killed in a car accident twenty-two years ago. It was you that led me to this conclusion in the first place. That woman I shared a cell with in the custody suite overnight, was drunk driving. That Santa train, in the shopping centre. So, in a roundabout way, we wouldn't be here if you hadn't arrested me. I have to thank you for that," Elizabeth smiles.

"What are you talking about woman?" the Oxford Inspector says.

Elizabeth continues crossly, "I hope you've let her go. All she did was drive a miniature train around some shops. Then, I thought about all the art. The art. It had to tie things together. Sandy Starborneck had some, Michael had some, Alexander had some. Even the cafe had some. Who was this artist? We found out that it was Alexander's daughter—"

"I'm arresting you for the murder—" the Oxford Inspector interrupts her.

"No, not again. I don't need anymore thinking time. I'm good. You misunderstand." Elizabeth holds up her hand, trying to stop the Oxford Inspector.

"Arresting you for the murder of Dr Sandy Starborneck, Dr Haven Usrey and Michael Pussett. You do not have to say anything, but it may harm your defence if you do not mention when questioned something which you later rely on in court. Anything you do say may be given in—"

"Have you finished? This young girl, Isla. Read the article unless you want to look stupid. She was killed in a car crash. Look at the piece. No doubt in the passenger seat," Elizabeth interrupts, "Killed, either intentionally or unintentionally. She was in a car driving to an art class in Wolvercote, run by a far-out hippy, Michael Pussett. Look. Look at Michael. There he is. Looking much younger but you can't mistake that face anywhere." Elizabeth points to the article. "They would paint in his house, that's why all the rooms are empty now, and he lives in his shed. He used to encourage drink and drugs as a way to improve the mind and paint. I read an article about it. He stopped teaching art after the poor girl died. He remembers the death, blames himself. That's why he kept one of Isla's paintings."

"And we were about to arrest him. But you murdered him before we could," the Oxford Inspector says.

"Are you listening? Just let me finish," Elizabeth pushes the article up under the Oxford Inspector's face.

"Oh, don't worry, we're taking note. Cuffs," the Oxford Inspector nods to the Constable, who is writing furiously, trying to keep up with everything Elizabeth says, while another gets out some handcuffs at the Oxford Inspector's request.

"Thank you. Please do take notes," Elizabeth adds. The Constable rolls his eyes. Elizabeth continues, "I remember Haven saying that Sandy hadn't drunk since she was last in the UK. And how she had gone mad with drink since she'd returned. She was also a painter. That's why she had a painting of Isla's. She had it there to remind her of her sin, perhaps to tell her not to drink.

She had likely kept it with her all these years as a warning to herself. Perhaps that's why it was on the floor smashed the first time we saw it. She must have recognised

Alexander when she attended the conference. What bad luck for her. The father of the girl she killed. Only, Alexander didn't recognise Sandy, to begin with, like I say. Sandy had grown older, and he was hardly at the conference. Missed her prize-giving, and really avoided people, preferring his research.

Maybe she thought she could get in and out of Oxford without bumping into him, but there he was. It was enough to drink again. She smashed Isla's painting, the reminder which had kept her sober all these years had now failed. All the ghosts had come back to haunt her. Maybe that's why Alexander went to get the painting. One can only surmise that he had gone up to Summertown to have it out with Dr Sandy Starborneck, but was too late, she was already dead. Maybe he went to pay his respects to Haven and saw the painting. He had to have Isla's painting from Sandy Starborneck's. You should interview Alexander about it."

The Oxford Inspector decides to pay more attention to the piece of paper Elizabeth has handed him and puts a hand up to stop the Constable from cuffing Elizabeth. He says nothing, now perhaps realising that he is out of his depth. So Elizabeth continues.

"Sandy Starborneck was a graduate student in Oxford. Decades ago. I checked."

"Oh, so we've jumped from Michael Pussett being an art teacher, to a young woman dying in a car from someone drink driving. What's that got to do with anything?" The Oxford Inspector says, now highly irritated due to being unable to understand fully the severity of what he's being told.

"I checked. It's in the records. They name Sandy Starborneck in that piece as driving the car and report it as a 'tragic accident'. But, if she was drinking, like I think she was, it was negligence at best."

"Wait. What? She was driving Michael when he had his crash? But she was dead already," the Oxford Inspector says.

"No, the crash twenty-two years ago. She was driving Isla, and her boyfriend, Dave. Dave from Kinder Habits."

"Who is Isla?" the Oxford Inspector asks.

"Professor Alexander Resander's daughter, Isla," one of the Constables chips in, behind the Oxford Inspector, reading back his notes, continuing, "You've got this Professor Alexander Resander who lost his daughter in a car crash, and the woman driving was this Sandy Starborneck. She was driving the car twenty-two years ago, but it was seen as an accident as for some reason she wasn't breathalysed. She left the country, probably running away and getting away with it. But then Professor Alexander Resander found out she'd returned many years later. He didn't spot her immediately because he didn't attend the conference much, staying in his laboratory, and also women change, you know, with age." The Constable immediately feels guilty reading that last line, looking at Professor Green and her wrinkly face, but continues. "Neither did the art teacher at the time, this Michael Pussett person. He didn't recognise Dr Sandy Starborneck, either. Men eh?" says the Constable, to Elizabeth, trying to be helpful, adding, "So then, if I understand it right. Dr Sandy Starborneck recognises the father, Professor Alexander Resander, blames herself for the daughter's death and starts drinking. She can't cope with the truth," the Constable adds, pleased with himself. Then he looks at the Oxford Inspector, who appears to have steam coming out of his ears. "Apparently, according to Professor Green here," the Constable finishes, quietly.

"Correct. Give that Constable a promotion." Elizabeth claps her hands.

"Just stick to taking notes, Constable," the Oxford Inspector says firmly.

"I looked into her history in America, and Sandy Starborneck had been giving money to alcoholics charities, since 1997, the year she returned. And, she hasn't been to any conferences in the UK since," Elizabeth adds.

"You mentioned the art. What cafe are you speaking about?" the Oxford Inspector asks.

"On Little Clarendon Street, Kinder Habits. They were engaged. The maître d', Dave, and Isla. They were on the same course. Look, you can see him in the article. After Isla's untimely death, Dave gave up his art studies. He couldn't get over that night when he'd been getting a lift to Wolvecote from Sandy Starborneck with Isla. They had stopped at a pub and drank, him, Isla and Sandy. Sandy crashed the car. There were no other cars involved. Isla wasn't wearing a seat belt and flew through the windscreen," Elizabeth says, adding, "Dave must have been sitting in the back."

"Just like Michael Pussett," the Oxford Inspector suggests, "flying through the windscreen."

"I presume Dr Starborneck wasn't breathalysed," Elizabeth continues, not answering the Oxford Inspector. "There was a mistake all those years ago. And Sandy Starborneck was allowed to go to the hospital to be treated. From the look of the report, they weren't found for some time. When they were, Isla was already pronounced dead. The other two were unconscious. Perhaps the drink was partly out of Sandy's system by then. She didn't have a criminal record, so she was able to slip out of the country without a fuss. Perhaps her face was bleeding too much when they picked her up in the field and they just wanted to fix that. Ignoring the breathalyzer. That's why she had a scar to the left of her eyebrow. When I first met her, she said she had it from a big mistake, and she was looking at Michael at the time, so I thought she meant he must have given it to her. She must have remembered him, even though he didn't her at first. Maybe she was trying to lay the ghost. Maybe Michael twigged, and that's when they started to fight? We will never know."

"So Dr Starborneck was responsible for the death of

Professor Alexander Resander's daughter, Isla. And she was drunk driving at the time?" the Oxford Inspector finally catches up. Elizabeth nods firmly.

"Isla was just eighteen. Sandy Starborneck was a little older, as I say, records show she was a graduate student." Elizabeth looks back at the computer, pointing. "See? Isla was accepted to Catte College. She must have been on a gap year, maybe pursuing her art. That's why Professor Alexander Resander was breaking into Sandy's house. To get the painting back by his daughter. That's what Gabriel handed him," Elizabeth says, almost to herself. "Professor Resander hadn't met Dr Starborneck before, all those years ago. And the crash, killing his daughter, happened pre-world wide web. I'm sure he's been following her career but was shocked when she came. You should talk to him, find out what he's been thinking."

"That's where I saw the image of Isla, in Professor Alexander Resander's home, that shrine he had for his daughter." Inspector Abley peeps his head around the stack, having been there for some time and choosing an opportune moment to make himself known and support Elizabeth. Elizabeth nods.

"Godric spoke to Alexander, and he is going on holiday to see the Northern Lights," Elizabeth informs the Oxford Inspector.

"Constable, let's get a car round there, straight away," the Oxford Inspector orders.

"I believe Sergeant Lemon should be there already as I phoned him earlier to go to question Alexander about his family," Elizabeth takes great joy in pointing out to the Oxford Inspector that they are, once again, one step ahead of him. "Do you still want to arrest me?" Elizabeth puts her hands together in mock gesture, waiting for handcuffs.

"Don't get smart, and don't leave Oxford, and stay out of the way," the Inspector says, as he points for the Constables to make a swift exit to go and speak with Professor Alexander Resander.

Then they are gone, not waiting for Elizabeth to finish what she was going to say.

"Shall we follow?" Bob Abley asks.

Elizabeth shakes her head.

"No, has it stopped snowing?"

"Yes, why?"

"He didn't let me finish, put two and two together and got five." Elizabeth shrugs. "Walk with me. Alexander has thrown himself into his studies ever since his daughter died, spending every waking hour in the laboratory, which is probably where he is now. He's a Professor, a big name. He won't be lounging in his home, where they're heading. He wants to forget."

"Ah, we shall go to the laboratory then," Abley replies, not quite understanding but wanting to appear knowing. Elizabeth puts her duffel coat on and walks to the help desk, where the librarian has gone back to stamping books and helping people with general enquiries.

"Arrests in the library, zero," she says to the librarian. "Solving another murder, three murders actually, three points to me. And, as for librarian points? Your printer needs more ink," and Elizabeth walks out, with Inspector Bob Abley in tow, picking up a pencil and thanking the librarian without paying, then putting it behind his ear.

58
THE ARREST

Three squad cars race up to Great Clarendon Street in Jericho, sirens blaring, and screech to a stop outside Professor Alexander Resander's home. The Oxford Inspector and his two Constables rush to the front door. The Oxford Inspector soon after peers through the windows and then indicates for one of them to go around the back. Not long after, a Constable opens the front door, a whippet standing by his side.

"Back door was open," he says, moving out of the way as the Oxford Inspector rushes in.

"Be careful. He's likely to be armed and dangerous," the Oxford Inspector warns. With that, they creep up the stairs and onto the landing. All the doors are shut. One of the Constables tries a door, but it is an airing cupboard. A towel falls out. The tension is palpable as the same Constable tries another door. It is the door to the Professor's bedroom. There is a suitcase on the bed, half packed. "Good, he hasn't left yet. We still have time," The Oxford Inspector says.

While looking around, a Constable sees an envelope on the dressing table, alongside some books. The Constable opens it, only to find numerous photographs of Sandy Starborneck, seemingly through all of her career. In some, she has her eyes painted with nail polish a bright red. In others, scribbles of horns and a devil's staff.

"Sir," the Constable offers the Oxford Inspector a photograph of Sandy Starborneck.

"Bag it up," the Oxford Inspector replies, still listening out for any movement in the house. He walks back out onto the landing and pushes open the second bedroom. Just as Elizabeth and Bob Abley saw it, the room hasn't changed. The Oxford Inspector takes out some tweezers from his pocket and picks a photograph of Isla off the wall. He indicates for a Constable to take out an evidence bag and pops it in. "I need everything you've got on this girl, and pronto." As the Oxford Inspector is pleased he has finally found the murderer, a Constable comes rushing up the stairs.

"Sir, there's been a call for all cars. An incident on Magdalen Bridge."

"What are you waiting for? Let's go." He waves at his Constables to get going. But he stops for a moment, looks around at the room and shuts the door respectfully. As he turns and sees his Constables charge down the stairs and out of the house, he walks a little slower, taking everything in. When he gets to the downstairs hallway, he strokes the whippet and takes a biscuit out of his pocket for the dog, then shuts the front door carefully, to make sure the dog is safe. The Constables have the engines running, he gets in, and they tear away.

59
ON THIN ICE

"I can't help it if he didn't let me finish." Elizabeth has her driving gloves on and is navigating the Talbot through some ice on the road, "How did you get your car clamped?"

"Having a Cambridge resident's permit on my windscreen may have swung it. How the hell did I know I couldn't park outside the Bodleian Library?" Bob Abley says, used to being able to park anywhere he likes, adding, "Why aren't we heading to Resander's?"

"It wasn't Alexander who murdered the Americans and Michael. We need to visit someone else first. And they live off the Cowley Road."

"What? But you said—"

"No," Elizabeth replies, driving slowly around Radcliffe Square. "I hope we're going to make it."

"Who did it?"

Just as Elizabeth is about to spill, Godric runs up to the car, dressed as Father Christmas carrying a sack over his back, and jumps in the back.

"Hello!"

"Where are the dogs?"

"With Mike."

"Mike?" Elizabeth looks at Godric in her rearview mirror.

"The concierge. Bellboy sounds so much better." He pats his Nanna on the shoulder as she pulls away again. "He's taken them for a walk while I picked up this Santa outfit. Good eh? Managed to procure it from Catte College Porter. Gave me it to borrow for the end of the pantomime. Someone's going to come up on stage and throw sweets out at the audience. He also said after all the hoo-ha the Porters weren't going to dress up as Father Christmas this year to give the Dons their presents," Godric replies. "I thought I'd wear it over to Jericho. Got a few other treats in here," he pats his sack, "I'm hugely popular on the High Street, you know," tapping Bob Abley on the shoulder. "Have you been good?"

"No. But that hasn't stopped Father Christmas bringing me gifts," Bob Abley replies, "tree lights, cakes, biscuits, snow globes. So the whole being good thing is hokum."

"Where are we going?" Godric asks. The three of them drive past Inspector Bob Abley's car as it is being put on a tow truck. He shouts at the team hoisting his car up onto a platform that he will be over and will want words with their bosses. "Maybe Santa made a note about you not being good after all," Godric adds.

"Raynott's going to have a field day with this. He'll put a copy of my clamping fine up on the wall for all to see." Abley is cross.

"We're going down the Cowley Road. To pay a visit to a relative of Professor Alexander Resander's, if either of you are not too preoccupied," Elizabeth says.

As they turn and enter Magdalen Bridge, they spot Professor Alexander Resander running on the pavement, shouting at someone to come back. He's ahead of them by fifty yards, but there is no mistaking it. And as they get closer, they can see that the person he's chasing is Linda.

"What in blazes?" Elizabeth is shocked to see them both.

They spot Linda running down the steps to the punts. A small crowd already on Magdalen Bridge looking down at the ducks and swans, are also now watching the commotion. Elizabeth pulls over, and they rush after them, Godric still in his Father Christmas suit. When they get half way down the steps, they see Linda has already jumped into the water, and Alexander is holding a punt pole out to try to reach her.

"Is he about to kill another woman?" Godric asks, shocked.

"Unless he's trying to kill the killer, then I don't think so," Elizabeth sagely replies. They hear footsteps behind them, and it is Sergeant Lemon, who rushes over to Professor Alexander Resander to arrest him. Elizabeth continues to explain to Godric and Bob Abley. "Linda is Isla's mother," she says matter of factly.

"Wait, she's Alexander's ex-partner?" Godric asks.

"More to the point, she's been working at the College for twenty-two years, since her daughter was accepted all that time ago. Isla must have been on a gap year when she was killed in the car crash with Dr Sandy Starborneck, just enjoying herself before beginning her studies. Or, that was the plan," then Elizabeth shouts to Sergeant Lemon, "He didn't do it!" as she watches the Sergeant struggle with Alexander some feet away.

"What's Lemon doing?" Godric asks, now at the bottom of the steps. But Elizabeth continues to explain, as they all run towards the river.

"Linda got a job in the alumni office and couldn't leave after Isla died, clung onto the memory, no doubt. It made me suspicious when all the graduate students still about before Christmas seemed to love Linda and help themselves to food from her kitchen. Why would they do this? My experience of caterers is they have to enforce strict rules, or the students take a mile. But Linda likes them. They remind her of Isla. So she's kind."

As they arrive by the water's edge, they are within arms length of Linda, splashing about in the freezing river, trying to get away from Alexander who is prodding the ice with a punt pole near her with one hand, while trying to shake Lemon off with the other.

"Shall I get her?" Godric looks at Linda, and is about to dive in himself.

"No. It's too cold. Let's get one of these." Bob Abley pulls the chains off a punt, and Godric grabs a pole, punching the ice to free the punt. A little out of breath Elizabeth continues to explain.

"Linda's relationship ended as she and Alexander, they both couldn't cope with losing their only daughter in the car crash. Alexander threw himself into work, while Linda grew bitter, perhaps plotting revenge against Dr Starborneck. I didn't work it out for a bit, as there wasn't the common surname. Though Isla had her father's, Linda has her own."

"What are they doing?" Sergeant Lemon shouts to Elizabeth, as Bob and Godric jump on a punt.

"Come back!" Elizabeth shouts to Linda who now appears to be swimming further out into the icy water. As Elizabeth reaches for a punt pole to try to pass it across the water to Linda, Lemon asks, having heard Elizabeth's explanation, "Linda is the killer? I was bringing Alexander in for questioning. You left me a message?"

"Yes, he's family. He needs to be questioned, thank you. I had to be sure about Linda, and I've only just had it confirmed. Dr Sandy Starborneck killed Alexander's daughter who was also Linda's daughter. Linda followed Sandy's developing career, as Sandy went back home to America Linda followed her success, always hoping she could get her revenge should Sandy ever set foot in England again. Isn't that right?" Elizabeth suddenly shouts to Linda, but Linda isn't listening. She is busy trying to swim away, so Elizabeth continues explaining the case to

Lemon, raising her voice in case Linda can hear. "But Sandy Starborneck wouldn't come back to the UK, no doubt haunted by what she'd done. Only recently, she finally couldn't refuse a trip when she won a prize for her research and the funding required her accepting the prize in Oxford. Sandy must have been torn. Well, Linda knew she could pounce. And the woman practically fell into her lap," Elizabeth says, as Godric helps her onto a snow-covered punt

"Sandy Starborneck was in the wrong place at the wrong time!" Elizabeth shouts back at Lemon, "And moving from alumni relations to catering, Linda thought it was fitting to poison her with yew. I remember when I first asked Linda about Sandy Starborneck, she said 'I don't know her,' which seemed an odd reply when being asked about what she'd seen the night of the scuffle with Father Christmas. I wasn't asking Linda about Sandy's character. Linda was protesting too much." Elizabeth sits down in the punt, looking at the clumps of ice bobbing about below where the river has frozen between the punts.

"She was in a relationship with this one?" Lemon asks as he struggles to cuff Alexander.

"Yes. Though Linda kept her distance from Alexander in College, despite working for decades in the alumni office. She only moved to catering recently, very recently, in fact, It's all in the College records. I was suspicious why the transfer to a more junior job, and so quickly. She heard about Sandy Starborneck coming." Elizabeth shouts over to Lemon, "You know, I think Alexander's just trying to save her."

"What are you doing here?" Lemon asks Inspector Abley.

"Catching a killer."

"Alexander isn't the killer?" Lemon asks.

Bob shakes his head.

"That's what I've been saying." Elizabeth throws her hands up in the air. "Linda's not in danger from her ex-partner." Elizabeth shouts.

"So they are married and had a child?" Lemon asks, grabbing Alexander's other hand, causing him to drop the pole.

"We never married, but yes, we had a daughter," Alexander finally speaks, looking at Linda in the water. "I'm not trying to kill Linda. I'm trying to save her. She's going to drown. Let me get her!" he screams, his eyes fixed on Linda.

"She killed them all. And now, she's doing a good job of trying to kill herself by the looks of it." Elizabeth says, adding, "Dr Starborneck was drunk driving with Linda and Alexander's daughter in the car. The daughter died. Linda got her revenge, and now she doesn't want to be rescued."

Linda continues to swim further out into the icy water of the Cherwell.

"Leave me alone!" Linda shouts and turns to swim towards the Magdalen Bridge.

"She's gone. Isla's gone. She wouldn't want you to do this!" Elizabeth shouts.

"My Isla! There's nothing left–" Linda shouts frantically, swimming away.

"Stop her! She's heading for the Thames!" Elizabeth shouts again, "Godric, your boat skills."

Godric pushes off faster with his pole, heading straight for Linda. Alexander sees what they are doing and how Linda is headed under Magdalen Bridge, breaks away from Lemon and jumps in a punt himself, grabbing a pole – one wrist still in a police cuff, the other cuff dangling. Lemon jumps in after him, not wanting to be left behind.

"Linda!" Elizabeth shouts.

"Stop following—" Linda looks back. Her arms flailing, and she starts to shout at Elizabeth, but her head temporarily dips under the water as she disappears under the bridge. Godric speeds up, his punt pole working overtime. Linda's body is being taken faster towards the Thames, as her head reappears, but the cold has got a grip, and she is uncommunicative, letting the water carry her away.

"Linda!" shouts Alexander. "Linda!"

Elizabeth hears sirens and looks back and sees uniformed police officers peering over the bridge. Being somewhat of an expert on a punt, Godric soon catches up with Linda and is alongside her limp body. Inspector Abley grabs her and manages to pull her into the punt. Linda is blue and unresponsive. Bob Abley starts to resuscitate her. Elizabeth takes off her duffel coat to cover Linda in warmth. Godric turns his punt towards the bank, which now has paramedics waiting, as well as police officers.

*

A short while after, Elizabeth is given her duffel coat back by a paramedic, and she puts the punt blanket down on a bench. Godric helps her on with the arms of her coat. She stands with Inspector Abley and Godric, beside Linda on the stretcher outside the ambulance, paramedics putting a drip into Linda's arm. Linda begins to come round.

"Are you okay?" Godric asks his Nanna.

"I'm fine," she brushes her duffel a little and turns to Lemon. "So you have your killer." Then Elizabeth speaks to Linda. "You poisoned Sandy Starborneck's drinks with yew needles, isn't that right?" Elizabeth tells Linda, adding, "I expect you asked Alexander to help, but he couldn't do it." Linda looks at Alexander, who is sitting on the floor of the ambulance with his feet hanging over the side, wearing a silver rescue blanket. He says nothing. Elizabeth continues, this time speaking directly to him. "When I saw you mixing something in the laboratory, you were cagey. For a moment, I thought it might have been the poison."

"It was banana seeds, *Musa itinerans*, they're important." Alexander takes Linda's hand, "stupid really. Just my distraction," he looks lovingly at Linda.

"My Inspector's here." Lemon nods over at the group

of police by a squad car, come to read Linda her rights. "He said they found this packet of photographs in your house. Of Sandy Starborneck, all defaced," Lemon says, looking at Alexander.

"I bet you find Linda's fingerprints are all over them. I'm right, aren't I?" Elizabeth leans over Linda, who is now being hooked up to a portable heart monitor by paramedics. "He hasn't got it in him, to kill. Not like you." Elizabeth stares at Linda, willing her to admit everything.

"What about Haven and Michael Pussett?" Inspector Abley asks.

"Haven found out what you were doing, didn't she," Elizabeth answers Inspector Abley, without taking her eyes off Linda, "and so you polished her off too with another Christmas-themed poison, mistletoe. It was just before Christmas that you lost Isla. You thought it apt, Christmas poison. She came into the kitchens after you, when the police took Michael away. She said it was for water. But I think she was having it out with you, as she came back very red-faced. She'd twigged, hadn't she? What you were doing. The note we found in Haven's hand up on Boars Hill? The "I'm sorry. I couldn't help it'? That was written by you wasn't it?" Elizabeth sees Linda break, something in her face releases the secrets she's been holding onto for years.

"I didn't want to kill her. I liked Haven. But she'd put two and two together. From the drinks. That night. She was suspicious and came into the kitchens. She kept saying that it was in her water, that the spirits told her what I'd done. But I knew that she'd found my glass. I used a special glass for Dr Starborneck. It had a tiny bit of nail polish on it, so I could tell which one had the poison. But no one noticed, except for Haven, that night of the dinner. She liked the polish. And then she saw me with the glass. I had to silence her."

Elizabeth looks at Lemon, who starts to take notes in his notebook.

"Oh, you well and truly did that, didn't you?" Elizabeth adds. "Drugging her with mistletoe and wine, then following her up to Boars Hill and waiting until she got hyperthermia and then leaving her there. What did you do? Share a peace offering? Perhaps if Inspector Abley hadn't left Boar's Hill early you might have knocked him off too," Elizabeth looks at Inspector Abley, who shudders at the thought. What if he had been there when Linda arrived and she had offered him a drink? Could he have taken one and be dead on the bench as well? "And as for Michael. You found out that he used to teach Isla. And you became close. But he forgot the name of the drunk driver. Something must have triggered him remembering."

"He came into the kitchen and saw the photographs in my locker," Linda replies, knowing the game is up.

"What was it? A fling? That you had with Michael? Did you split with Alexander over this?"

"No. I was never close to Michael," Linda says, shaking her head from her paramedic bed, looking at Alexander. "I didn't like him. He eventually told me he'd taught my daughter, said he'd done a bit of digging. Apparently, Starborneck confessed to him about killing Isla, when she finally admitted to Michael they'd met before. Haven knew too. I think Michael was blackmailing Haven. Of course, with Sandy dying in suspicious circumstances, Michael said he'd go to the police about my daughter and what Sandy had done. Haven was protecting her friend's memory. His blackmail worked on Haven. That is, until I killed him. Really enjoyed that one. Told him I'd got a new car and I had some money in Whytam Woods. Was going to collect. That he could have some if he kept his mouth shut," Linda looks at Alexander, "It was your car." Alexander lets go of her hand. Linda continues, "I didn't mean to implicate you. I was angry. If you'd driven my darling Isla to class that day, instead of her taking a lift from that evil woman, she'd still be here," Linda says, hurt that Alexander has now moved away.

"That's why you cycle everywhere. Because a car took your daughter," Elizabeth says.

"How could you? And you know I haven't been able to get behind the wheel since, since our Isla. I'm hurting too you know. Every day," Alexander whispers, dipping his head. But Linda's face is now cold.

Linda continues explaining to Elizabeth, "Only, made sure the seatbelt on the driver's seat didn't work. Met Michael up there in a lay-by. Told him where to find the money and cycled back. I cut the brakes. Had to research that. Had to get my own back."

"And as for Michael. That's why his hat was at Haven's," Elizabeth explains, adding, "He was looking for money. Haven's bag was at Michael's. She went to have it out with him, and he must have confiscated it, as it had her passport in and her phone. Now she couldn't leave to her dream Santa Fe."

Elizabeth continues. "The Sergeant informed us that Michael told the police that Haven had said she was in love with him. Showed some texts. But Michael had Haven's phone. It was Michael who sent those love texts from Haven's phone to his, to try to deflect any guilt from his door. The police were able to trace Haven's phone to a ditch at the back of Michael's garden," Elizabeth tells Bob and Godric, adding "she hit him with her porcupine ring at some point, no doubt to try to end his blackmailing ways."

"That was the mark on his cheek?" Abley asks.

"Exactly, I've told the police to check Haven's ring in the snow against the imprints on Michael's cheek. And, I'm sure he freaked out when he heard she'd died. All that potential extortion ended. Michael was broke, and the College had just cancelled his conference, wanting no more. He was not too happy with the Master – the dartboard in his shed would lend evidence that was the case."

Then, Elizabeth looks to Linda, "I always wondered why you liked Gabriel, if he was in on it with you, helping you. But no, it was just because he has lost his wife. You understood what he was going through. You felt he was like you. I wonder if he knew about your daughter? You know, you spun a tangled web. You threw me for a while when you took that watch. I kept wondering why, whose watch. Then I saw a magpie. You're a magpie, to fill your empty nest. Turned thief to deal with your grief. I can only imagine."

"My daughter. That bitch took my daughter away from me."

*

The Oxford Inspector walks over and joins Elizabeth, Lemon and Abley, as they all watch the ambulance with Linda drive away and Professor Alexander Resander being led towards a police car, with his silver recovery blanket still wrapped around his shoulders.

"Professor Elizabeth Green, thank you for solving the case," Sergeant Lemon says deliberately loudly in front of his Oxford Inspector.

"The pleasure was all mine. I found my visits to your police station most illuminating too. Though, I shan't be hurrying back."

"I'm sure my Inspector would like to thank you as well?" Lemon looks from his Oxford Inspector to Elizabeth.

"You've done a good job for the both of us, lad." the Oxford Inspector pats Sergeant Lemon on the arm and walks off.

"Ha!" Elizabeth smiles. What did she expect? A big thank you? Lemon flaps his arms in exasperation.

"Well, you did it again," Inspector Abley grabs Elizabeth's arm for a squeeze. "And Oxford is all the safer for having had you here." Bob Abley smiles at Elizabeth and shakes her a little until she finally laughs, half from relief it is over this time.

Sergeant Lemon looks at the two of them, as Bob Abley continues to pretend to shake Elizabeth hard, but is really just making her sway. Lemon appreciates that deep down, although Elizabeth professes to be as tough as nails, his old Inspector knows exactly what to say to get the best out of her. But, most importantly, what to do to make her happy. Lemon understands this complicated woman a little, and appreciates she is somehow using puzzles to bury her loss. He observes his old Inspector's face. Something about the creases in the corner of his face up to his eyes makes him miss the old bugger. He sighs, as the pain of missing Cambridge grows, as the pain of missing working with these two crazy individuals almost consumes him as he stands in the cold. What has he done?

60
THE FOUR AMIGOS

Professor Elizabeth Green and Godric sit by a window in the Victoria Arms pub, Old Marston. The public house is busy, and two fires roar at different ends of the room. A Christmas tree sparkles, and the bartender looks jolly as he wears a Father Christmas hat, while he distributes more treats to the dogs.

"We're setting up for a quiz soon. So you can stay there, but you'll have to play. Or, you can move tables further away," the bartender explains.

"But we wouldn't be able to see the river from there?" Elizabeth replies.

"Just the rules. This is a quiz table. Not yet, but in half an hour," the bartender says.

"Okay, thank you." Godric tries to be the peacemaker before Elizabeth starts her usual argument, "we will be gone by then." The bartender nods, smiles, then leaves.

"Will we?" Elizabeth corrects Godric, "I might like another stout."

"But you're driving, and I have to leave for the panto soon. Three more nights," Godric replies.

"You can keep the suite, but I have to get back. Bertie

and Soot will be wondering where I am," Elizabeth smiles for the first time, knowing it won't be long before she is home.

"I will be back before you know it," Godric hugs his Nanna.

"Thank you, Goddy, for being here." Elizabeth grabs his hand briefly. "When I was inside, to see your cheerful face… Well, it's nice to have a family."

"You've always got me, Bunny. And Hector, Monty, Clive, Bertie and Soot!"

"I was wrong about Dr Gabriel Deersman. He is a decent chap. He was just in Summertown to help his friend. He knew Alexander had lost his daughter, and he himself had lost his wife," Elizabeth says.

"Ah, forget about it," Godric replies.

"Oh god, I accused him of killing his own wife who died of natural causes. He was just helping Alexander get back the thing that was precious to him. The painting Isla had done. He is a good man. He didn't know the half of it, what was going on. He was just worried that Alexander might get arrested for breaking and entering. But he hasn't forgiven me for suspecting him. He uninvited me to his Chapel concert," Elizabeth says, feeling a little sad about it.

"Just because someone isn't a murderer, it doesn't make them boyfriend material. He was way too cheerful for you, no sense of sarcasm or irony," Godric replies, half relieved Elizabeth hasn't come back with a new man, as he'd have to share, and half disappointed for her, as Gabriel did seem nice.

"Please don't go leaping to hugely inaccurate conclusions."

"Whatever you say," Godric touches his favourite Nanna's nose with his finger.

The two of them sit in peace, but not for long when Lemon enters the bar.

"Hello! What a good idea. A celebratory drink! You just solved a triple murder," Lemon smiles.

"And got arrested to boot," Elizabeth huffs.

"No charges were made, and the caution dropped," Lemon says shrugging, then looking at Elizabeth fondly.

"Yes, but not without wrongful arrest. Bunny should sue," Godric replies.

"Godric," Elizabeth shakes her head. "I met a charming lady in prison. And, I've grown quite fond of Oxford again. I won't leave it so long. Will I get an apology from your Oxford Inspector?"

"Pigs might fly," Lemon replies.

"Snowy pigs," Godric says, looking out the window and seeing that it has started to snow again.

"I'll get them in." Lemon looks at their drinks. "Same again?"

"I think I'll have one more stout, please. Thank you, I'm not off yet," Elizabeth smiles. As Lemon goes to the bar, Inspector Bob Abley turns up.

"You need me to take the dogs back home? I need to get the car valeted when I get home anyway. You need to buy a car where you all fit, Elizabeth."

"They'll fit in mine, it's fine." Elizabeth rubs the dogs' backs.

"Hello. Can I get you a pint?" Lemon offers Inspector Abley, happy just to have the case solved and be off duty. And determined for one night not to worry about Inspector Abley's drinking habits.

"No, let me," Abley says.

"It's okay," Lemon replies and walks back to the bar.

"Isn't this nice. Everyone together," Elizabeth sighs, sipping her drink.

"It's a start, I guess," Bob replies. "But, can you not force this?"

"Do you want him back or not?" Elizabeth hisses.

"Of course I do, but pressuring him isn't going to work," Bob replies.

"He's not happy here. That Oxford Inspector has him on double shifts all through Christmas," Elizabeth says.

"This is relaxing," Godric chips in, sarcastically, checking his phone and waving at Lemon to buy him crisps.

"If he came back, he'd be working Christmas with me, I expect. Raynott hasn't exactly welcomed me back with open arms." Inspector Bob Abley sits down next to Godric.

"You have one shot. Once we leave, it will get less likely and harder to ask. What are you going to do? Wait until you can send him an email? Write him a letter?"

"I agree with Bunny, the direct approach does tend to cut through all the niceties," Godric suggests. "Just go for it."

"It is the niceties I'm trying to preserve," Abley replies, watching Lemon come back with his pint. Something makes Abley throw caution to the wind. "Will you come back, Lemon? To work for us, in Cambridge, I mean. You're greatly missed. People are always talking about you to me. Where's Lemon? You lost your strongest man? Where is Bells?"

"Of Saint Clements. I owe you five farthings, say the bells of Saint Martins," sings Godric.

"Not helping," Inspector Abley interrupts. "Everyone would be so pleased if you'd come back, and Elizabeth, and Godric."

"Hey! Don't drag me into this." Elizabeth takes a glug of her stout.

"Yeah, don't drag us into this." Godric winks at Bob Abley, who shakes his head. Lemon looks ahead, not sure his old Inspector's little speech convinces him.

"I'm working with a Sergeant who is into watches and clocks and wants to show me his collection of trains in his loft. You must meet him. He's such a good lad. But I need someone to complain that I talk about golf too much."

"You do, and I never complained much." Lemon is looking annoyed. "I need to think there is something in it for me."

"I'll recommend you for the Inspector's course. You can't enjoy working with that man here. He's more than useless," Bob Abley adds.

"He has some good people around him," Lemon says defensively.

"And so do I." Abley indicates Elizabeth, with a look. Lemon smiles for the first time.

"That was pretty cool, the way you solved that," Lemon tells Elizabeth. But Elizabeth keeps quiet, this is Abley's opportunity to speak.

"Come back to where it's flat, and you can run along Midsummer and Stourbridge Commons in the morning," Abley says.

"They have the University Parks here."

"Come back to piss off the Super. Raynott is delighted everyone thinks you left because of me."

"I did."

"If you won't come back for me," Bob Abley tries to suck up the punch to the stomach, "come back for the city you grew up in, the one where your parents live. Come back and help."

"I'll think about it," Lemon finally says. Godric has been keeping quiet, but when he hears these words, he grabs Lemon and shakes him.

"Yay! While you're thinking about it, you can come and see me in the panto."

The bartender comes back over and says, "You playing? Or you moving?"

"We're not moving. We have our drinks," Elizabeth says threateningly.

"We might need to move," Lemon replies.

"Let's play?" Abley suggests.

"I'm tired," Elizabeth says.

"You're good. And I'm better." Godric strokes his Nanna's hair.

"Hand us some of those pencils. He's paying," Sergeant Lemon says, then points to Inspector Abley to get out his wallet.

"Ten pounds," the bartender says dryly, holding out a hand ready to move off. "What you called?"

"Eh?" Abley says.

"Team name?"

"The Cambridge Quizzicals Away Team," Godric offers without missing a beat.

"Cambridge? Boo!" a competing team on the next table show their displeasure. The four of them laugh and lift their glasses to clink together.

"Okay, I can take contemporary culture, science, maths, art, theatre, sport, well, mainly rowing," Godric says to his Nanna. "You can take science, music, animals, gardening, modern British landscape, Bunny." Godric looks at Bob Abley and Lemon. "You two. What are you good for?"

"Golf and running." Lemon points at Abley and then himself.

"Is that it?" Godric waits to see if there are any other areas of expertise.

"I had a flying lesson for my birthday," Lemon shrugs.

"One flying lesson," Godric replies. "Right, now we have an aeronautical expert. Who knew?" Godric opens his eyes wide.

*

The pub quiz goes on for far too long. The dogs are fast asleep under the table as the final questions and answers are read out by the quizmaster.

"We had a tie break with Universally Challenged and The Cambridge Quizzicals Away Team up to the last question, which was, 'Apart from astronauts, who else has seen the curvature of the earth?' The Quizzicals had it, with Concorde passengers!" the quizmaster shouts.

"It flew eleven miles up, at 1,350 miles per hour too. I might have had a book with my birthday present," Lemon explains, as cool as a cucumber.

"So, the Quizzicals win. Well done, Cambridge!" The quizmaster shouts. There are some boos, followed by a lot of cheers, applause and general appreciation of worthy competitors from the other team tables around the room.

"Whoop, whoop!" Godric shouts. "It's going to be a good Christmas, I can feel it. Whose round?" Then Godric remembers he's on juice as he has a performance later, so adds, "get me some more crisps while you're there."

"You make a good team after all," the bartender comes over to bring the winnings and the small sash with 'OXFORD WINNERS' on it.

"Only one sash?" Abley asks. Godric wastes no time in putting it on and then also putting it over Lemon's head. The two are squashed.

"Take it off, or I'm not even thinking about coming back," Lemon replies. Godric takes it off quickly to everyone's relief, then hugs Lemon and winks at Abley.

"I know someone who might like this for his Christmas present. A certain Superintendent will be so proud of everything we've done in Oxford. Don't you think?" Abley says, who is then gladly given the sash by Godric for Raynott.

"It's time, I think. Home James, and don't spare the horses." Elizabeth gets up and looks out of the window at the view towards the river. She decides to take the dogs out to stretch their legs. They see the sun setting over the hills on the horizon, as the Victoria Arms garden sweeps down to the river. She leans against the wall and turns to Inspector Abley who has followed her out.

"Thank you," Elizabeth says.

"For what?" Bob Abley looks at Elizabeth, smirking as if she needs to spell it out. "Thank you too," he adds, "I've got everything I need for Christmas. Fairy lights and a snow globe. And maybe my Sergeant back."

The two of them look out as the sun sets.

"You'd better hire me," Elizabeth insists.

"There may be no murders."
"When the time comes."
"When the time comes."

61
HOME

Inspector Abley opens the front door to his flat. There are several bills, but more Christmas cards on the mat. He brings in a box that was hidden in his outdoor basement cupboard. He opens it. It is the loud cuckoo clock that Sergeant Goodey threatened to give him as a Christmas present.

"Time for re-gifting I think." Inspector Bob Abley looks at the snow globe that he couldn't turn off last time he was home. "And I know just the perfect person to give this to." He smiles and looks at the burnt gingerbread man perched on top of the now cold fire. He turns the fire on and moves the biscuit to the table. He sees his landline answerphone flashing. No one uses it apart from Elizabeth, so he is half-thinking about ignoring it. But his curiosity is too much, so he presses the button.

"Hello." Inspector Abley recognises the voice immediately. "I thought if I rang this, you'd think it was Professor Green pulling you back to Oxford or something. Ha ha." Lemon speaks, then there is a long pause on the message, which Bob Abley hangs on, eyes wide. Lemon continues, "I just wanted to say that it was good to see you. And, well. I'm coming back! I spoke to the Superintendent, and he said yes, but not before the New Year. Budgets, or something. So you're on your own until then. Right, well. I just wanted to say don't do anything stupid before then. And I'm not playing golf." Lemon laughs at the end, and then the phone goes dead. Inspector Abley beams and shuts his eyes. Then he goes to the fridge, pulls out a beer, and finds some golf on the box, throwing himself on the sofa.

*

A week later, and Elizabeth and Godric walk through the front court of St Bene't's College towards the Chapel, just in time for Christmas Eve Carols. They spot Emily with her husband Cuthbert in the queue and head over to join them. The snow is thick on the ground, and Elizabeth smiles and says hello to many locals. It is good to be back. She enters the Chapel, the carols about to begin. Elizabeth bumps into her Head of Department also walking in.

"That is the very last one of those wretched networking events I go to for you. Ever," Elizabeth says, accentuating the weight with which she carries this point.

"It's lovely to see you too. I did hear all about it. And there you were earlier saying conferences were dull. See, I told you." The Head spots someone else and leaves Elizabeth to bore her eyes into his back.

Godric and Elizabeth continue to find a pew and sit down next to Emily and Cuthbert, as the first carol washes over them. Elizabeth takes hold of Godric's hand as they sit and listen.

"Happy Christmas, Goddy," Elizabeth says, looking up at the fan vaulted ceiling, very glad to be back home, as Godric puts his arm around his favourite Nanna.

THE END

Thank you so much for reading 'A Christmas Mystery', book four of the series Cambridge Murder Mysteries.

Titles available in the Cambridge Murder Mystery Series:

Book 1: Poison

Book 2: Cursed

Book 3: Blood Moon

Book 4: A Christmas Mystery

Book 5: Valentine's Day – Kiss of Death *(coming soon!)*

Short Stories in the Cambridge Murder Mystery Series:

Christmas Eve Mystery *(coming soon!)*

Green *(available by subscribing to my newsletter)*

Other titles by Charlot King:

Animal Tales: Woof

Animal Tales: Pup

For more information on the other books in the series please do visit www.charlotking.com If you'd like to follow what Charlot King is up to, you can find her on Twitter: @queencharlot. And, if you enjoyed this book, Charlot would be very grateful for a review on Amazon as well as telling all your friends. Much appreciated. Thanks again, and happy reading, and Merry Christmas!

Printed in Great Britain
by Amazon

51000131R00194